What readers think of The Billion Dollar Embezzlement Murders

IT WILL KEEP YOU UP ALL NIGHT.
Move over Elvirah and Willie. Frank Hopkins has created a pair of sleuths to rival the Higgins-Clark duo, adding the distinction of their being published authors. If you follow Margaret and Paul through this embezzlement scam, you will not only be rewarded with a gripping thriller, but you'll also take away an education in Finance and Geography. Hopkins's Ph.D. in Economics gives him the authority to fine-tune the shenanigans of his characters so as to distill them down to the understanding of everyman... You don't want to miss this one. Mary D. on June 22, 2019

Take a Ride with Hoffman and O'Hare
They met in Abandoned Homes, and now they're back for more action. The Billion Dollar Embezzlement Murders takes us for a ride with Hoffman and O'Hare, the best pair of sleuths since Nick and Nora. The stakes are high. Bad guys get testy when there's a billion dollars at stake. Hopkins does a good job in describing action and in setting scenes and this book has plenty of action. Take a read and get involved with Hoffman and O'Hare. Jackson Coppley on June 8, 2019

Great Read
Margaret and Paul are back: married, happy and enjoying the good life in Greece. But, their bliss gets blitzed when a massive embezzlement scheme in their native Delaware is uncovered and follows them to Greece. As they assist their friend, they find themselves targets for elimination also. Frank Hopkins continues the fast-paced action for this pair we first met in "Abandoned Homes: The Vietnam Revenge Murders." William Kennedy on July 22, 2019.

D1458004

Another great novel from Frank Hopkins!

I was most impressed with the amount of research that Frank Hopkins must have done to write The Billion Dollar Embezzlement Murders. The technical aspects of embezzling that amount of money were well described. His depiction of Greece and its many islands made you feel you were there. Being a Delawarean, I was familiar with many of the other locales throughout the book, which added to the verisimilitude. And, of course, the plot was spot-on and moved quickly. Highly recommended! by F. Weldon Burge on July 4, 2019

A good read

The Billion Dollar Embezzlement Murders held my attention from the first page to the very end. I liked the flipping between the different characters trying to solve the crimes to the perpetrators still committing them. The description of the scenery only adds to the enjoyment as the story journeys across the world. Amy on June 14, 2019

Unique mystery !

Just finished reading Frank Hopkins latest novel "The Billion Dollar Embezzlement Murders" . This mystery is filled with high-tech crime -- murder -- back stabbing intrigues and Greece. No putting this story down as it is a straight read through. Bill on September 20 2019

They're Back!

May 28, 2019

An unlikely pair at first, Frank Hopkins new dynamic duo, Hoffman and O'Hare are fast becoming super-sleuths. Professor and cop, now writers, travel to Greece and uncover the crooks behind the Billion Dollar Embezzlement. Crooks who also happen to be murderers. Frank Hopkins second novel featuring Hoffman and O'Hare has them in a fast-paced race to discover the murderers before they become the next victims. Amazon Customer on May 28,2019.

Thank you for reading *The Billion Dollar Embezzlement Murders*. If you liked the book, or my other books, please write an Amazon review to inform other potential readers they will enjoy the book. Please open my Amazon author page to access the forms to write your review.

https://www.amazon.com/Frank-E.-Hopkins/e/B0028AR904

Check on the book cover of the book you want to review and the review option will appear toward the bottom of the page.

FRANK E HOPKINS

The Billion Dollar Embezzlement Murders

Frank E Hopkins

Books by Frank E Hopkins

Fiction:

The Billion Dollar Embezzlement Murders

Abandoned Homes: Vietnam Revenge Murders

First Time

The Opportunity

Unplanned Choices

Non-fiction:

Locational Analysis: An Interregional Econometric Model of Agriculture, Mining, Manufacturing and Services, with Curtis Harris.

ISBN 13: 978-0-9988200-2-6

Ocean View Publishing
Ocean View, Delaware 19970

DEDICATION

To Greece and its citizens, who provided a perfect setting for this international thriller. The rugged scenery and clear blue water of its seas is unparalleled in Europe. Its people are friendly and helpful to the tourist, since the English language is taught in Greek schools, eliminating most communication problems between Greeks and English speaking tourists. The food is fresh, healthy, and always tastes great. The efficient and entertaining ferry transportation system between its mountainous islands should be experienced by all. One can spend a satisfied lifetime visiting its archeological ruins and museums, and studying its history.

.

ACKNOWLEDGMENTS

I would like to thank the Maryland Writers Association Southeastern Chapter Critique Group and the Rehoboth Critique Group of the Rehoboth Beach Writers Guild for reading and advising me on how to improve the book. Thanks to Mary-Margaret Pauer who performed the development editing to improve the rhythm of the novel. Thanks to the beta readers who read late drafts and provided comments that significantly improved the novel: Patty Apostolides, John Bacon, Karl Braungart, Leslie Cooney, Jeff Smith, and Susan Wimbrow. Suzi Peel performed the final copyediting, identifying errors, and suggesting improvements in the novel. Stephanie Fowler of Salt Water Media produced the excellent book cover that portrays the themes of the book.

PART 1 - SUNDAY, JANUARY 3, 2010

Chapter 1 The Event

Sunday afternoon, January 3, 2010

Steve looked around Hank's large study with its mahogany desk, bookcases, dark brown carpeted floor, its walls adorned with pictures of the foreign lands Hank had visited. Steve pressed the return key on his laptop to start a series of programs that checked the balances of a hundred and twenty offshore accounts. Their total value equaled $1,048,432,987. Steve thought he would soon be able to afford Hank's high-class life style. He could move out of his apartment with its beer-stained wooden floor to an exotic country populated with sensual women who appreciated a man with money.

Hank had said, "Access the program file, *Your Share*, and execute it." Steve knew his share should be twenty percent.

Once the program finished running Hank asked, "Is your take satisfactory?"

Steve nodded, "Yes," and found it had equaled his expectations.

"Did you tell anyone you were coming here to my Bethany Beach house tonight?"

"No, you told me not to. I'm taking a two-week sailing vacation in the Caribbean, so no one can ask me about the withdrawals if they're discovered early. My cell phone doesn't work there." Steve liked visiting Hank's five-thousand square foot beach house on the Atlantic Ocean in a gated community just north of the village of Bethany Beach. He wanted to buy a larger house in the Caribbean in the spring once he had permanently left the country.

"Good, we can't be too careful. We don't want anyone to connect us even though we can't be traced electronically." Hank handed Steve a glass of Johnny Walker Black Label neat and said, "Time to celebrate."

Steve took a large gulp while Hank sampled a glass of Cabernet Sauvignon.

After raising his glass two more times, he handed it to Hank. Though slightly dizzy and nauseous Steve said, "I'll have another."

Hank poured a larger drink for Steve, then tasted his wine and waited.

Half way through the second drink the benzodiazepine sedative in Steve's glass kicked in. He passed out and fell forward on the desk.

Hank smiled.

PART 2 - EIGHTEEN MONTHS EARLIER

Chapter 2 Dinner at Margaret's House

Monday, June 16, 2008

Detective Margaret Hoffman called Paul O'Hare at the police safe house. "The case is over. Come to dinner at my home tonight and I'll explain. Bring your outline of our book. My boss Lt. Nelson is looking forward to reading it. An officer will drive you to your home from the police safe house. I'll see you at 6:00."

"I'm looking forward to seeing you again. Solving the skeleton murders crime was fast. You said it might take several months." Paul remembered her lying in bed after they first made love four days ago. Only eight years younger than his sixty-three, she had a perfect body for a woman of any age, and sensual long flowing blond tresses.

"No, we were lucky. You'll love the sights of Indian River Bay."

Paul left his home in Ocean View, Delaware to drive through the clear warm spring evening to Margaret's home on the south side of Whites Creek a hundred yards from the Veterans of Foreign Wars facility. Paul had never visited her house. Margaret had emailed him a map so he wouldn't miss it since he had to drive on rural roads. He looked forward to the bay scenery, hoping to watch the sun set that evening. The fifty-year old homes shaded by large trees impressed Paul. He found her redwood split-level home, on Woods Edge Drive, and parked in her driveway.

Margaret opened the door. Paul handed her a manila envelope and a bottle of chilled Chardonnay. She looked at the envelope and said, "I know you're eager to show me the outline, but when you come to my door, I expect a kiss, not just a document to review."

Paul beaming, took her in his arms and kissed her passionately. She responded in kind, dropping the envelope as she did, but wisely holding on to the wine. Paul bent down and picked up the document as Margaret pulled him into the living room. Their hunger for each other had grown since their first time in bed last week. After putting the wine in the cooler, she led him into her bedroom.

Lying in bed feeling satisfied, Margaret looked at him and said, "We could have waited until after dinner and discussing your book, but I'm glad we didn't."

Paul gazed lovingly at her body, realizing her perfection, which he planned to experience as often as possible. "So am I. You are all I thought about in the safe house."

"Paul, you're staring at me. Haven't you ever seen a naked woman?" Margaret teased, soaking in the unspoken compliment.

"Not like you."

"Well, get used to it. But you haven't seen the bay from here, which impresses me every day." While touting the bay, she loved his words of affection, athletic body, blue eyes, a full head of white hair, and his passion for her. She rose and reached for her clothes.

Paul said, "I'd rather stay in bed, but I'll follow you." He watched and savored her as she dressed. He knew he'd always enjoy looking at her.

"It's only 6:30. Let's eat first. We can see the sun setting after 8:00. Have a few grapes, olives, and cheddar cheese while I cook."

Margaret took Paul's wine from the cooler and the appetizers from the stainless-steel two-door refrigerator. Paul accepted the plate and bottle and asked, "I'm curious. What's for dinner?"

"This afternoon, I purchased two lobsters from a local fisherman. The water has been simmering so it will take less than five minutes to boil," she said as she turned up the heat on the stove. "We will also have salad and corn on the cob. I only have to cook the lobsters for ten minutes and the corn for five."

"Love lobster. Being in upstate New York for so long, it shocked me to find Delaware has its own lobsters. Like many Americans I believed they only lived in New England."

She said, "Another great reason for living in Delaware with its cold-water, deep-sea canyons that harbor sea life from northern climates. Can you open the wine?"

After Margaret drank a taste of wine from her glass, she began, "Let me tell you how the Abandoned Homes Skeleton case ended."

Then she retrieved the cooked lobsters, asking, "Do you want to wait until we finish eating before I continue my summary?"

"No, it's too exciting to stop now."

As she talked, Paul removed a claw from his lobster and cracked it, spilling lobster water on to the bib Margaret had provided. He pulled out the lobster meat with a small fork and dipped it into butter. His face expressed his appreciation for its exotic taste, which had seemed strange to him as a child.

Margaret asked, "Is it okay?"

"Dinner's perfect," Paul said thinking of the lobster and her.

Margaret ate, happy to see Paul's response to her first home-cooked meal for him, and continued her story.

Paul opened the manila folder and made notes and additions to his book outline between savoring the fresh salad, early corn, and the seafood.

Margaret talked through dinner and for twenty minutes after. She discussed aspects of the crime and investigation that didn't involve Paul to help him expand his book's outline. She elaborated on the police chase of several of the criminals. When Margaret stopped talking she said, "That's it."

They both took the dishes to the dishwasher which she started.

"Let me show you my beautiful view before it gets too dark. It's a short walk to the VFW parking lot where we can see across the bay to the Indian River Bridge."

They walked out her front door into a windless warm evening, and arrived at a path leading to the parking lot. While Paul had seen the bay before, he enjoyed it more with Margaret holding his hand.

Paul looked west to take in the panoramic vista of the flat, wide bay opening toward the electric power plant. He turned his head right to the northern boundary of the bay and continued to scan to the east to the barrier islands connected by the Indian River Bridge. "I wish I had my camera."

"You will have plenty of time to take pictures. The view differs seasonally and by the time of day. I sometimes come here early in the morning to watch the sunrise. We could do that when you stay here."

"I'd like that."

"The shadows are getting long. It's time to watch the sunset." Margaret led him up the path edged by blooming spring daisies. They returned to her house and walked to her back yard, bordering on the riprap rocks of the eastern shore of Whites Creek. Paul noticed several kayaks on a small dock protruding from the downward sloping grass yard along the water.

"The blue one is mine," Margaret said pointing.

"I didn't know you kayaked. It's one of my favorite activities."

"I have lots of surprises. It'll take time for you to learn them all. You're welcome to join me."

"I'd love to," he said, hoping this would be the start of developing joint memories of activities besides sex and eating to help bind them into a permanent relationship.

They sat facing west on a refinished dark green park bench Margaret had purchased from an antique store in Selbyville. Paul could hear the crickets and frogs begin their evening mating calls, knowing the sound was appropriate for the evening.

"Let's not talk, but just enjoy the beauty of the sun disappearing," Margaret said.

Paul nodded and reached out for her hand. Trying not to stare at her, he kept his eyes focused on the red and orange colors to the west.

A few minutes later, Margaret said. "Let's go to my study and review your outline."

The room impressed Paul. It contained built-in walnut book cases on two walls, a large oak desk, and an oak table, surrounded by four chairs. They sat at the table and Paul handed her the outline. "Can you read my handwriting? I attached the notes from listening to your summary."

"If I can't, I'll ask."

Paul looked at her concerned as she quietly read, hoping for her approval.

When she finished, she smiled and said, "It's great. It's more than a chapter outline. It divides each chapter into scenes. You have fifty chapters and at least two hundred scenes."

"Two hundred and twenty-six." Paul knew he had impressed Margaret.

They talked for two hours commenting on and improving Paul's outline. Margaret noticed Paul yawning. "Paul, you look exhausted. You can sleep here rather than drive home this late."

"Thanks. Let me go to my car and get a toothbrush and pajamas," Paul replied, elated she had invited him.

"I'm off the rest of this week. Stay here. We can work together," Margaret said. Was she going too fast? She didn't want to scare Paul away.

"I will as long as you come to my house at five for tennis and dinner on Wednesday. Meet me at the tennis courts."

Margaret asked, "Do you think we'd get together if we didn't write the book?"

"Yes, we liked each other as soon as we met at the abandoned home." Paul neglected to tell her he planned the book to entice her to become involved.

"We'll need to spend a lot of time together," Margaret said.

Paul understood from the way they had greeted each other that evening that would be no trouble.

Margaret said, "I'm afraid the book will become a second job and detract from our relationship."

"Let's make sure it doesn't," Paul said. As he fell asleep, Paul hoped tomorrow would be the beginning of the second phase of his life.

Margaret looked at Paul while he slept as the early morning light entered the room around the curtain borders. She wondered how she should start the day. She left the bed without making a sound to walk into the kitchen and turn on the prepared coffee brewer.

A few minutes later Paul wandered in.

"What do you want for breakfast?" Margaret asked.

"Normally, I have bacon and eggs. Why don't we go to the Veterans of Foreign Wars restaurant? I have fond memories of that restaurant."

"I want to keep my figure so you hang around. I don't make a regular practice of all-you-can eat restaurants. Why don't I surprise you? Drink some coffee."

While Paul reread their work, Margaret prepared French toast, sliced honeydew melon, and sausage links. The smell of the sausage cooking made it hard for him to concentrate.

Chapter 3 Cementing the Relationship

Tuesday, June 16, 2008

After breakfast, Paul went to his car and returned with his laptop. They wrote a list and description of characters, settings, and the revised outline, which they completed by Tuesday evening.

Margaret met him at the courts a few minutes before five on Wednesday. As they warmed up for the match, she noticed Paul's speed and reactions didn't match his performance last year before they began their relationship. He had not recovered from his three-week stay in the hospital for the hantavirus infection. Margaret decided to go easy on him.

When Paul started hitting the ball, his lack of stamina surprised him. After five minutes, he said, "I don't think I can play. Let's practice for a while."

Margaret said, "Okay. Don't stress yourself. You need to recover your health. I'd rather work on the book than play tennis."

They hit for fifteen more minutes before Paul said, "It's time to quit. I'll go to the gym and work on the treadmill before our next match."

Arriving at Paul's house, he said, "Let's have wine and eat before we shower." He poured them a glass of Chardonnay.

"I'll review what you've written while you cook."

Paul had prepared the eggplant parmesan in the morning in a square oven-baking dish. He placed the dish in the refrigerator before he went to play tennis. It was one of Paul's favorites, and he hoped to impress Margaret with his culinary skills.

When Margaret started reading, he took the plate out and placed it in the 350 degree oven. He anxiously watched her. When she grinned, he relaxed and tossed the salad. He popped a piece of sliced tomato into his mouth.

After dinner they showered together. Paul kissed her as they were drying each other and said, "I want to take a short nap before we return to writing."

Margaret looked into his eyes, and asked beaming, "Will this happen after every shower?"

"That's a good plan." They walked hand in hand to the bedroom and didn't return to the book that evening.

For the next two days, they continued working on the manuscript. At 7:00 on Saturday morning Paul said, "I have my camera. Would you like to join me while I take some early morning pictures of Indian River Bay?"

She responded by holding his hand, "Lead the way."

Paul retraced the tour Margaret had given him on Monday evening. He took twenty pictures of the east, north, and south sections of the bay.

At breakfast Margaret said, "Writing a book and making love is delightful. After I return to work, let's meet three times a week to work on the book."

Paul agreed, hoping that would be the minimum frequency. They spent the morning kayaking and enjoyed a picnic on Margaret's deck. They celebrated their writing and bonding progress by eating at Fager's Island in Ocean City on Saturday night.

They made love Sunday morning and continued writing the scenes during the day. Margaret retired early since she had to return to work at 8:00 a.m. at the State Trooper's Barracks 4 in Georgetown, Delaware.

Although Paul worked out on Margaret's treadmill the next week, he had not regained enough strength to play tennis. He had difficulty communicating with Margaret over investigative techniques, police procedures, and its specialized vocabulary. To learn more about the topics, he enrolled in two courses at the Georgetown campus of Delaware Tech, recommended by Margaret: "Introduction to Criminal Justice" and "Essentials of Interviewing and Counseling."

On Saturday afternoon, Margaret decided she needed to learn more about writing and discovered the Eastern Shore Writers Association through the Internet. She called the president, and told him the topic of the book she and Paul were writing. Margaret asked for advice on how to get it published. He explained, "The normal procedure for non-fiction work is to prepare an outline and market the outline to a publisher. However, with your topic and the two authors having participated in the case, you should have no problem selling the book. I'll call my agent and tell her to contact you."

The agent, Doris Powers, had a law degree. She specialized in author contracts and called Margaret an hour later and suggested they meet. Margaret said, "I'll have to call my writing partner to find a time convenient for him."

They agreed to meet at his house at 4:00 on Sunday. Doris suggested they "bring no more than a two hundred and fifty word summary of the book, as well as short bios and an outline."

Paul volunteered to write the summary, his bio, and bring the outline.

At the meeting, Doris summarized the publication process, reviewed their documents, suggested changes, and told them of six publishers she'd call, as soon as they both signed her as their agent.

Doris left the meeting smiling with the signed contract. On Monday, she arranged all the publisher meetings. They had each expressed interest in the book and stated they'd send in a bid including an advance if they decided to publish it. The highest bidder offered $250,000. Doris arranged to meet with Margaret and Paul on the next Friday. Doris presented the bids and recommended they accept the highest offer.

They agreed to submit the first draft within seven months by February 2009. Soon they'd be published authors.

June 2008 to June 2009

Since Margaret's police workload had decreased from the heady days of the abandoned home skeletons case. Margaret's current caseload consisted of standard house robberies, car thefts, small business fraud, but no murders. None required extensive overtime or weekend commitments, enabling her to devote more time to their shared activities.

Six months after they started writing, Margaret enjoyed her time with Paul: indeed time spent without him seemed wasted. Margaret loved having him next to her, his warmth, sensual male aroma, and the quiet rhythm of his breathing as he lay in her bed. Occasionally, they would wake up together in the middle of the night, have a short conversation, and sometimes make love. Her life now had improved after the loneliness of her five years as a widow. Margaret couldn't imagine living without Paul, thankful she had followed her husband, Josh's advice on his deathbed to find a new lover after he died.

Besides sex, she enjoyed his companionship, someone to play tennis with, and kayak, hike, talk to, and go on weekend trips. They always launched their kayaks before 7:30 in the morning before it became too hot. They usually returned to her dock by 9:00 a.m.

While she still remembered the happiness she shared with her deceased husband, with Paul she again had something to look forward to every day, not just work, eating and sleeping. Margaret had fallen deeply in love with Paul.

She first expressed her love verbally on a hot July day when they kayaked from her dock into a west breeze for several miles.

Paul's stamina had increased, but Margaret always had to be careful not to out distance him. While Paul stowed the kayaks on Margaret's dock, she said. "Paul, I love kayaking with you. I love our life together, and I love you no matter what we are doing or when we're alone."

Hearing her last words, Paul dropped his kayak on his unprotected

16

foot. "Christ that hurts."

"Paul, I expected a different response."

Examining his foot and feeling embarrassed, Paul replied, "I'm talking about my foot, not us. I love you too." Paul had loved her since the day they met, but feared to express it, worrying she'd reject him. He sighed with relief that they had conquered that hurdle.

They stared into each others' eyes, and he leaned forward, gazing at her lips. They kissed.

With the uncertainty about commitment that each experienced gone, their relationship entered a new phase. While working at writing the book that day, they devoted most of their time to privately speculating about their future together. They celebrated that evening by eating healthy seafood at the Cafe on Route 26.

Paul spent his evenings and weekends with Margaret, engaged in athletic activities when not writing or making love. As his love for her and their life together deepened during the fall, he detested the trips to exchange sleeping locations. By December 2008, he decided to suggest they live together in one home.

On a mid-December evening after three days of a heavy cold rain, Paul said, "Driving in the rain isn't fun."

"I felt the same way."

Paul asked, with trepidation, "Is it time we move in together?"

"Yes," Margaret said, reaching for his hand across the table, apprehensive Paul wouldn't want to leave his house. "Where?"

"Here, of course. I can't match your beautiful views of the bay and the convenience of your kitchen. Besides my kids told me they plan to come to the beach every weekend next summer and take a two-week joint summer vacation there. I might just be in the way. There wouldn't be room for us." Paul replied.

"Nonsense, you love them and your grandchildren. Don't you want to spend time with them?" Margaret replied thankful she didn't have to discuss the relative merits of each home before she had to convince him, she had a better house.

"Margaret, I'd like to spend more time together. When they invite us for dinner, we'll visit them. They're old enough to cook for us."

"Living together would help us finish the book sooner. This weekend I'll move my clothes from your house and you can bring all your winter clothes here." Margaret said.

"We've almost finished the first draft. Editing shouldn't take much time."

They followed the advice of the president of Eastern Shore Writers Association and had five friends read and comment on the book draft in January. The three hundred and fifteen comments shocked them. They both read each comment and decided which ones to incorporate into the document. After five days of intensive work, they completed the changes.

At ten in the evening once they had finished the second draft, Margaret said, "Let's follow the advice of two of the reviewers and read the book out loud to each other, to find out if we have realistic dialogue."

Both liked reading to each other. They enjoyed discovering where they should eliminate redundant dialogue and narrative, and where adding text would improve the book. They sent the book to the publisher on February 16, 2009, meeting their contractually required deadline.

The publisher returned an edited version of the book in March with a book cover for their review. Margaret took a two-week vacation in late March to accommodate the publisher's demands. Their agent explained the publisher required this process because of the pressure to release the book rapidly before the competition published on the same topic. While at first complaining about the editor's comments, they realized the edits improved the book and eliminated grammatical mistakes. They received proofs of the book to review in the middle of April and returned their corrections on April 30.

The publisher released *The Abandoned Homes Serial Murders* on Monday, May 25, 2009.

On the last Sunday morning in May, their agent emailed them a copy of a glowing New York Times review.

To celebrate their meeting at the abandoned home in 2008, the book's publication, and their release from the drudgery of writing and editing, Paul proposed a hiking trip to the top of the 3,284 foot high summit of Old Mountain, in Shenandoah National Park in Virginia. To avoid crowds, they decided to hike on Thursday in the last week in May.

Paul told Margaret, "A day climbing Old Rag Mountain in the Blue Ridge would be a perfect vacation. We can leave our laptops home and forget writing and editing."

"Have you ever climbed it? The trail is a nine-mile strenuous hike."

"No, but I've hiked the mountains in upstate New York. It shouldn't be much different." Paul often thought of his deceased wife, Janet, their many hiking and climbing outings. He hoped he could revive that activity with Margaret.

"I climbed it many times years ago. We'll start by 8:00 a.m. to avoid the heat of the afternoon."

He booked a motel for two nights in Sperryville, Virginia, eleven miles north of the mountain and a ten mile drive south of Little Washington. Paul had also secretly called the Inn at Little Washington restaurant two months earlier for reservations to celebrate the first anniversary of the start of their relationship.

They drove out Wednesday night with hiking and dress clothes in their luggage. Paul did not tell Margaret the real purpose of the trip. He carried a small box containing a full karat diamond engagement ring. While he knew marrying Margaret would ensure perfection in his life, he wasn't certain how she felt about the permanence of marriage.

The hike started well. Paul and Margaret approached the summit via the shorter and steeper Ridge Trail than the longer and easier Saddle Trail. At one and a half miles, Paul felt tired and slowed his pace particularly when he had to scamper over granite rocks. Margaret sweated, but her breathing was unhurried.

Paul had hoped to propose at the summit, but changed his mind observing his perspiration and shortness of breath. He thought his imperfect physical condition, while sufficient for tennis, might cause Margaret to turn down his proposal.

When they reached the top, he rested, while Margaret reached into her pack and pulled out two cold beers in a small insulated carrying case and gave Paul one. "It's a traditional reward for reaching the summit."

Paul felt better as he drank the beer. "Didn't know you had two beers. How did you do that?"

"A woman never tells all her secrets. It restores electrolytes. When runners finish the Marine Corp marathon in DC, they're offered orange juice or beer for the same reason."

"I can guess which is the more popular," Paul said.

They returned to the motel and dressed for the evening: Both looked forward to dining in the highly awarded restaurant. As they entered, the restaurant's ambiance impressed them. The Delmarva shore had nothing like it.

They tasted the wine as they examined the impressive menu. Margaret ordered Pan-Seared Peking Duck Breast, while Paul chose a Grilled King Lamb Chop Perfumed with Rosemary on Lentils Dijonnaise with Minted Béarnaise. After sampling each other's entrees, they agreed they had never had a better meal.

When Margaret left for the restroom, Paul placed the open ring box next to her dessert plate of Warm Granny Smith Apple Tart with Buttermilk Ice Cream. After returning she gazed in wonderment at the dessert, exclaiming, "That looks great."

Paul, disappointed she had not seen the ring remained quiet. Margaret went to pick up a dessert fork and knocked over the small box and watched as it dropped toward the floor. She knelt down to pick it up. The sparkling of the diamond transfixed her. Margaret looked at Paul and said, "Aren't you supposed to be the one kneeling?"

"Yes, but you beat me to it," he said, thankfully he didn't have to worry his tired legs would prevent him from standing.

She stared at him, smiling.

"What's your answer?" Paul asked.

"I haven't heard a question."

"Oh. Will you make me the happiest man in the world? Marry me?"

Margaret jumped up, said, "Yes" and embraced him. The rest of the diners curious about the noise turned toward the beaming couple. Paul put the ring on her, and they understood the excitement when Margaret flashed her hand to all corners of the dining room.

They discussed the wedding on the drive home. Margaret said, "I don't want to wait long."

"I agree." They set the date for June 20, 2009 four days after the first year anniversary of solving the abandoned home skeletons case.

Margaret said, "Let's have a small family wedding at Veterans of Foreign Wars Hall where we enjoyed our first brunch together."

"You mean my first police interrogation?" Paul asked grinning.

"Don't complain. It worked out well."

"Yes it did. I agree."

"Were you aware Walter Nelson has a certificate from the Universal Life Church to be an officiant in a non-religious marriage ceremony?"

"Yes, he told me over six months ago. Walter officiated at his youngest son's wedding. I think he was marketing himself if we became engaged."

"Let's have him marry us."

They had settled on the major aspects of their wedding by the time they returned to Margaret's house. The wedding guests included their family and friends. Paul insisted they invite a former colleague of his, Kostas Canakis, a Greek who had retired to the island of Mykonos. Both agreed to have a month-long honeymoon in Greece with Kostas' guidance. Paul promised to bring his camera to record their honeymoon.

June 2009

After the book's initial success, their publisher scheduled a cross-country trip for book signings in the major book stores in forty-five cities through the summer and fall. They appeared on thirty-three local TV stations the day before the book signings. The signings and associated publicity kept the book in the top ten of the New York Times bestseller list. Unfortunately, because of her police work, Margaret could not attend all the signings and TV appearances. She only went to those on weekends.

When told of their book signing schedule Professor Canakis advised them to postpone the honeymoon until mid-April 2009 since the winter in Mykonos differed little from that in coastal Delaware.

PART 3 THE CREDIT CARD CRIME - SEPTEMBER 2009 TO JANUARY 2010

Chapter 4 The Seduction

Friday, September 18, 2009

Hank met Steve at the Hang Out, a singles establishment with a long bar, twenty small tables and booths, a dance floor, and space for a band or a DJ on a Friday night in Long Neck, Delaware. Steve recognized him from work and Hank's greeting surprised him.

Hank walked over to Steve, who sat on a bar stool drinking a Dogfish Head Pale Ale. He said, "I'm Hank Strong. You work at Liberty Credit. I've seen you in the halls. What do you do?"

Steve, who was a slender five-foot six, looked up at the large six foot two inch bald heavy-set man who towered over him.

"That's right. I'm Steve Haven, the administrator for the credit card database.

"That must keep you busy. I head up Finance. You IT guys keep our company functioning and our data secure."

They talked for an hour, with Hank getting Steve to confess, his divorce had financially drained him, something Hank knew before he approached Steve.

"Her lawyer screwed me on alimony and child support. I had to move from a riverfront house in Seaford to a one bedroom basement apartment in a run-down house in Laurel."

Steve's unhappiness festered on his declining take home pay. He had been proud of his six-figure income before his wife Maria left him because of his drinking, violent behavior, and cheating. He blamed her for his discontent. His life imitated his father's. Steve saw nothing wrong with getting drunk and passing out in front of his wife. Slapping her to keep her in line when she criticized his drinking was acceptable since his father did it and he stayed married for over forty years.

The financial shock mentally disabled Steve. While he kept his job, his life changed. His girlfriends left when they realized he couldn't entertain them for dinner, buy them jewelry and clothes, and take them on weekend trips. He stopped ordering expensive scotch at bars and settled for rail brands. His one-bedroom basement apartment depressed him each time he entered it, making him ripe for Hank's proposal.

They parted, shaking hands with Hank suggesting to Steve, "Let's meet for breakfast tomorrow at 9:00 at Jimmy's Grill in Bridgeville. There's something I'd like to talk to you about that will help you with your financial problems. But listen, you can't tell anyone about this conversation and our meeting tomorrow. You'll realize why when we talk."

The next morning, Steve, hung over, wore wrinkled black shorts, a gray tee shirt and blue sneakers. He arrived at the restaurant a few minutes before 9:00, saw Hank sitting at a table, and joined him.

Hank stood up, dressed in a blue blazer, pressed white shorts and shirt, offered his hand and said, "Thanks for coming. I'm playing tennis later and have to leave by ten."

"I'm curious. Why are we meeting?" Steve said craving a glass of orange juice.

"Let's order before we talk. I'm starving."

Steve told the waitress, "I'll have pancakes, sausage, a large orange juice, and coffee," thinking the pancakes might quell his nausea.

Hank looked at the waitress, "A mushroom and cheddar cheese omelet and coffee, please."

Then Hank began the main conversation. "You'll know why we're meeting after I tell you my proposition. All our meetings must be confidential."

Steve thought, this guy scares me. He talks like we're in a spy movie. "I'll keep quiet, but why?"

"I'm sure you're aware of the national IT security breaches such as the TJ Maxx hack of 94 million customer IDs in 2007 and the Heartland hack of 130 million IDs in 2009 and. As VP of Finance, I'm responsible for ensuring we minimize financial risks. I know little about our IT security system, and I want you to brief me."

"Now? I don't have the security regulations with me."

"Brief me from memory. I'll break in when I need clarification. I'll retain most of what you tell me." Hank reached into a pocket of his jacket and handed an envelope to Steve. "Please don't open it until you're in your car." Then he reached into his left front pants' pocket and discreetly turned on a solid state silent recording device.

Steve talked, interrupted several times by Hank asking questions.

At 9:50 Hank picked up the check and said, "Steve, I have to go. I realize you haven't finished talking and I expect I'll have questions. Let's meet here next Saturday at 9:00 to continue our discussion. I'll leave after you and pay the bill."

At first Hank's proposition scared Steve. However, holding the envelope filled with cash helped him overcome his fear. When he closed the door to his 2002 Silver Celica Toyota, he ripped open the envelope and found twelve wrinkled twenties and a ten-dollar bill. Smiling, he thought I'm doing nothing wrong, the VP has a right to know, and he appreciates my knowledge.

The next Saturday Steve, more comfortable with this new relationship, looked forward to delivering his briefing. Before they started the discussion, just after ordering, Hank handed Steve an envelope. "The information you gave me exceeded my expectations."

Then Hank asked more detailed questions.

Steve, excited by the fatter package, didn't want to wait to open it, but he realized he couldn't until he had answered Hank's questions. Safe in his car, he opened the envelope discovering twenty-five aged twenty-dollar bills. "Christ," he said out loud to the interior of his car. "I hope this never ends."

They met two more times at Jimmy's Grille. Steve pocketed the money and used it to reclaim his former lifestyle of wearing fancy clothes, frequenting bars, and scoring with loose women who loved big spenders.

Steve looked forward to the fifth meeting, but wondered how much more he had to say about the company's IT security. He feared the end of the money and a return to poverty.

"I should tell you, I've been talking to others about our IT security. While you all confirm each other's answers stressing the system is secure, there's only one way I could be convinced. I'm offering $100,000 to anyone who can write a program to hack into Liberty's computers, charge a real customer's credit card, credit the seller's account, not send out the charge on a customer bill until a specific date a month after the transaction, and deposit the charge into a private offshore account," Hank said.

"Are you serious?"

"If no one can do it, I'll consider the system secure."

"That's a lot of effort if the program can't break the system," Steve replied, thinking, I could use the 100K, but don't want to waste my time and get nothing.

"I agree. You have five weeks to try. We'll meet every week. You can brief me on your progress. The envelope will contain $2,000 each week. If you're successful, you can keep what you have, and I'll deposit the $100,000 in an offshore account in your name."

Steve, stunned, realized this year's financial problems would finally end. More clothes, bars, and women. Perhaps he'd buy a new car.

"What if I get caught?"

"Don't worry, I authorized your actions. I'll give you a customer who won't complain, and an offshore account. Failing to break into the database is your only worry."

"Why won't the customer be billed until four weeks after the transaction?" Steve asked.

"If a customer receives a bill earlier than four weeks, and examines it and finds the transaction you initiated, the customer will alert the bank that someone has broken into the system. If you wait four weeks the break will go undetected for that period of time."

Steve wondered about his competition, but thought, no one has more expertise on the IT system than the DBA. Steve wanted to go home and start.

"A few warnings," Hank said. "If you are successful, you have to develop counter measures to defend against the security weaknesses you discover. Don't try to find who else I've talked to. If you do, and I find out, the money ends. I told the others the same. There might be more than one way to hack the computers. I need to know. Hopefully, everyone will fail, and I'll have no trouble sleeping at night."

"That sounds reasonable. Do we have anything else to talk about?" Steve said.

"No," Hank slid the envelope to Steve who had started to leave the table and said, "Good luck."

Steve rushed to his car to examine the money. Twenty used $100 bills. A down payment. Then he worried. How can I hide the money from the IRS? I have to save it and not waste it on drinking and women as I usually do. I'll postpone buying a new car. Besides, I'll need my spare time to write the code.

Steve worked eighty hard hours at his new assignment before the next meeting. He had prepared a document detailing how he would use the testing database to develop and validate his new code to ensure real data would not be corrupted, and his work not be detected. He wrote his approach for circumventing the security traps in the existing system and breaking into the database.

When they met, Steve handed a manila folder containing the document to Hank as he said hello.

"What's this?"

Steve explained the document's contents.

Hank returned them, "Just report verbally. I want nothing in writing. If I lost them, and a hacker found them, they could use the information to steal from the company."

Steve thought that's improbable, but accepted the returned documents and briefed Hank on his work.

When he finished, Hank just said "Great work," as he handed him the promised envelope. "It's none of my business, but the income you're receiving is taxable, and I'm not withholding any amount for income tax payments. You'll have to do that yourself, but it might be tricky to explain the extra income to the IRS. Do what other consultants do to avoid taxes."

"What's that?"

"They send the money to an offshore Cayman Islands account. The IRS never discovers their illegal transactions."

"How do I do that?"

"Here's information on a bank I use. Read the instructions on how to access the account. Sign this card, and I'll set it up for you. When it's operational, I'll wire your earnings to the account."

Steve agreed.

At the end of the five week development period he explained to Hank how he successfully accessed and charged the fake user IDs account. Steve now had $8,000 in the off shore account.

Hank said, "That sounds good. But I'd need to see it in operation." Hank, handed him his personal card listing his home address, "Come to my house in Bethany Beach next Sunday morning at 9:00 and show it to me. It's in a gated community, north of the village. I've written the gate password on the card. Drive to the ocean, my house faces the beach. I'll leave a garage door open so you can park out of sight and we can be discreet."

Steve drove into an almost deserted Bethany Beach on a cold November morning. Steve's first view of the three-story, rectangular five-thousand square foot, gray-siding home shocked him. While he knew he could never afford this level of luxury, he hoped his association with Hank would help him move from a rented room into his own home. The first floor had no living quarters, only a three-car enclosed garage. Steve carried a briefcase with his laptop and rang the doorbell on a small enclosure in the center with stairs to the second floor.

Hank escorted him into the study. A coffee pot steamed on a table next to a plate of donuts. He noticed Steve's hungry eyes, and said "Have some."

Steve did, devouring one in two bites and setting two more donuts and a steaming full mug of coffee on the table. He placed his laptop next to the donuts and turned it on. After Steve logged into Liberty Credit's account, Hank asked, "Can the access be traced to my house?"

"No, I'm going through a covert route that places your access point somewhere in Chile."

Steve explained the execution of the program and sent $46 to the provided offshore account.

Hank opened and logged on to his PC. "I'll check to see if the transfer was successful." After a minute, Hank read the account balance $10,046. "Congratulations, it worked. I'll transfer the reward to your Cayman account." After the payment had moved, Hank said, "Check it now."

Steve beamed when he read $100,000 had been added.

"What will you do with the money?"

"I'm not sure. If I spend it, the IRS might ask for proof of income. I'll just leave it there for a while."

"Wise move. Do you like my beach house?"

"Yes."

"Do you want to own one in Delaware or in the Caribbean?"

"Of course, but I can't afford one, even with the $100,000."

"Steve, you should have transferred $100 million instead of only $46."

"If I made a large withdrawal, the bank's IT security software would have flagged it, and we'd get caught."

"Not if you kept the withdrawals at less than a hundred dollars."

"That would take years. What are you proposing?"

"To make us both rich. You've already violated the law by sheltering your income offshore without paying taxes. The penalty isn't much larger if you steal a fortune for yourself. You'll never have to work again. No one has discovered your withdrawal program. Why should they in the future?"

Steve, shocked at the proposition, remained quiet for a few minutes wondering should he go for it and retire or return to his old life with a large bank account he couldn't spend.

When Hank saw a smile develop on Steve's face and his eyes sparkle, he said, "I can get us false IDs so no one can find us if we disappear overseas."

"Let's go for it."

"How long will it take you to write and test the code to withdraw one billion in small amounts over a month's time and deposit them into one hundred and twenty offshore accounts? Your cut will be twenty percent of the total."

"Three weeks." Steve thought he might do it in less time, but he knew underestimating software completion time was a major cause of project failure.

"Good, in the meantime I'll set up the offshore accounts and get us fake passports and identities. There is one change to the scenario you used in your program. Construct the program using a month's difference between the transaction and billing date for the first customer. Structure the billing dates for the other customers to equal the first customers billing date plus add a random time chosen from between one day and a month. That will avoid a fixed pattern under your original system that could be detected by someone investigating the company's losses."

Saturday, December 5, 2009

Steve parked in Hank's garage. They greeted each other briefly and entered Hank's kitchen.

Steve placed the laptop on the table, logged in, and accessed his withdrawal program. He pressed the return key, the program, charging Liberty Credit card customers, variable amounts, less than $100 but more than $50 during the Christmas shopping season, so as not to alert the IT system of an abnormal number of transactions.

Hank asked, "It's started. You sure we won't be detected?"

"Yes, the return command executes the program on multiple overseas servers, one for each deposit account. We used fake overseas IP addresses, untraceable to this laptop, to execute each program." Steve paused for a sip of coffee. "In four weeks we'll be rich."

"Then let's meet at my beach house in a month, to see how successful we were. I'll have our fake passports and airline reservations. You'll tell me then where you want to go." He handed Steve a list of countries without U.S. extradition treaties.

Steve gloated, driving home. In four weeks he'd be worth over $200 million, which Maria, his bitch of an ex-wife couldn't touch.

Chapter 5 Margaret's Retirement

Thursday, December 10, 2009

Paul retrieved the mail and opened the first of their royalty checks which would be paid in six-month intervals. He grinned when he read they had sold over two hundred thousand books. The $3 royalties per book paid off the advance of $250,000, and even minus their agent's fifteen percent cut of $90,000 left them with a check of $260,000.

Paul, like a child, didn't want to wait the three hours before Margaret returned home. He wouldn't let himself call her as he hoped to see the look on her face when she read the letter.

When Margaret opened the front door, he greeted her with a cold glass of champagne and an opened envelope containing the letter on a silver tray. "Here, you'll enjoy both."

"What are we celebrating?" Margaret asked.

Paul remained silent as she drank the champagne and retrieved the letter from the envelope.

Margaret had an infectious look when she read the letter. She pretended to pout as she said, "I'm jealous you always get to read the good news first." She put her glass on the foyer table and slid into his arms and kissed him like they were teenagers. "Are we rich?"

"Yes, since we saved the advance. And we were financially secure even before this letter, given our pensions. If these checks continue and we don't spend them, we'll be excessively rich."

"Paul, you and I don't have the lifestyles to spend it on a good time. I've been thinking since the abandoned homes case has ended, work is boring. I'm not only jealous of you opening the mail first, but I miss spending the day with you. This check convinces me, I'll retire. Is that okay with you?" Margaret said.

"Yes, I'd rather spend time with you than play tennis or golf without you." Paul said.

"Good, you should still play sports with your male friends. It'll keep you young and virile," she said, with a sensuous wink.

"If we're together, we could write the next book in less time than we took for the first," Paul said.

"And we could make love any time." Margaret took his hand and walked him into the bedroom.

While both cuddled in bed, smiling at each other, Paul asked, "Hon, when are you going to tell Lt. Nelson, you will be spending every morning in bed, making love to your husband?"

"I'll talk to him tomorrow and turn in my retirement papers, but I won't use your words. You should be careful what you promise. I might hold you to it, which could be embarrassing for you."

"Be nice to Lt. Nelson. I'm playing golf with him and Senator Downing on Sunday."

"Okay."

Detective Margaret Hoffman knocked on Lt. Nelson's open door at 9:00 a.m., and cheerfully handed him a manila folder containing the resignation.

"Margaret, you look happy this morning," Nelson said as he read the document. He looked up and stared at her, "Are you resigning because the Senator and I took $10 from Paul and his partner last Sunday?"

"No, we have enough money to lose $10 every weekend and still live well for the rest of our lives. Walt, you're a great boss, but the job is getting dull since the skeleton case. I decided it's time to relax and spend more time with Paul."

"Too bad. I learned over the weekend they've promoted me to Captain. You're my choice to replace me. My job is always exciting."

Shocked, Margaret realized she didn't expect to hear this. She contemplated having Nelson's job. If she was still a Marine, she knew she'd take it. Then her potential promotions motivated her performance. But she had left the Marines years ago, had enough medals, and retired as a Colonel. Margaret knew she had a different life now, and although tempted she said, "Thanks, I'm flattered. If I hadn't met Paul, I'd take the job. Now I'm sure I want to quit and spend more time with him. I won't object to his playing golf with you and the Senator."

"Won't you two get tired of each other spending all that time together?"

"You're not bored with your wife, Barbara."

"No. I still get excited going home at night and waking up in the morning next to her, and we married many decades ago. But we don't spend every hour of every day together."

"I'm sure we won't either. He'll still play golf and tennis. Besides, we have decided to write another book. Writers work for hours alone before they show their co-author their work."

"I'm surprised you kept working this long. What's the book's topic?"

"Don't know yet."

"Will you leave in two weeks?"

Margaret paused before answering, realizing two weeks wasn't long enough for Nelson to find replacements for her and for himself, "Since you're taking a new job, I'll stay for four weeks to make sure we have a smooth transition."

"Thanks."

Margaret asked her two detective staff, Helen Jenson and Bill Norse, to meet in her office at 9:30. She also called Ben Johnson, head forensic investigator at Troop 4 in Georgetown, and asked him to attend.

When they had assembled, Helen asked, "Do we have another case?"

"No, continue our current investigations. I came from Nelson's office where I submitted my resignation, which he accepted. I'll be leaving in four weeks. The three of you are well qualified to solve our open cases."

"We're surprised you stayed this long, with your marriage and success as an author," Bill said.

"So am I. I love the job, but don't need the money. I want to spend more time with Paul. We're looking for a topic for another book," Margaret said.

"Perhaps you and Paul can help us solve the next big one. However, I expect nothing as big as the abandoned homes skeleton case to occur for a long time in Sussex County," Helen said.

Just as they ended the meeting Lt. Nelson walked into Margaret's office announcing, "I've talked to Paul, and the VFW hall. The retirement party will be on Sunday, January 17."

"I have no choice?"

"No you still work for me! I hope to get you and Paul drunk."

"No chance."

Chapter 6 Protecting Hank

Sunday afternoon, January 3, 2010

Hank continued to smile as he watched the drugged Steve Haven sleep.

He poured another glass of Cabernet Sauvignon to replace the wine that had warmed as the drug took effect rendering Steve unconscious. He looked at the comatose body and finished his drink. After logging on to the laptop he accessed Steve's Cayman Islands account, and transferred ninety-five percent to his own off-shore accounts. He left five percent to confuse the police about his involvement in the crime.

To remove the electronic hardware evidence, he carried the laptop to his garage and placed it on a workbench and took it apart. He feared placing it in the garbage, since an electronics-smart individual might find the laptop, access the files, and notify the police. He used a vice to crush the disk drive, memory, and CPU. Hank placed the flammable components in a foot-high steel drum, doused them with gasoline, and walked out to his back yard. He took a butane lighter, aimed it over the gasoline fumes and ignited the mixture of gas and computer parts. The non-metallic elements caught fire or melted becoming useless and Hank hoped untraceable.

After the fire burned out, and the residue cooled, he placed the ashes in a water-tight black plastic bag, carried it into the garage, and picked up a shovel. After looking at each of his neighbor's homes finding all but one dark and empty, he walked to a group of five Crepe Myrtle trees in the backyard. His house blocked the view from the one lit home and he dug a three-foot deep hole. He retrieved the bag of the untraceable computer parts and buried it.

Hank went to his bedroom and dressed in warm hiking clothes. After putting on gloves he carried Steve's body to his garage, and placed it in the trunk of Steve's car. Hank checked the gas tank gauge and finding the tank half full, said to the sleeping Steve, "That should be enough to get you where I want."

He opened his garage door, and drove to an abandoned home with an old barn on an empty stretch of road in Clarksville, Delaware. He walked over the dry ground and examined both the home and the barn. As expected, he found them empty. After opening the large door to the barn he returned to Steve's car smiling and drove it into the barn. Hank opened the trunk and carried Steve's body to the driver's side and placed him in front of the wheel in a driving position. He slowly poured half a fifth of Black Label Scotch in Steve's mouth, most of which dribbled out of his mouth onto his face, neck and chest. He spilled the rest over Steve's clothes.

Hank turned on the car's ignition. He left the barn with the door closed, and walked to the house. After staying there for an hour he returned to the garage, covered his face with a wet towel and examined Steve. He wasn't breathing. So Hank felt safe and started the eight-mile walk to Bethany Beach.

Hank arrived at his beach house tired but refreshed after disposing of Steve. He knew he would never get caught. He showered then watched a movie on Netflix.

He left at 7:30 a.m. the next day, arrived at his office a half-hour later, and began an uneventful day. Hank and his staff worked on closing the books for the 2009 calendar year. No one had alerted the company of any illegal withdrawal throughout December.

Chapter 7 Discovery of the Crime

Friday, January 8, 2010

Jeanne Baker noticed an unfamiliar entry on her December credit card bill, a charge of $78 from the Seaside Boutique in Rehoboth Beach, Delaware on December 9, 2009. She called the credit card company's help desk informing them she was in California at the time. They forwarded the message to Joann Cummings, Information Technology Director.

With Steve Haven, the Database Administrator (DBA) not scheduled to return from vacation until Monday, January 18, 2010, she did the research herself and voided the transaction, which she believed was a simple case of credit card fraud. She canceled Baker's current credit card and issued a new card, standard company procedure to end illegal purchases. In the next two days she received similar help desk references from 112 individuals. While a small number for their thirty-five million customers, Joann became suspicious and notified her boss, Ed Davis the Director of Operations that she believed a fraud attack of grave proportions might have started.

Per company policy, Liberty Credit Inc. did not call the police or notify the U.S. Secret Service or the Federal Trade Commission (FTC) at the beginning of a credit card fraud event.

Joann Cummings met with Ed Davis three days after the first help desk call. Before the meeting Joann developed a summary table of the 342 illegal transactions valued at $16,360. She handed it to Ed. "I find three similarities between them. They're all less than $100 and more than $50.

No customers made more than one transaction. They were randomly distributed throughout the U.S."

"I'll call our IT Security Manager, George Belford, to join us and give us his opinion," Davis said. Once he arrived, Joann handed him the table and explained her findings.

"This sounds like an attack by a professional hacking group. They know how to avoid making the IT system send out alerts and stop processing the phony charges," Belford said.

"How do we stop them before they steal over $100,000?" Joann asked.

"For small amounts of credit card fraud, we remove the charge from the customer's account and ask our insurance company for reimbursement. If the fraud is large, I will report it to the FTC and open a formal investigation. I'll work with your DBA to execute the queries I need to analyze the theft. Is this the only fraud impacting Liberty this week?" Belford said.

"Here's the problem. Steve Haven went on a sailing vacation in the Caribbean and hasn't answered his cell phone. George, you'll work with me. There were one hundred and twenty-four other cases, where our automatic controls worked and stopped them, but these transactions were the only ones reported by our customers through the help desk," Joann said.

"Let me get started. I'll need access to all the help desk calls and the full fraud data."

"You'll get them this afternoon," Joann said.

George Belford walked into Joann's office with a summary report of his investigation the next morning.

"Before you start, it's getting more serious. We have had over 1,200 help desk calls for illegal charges of $91,242 as of today." Joann said.

"The criminals must have been well organized to coordinate an attack this large that took place over a long time period. There are only three ways the criminals could have gotten the credit card numbers and their passwords. First, phishing, by emailing a phony offer mimicking a well-known establishment to obtain the naïve customer's ID and password. Second, by collecting information on unsecure internet transactions. Third, by placing physical devices on ATMs, gas pumps, and so on, to collect credit card information, undetectable by a customer when they make a legitimate charge. The criminals may have used one or all three techniques to amass IDs and passwords over a long time period. They then executed them in a short period in small amounts so we wouldn't find out until they had finished. They might perform the same fraud on other companies. We should alert the FTC, so they can notify other credit card institutions of the risk of a similar attack," Belford said.

"You don't think someone hacked our database and downloaded the IDs and passwords?" Joann asked.

"It's always possible, but unlikely. We have strong security protection. I examined that possibility and found no evidence of hacking. However, it doesn't mean it didn't happen. We'll need to hire an outside computer fraud investigation firm to audit our system to make sure."

"How expensive is that?"

"Very. I suggest we wait a few weeks. If it stops that will confirm my theory. However, I recommend we change every customer's password and card numbers as a precaution. We should keep the attack secret from our customers to avoid panic. We might want to wait to tell the FTC after we have changed all the credit cards." Belford said.

"I agree. I'll ensure we mail new cards with new passwords asking our customers to activate the cards. We'll give them a week. If they don't notify us, I'll mail them again with a new deadline," Joann stated, feeling relieved that Belford's proposal should stop the bleeding.

"Let's get Ed Davis's approval before starting," Belford said.

They met with Davis late in the afternoon, and Belford explained his analysis and recommendations.

"That might be expensive given we don't have an estimate of the size of the problem. Joann, did you issue new credit cards to those who complained of the incorrect charges?" Davis asked.

"Yes."

"Let's wait for two days before we issue new credit cards to all our customers. If the calls stop, we won't need to react further. If they increase, I'll approve Belford's recommendation."

At their Thursday meeting, Davis said, "I hear you have bad news."

"Yes, the number of help desk calls exceeds ten thousand, with a total value over $750,000 in fraudulent charges. Our help desk is swamped. We can't wait to carry out Belford's recommendations," Joann said.

"Go ahead. I'll need a cost estimate by tomorrow to explain to my boss," Davis said.

"We're restricting the card reissue to our 30 million U.S. customers. We haven't seen the same fraud with our foreign customers. That will reduce costs," Belford said.

"We have set up the program and alerted the staff to prepare a mass mailing. We'll start as soon as I can get to my office," Joann said. "Finally, we should tell the FTC of the problem."

"I agree, otherwise the newspapers will kill us. Let me know if the rate of credit card fraud increases," Davis said with a frown on his face.

PART 4: INVESTIGATING THE CRIME

Chapter 8 Margaret's Retirement Party

Sunday, January 17, 2010

A full moon adorned the sky above the Indian River Bay creating great views of the horizon as the party started at 7:00 p.m. The cold weather created clear air and beautiful views.

Over one hundred guests attended Margaret's retirement party. Most of the Delaware State Police assigned to the Georgetown barracks, twenty of Paul's tennis and golf friends, and Paul's children came to wish her well.

Walt Nelson had arranged a buffet with fish, chicken, and roast beef, salads, rolls, and vegetables. He had also set up an open bar for the guests. Since so many troopers attended, he assumed the guests would have arranged for a designated driver to avoid accidents and arrests.

Margaret and Paul enjoyed the party, drinking only two glasses of wine, not wanting the efficient and courteous Ocean View police to stop them on the short trip home. They switched to sparkling water even though Captain Nelson tried to ply them with martinis.

Around 10:00 when everyone at their table had left or occupied the dance floor except Margaret, Paul, Senator George Downing, and Captain Nelson, Nelson asked, "Have you chosen the next book's topic?"

"No, we're in no rush," Paul said.

"On Thursday I learned of a major crime that might interest you," Senator Downing said, looking at Margaret and Paul to gauge their curiosity. "The Liberty Credit Card Company reported they discovered over twenty thousand unauthorized credit card expenditures by their clients. By law the Federal Trade Commission has to take the lead in the investigation.

"The FTC called me to let me know about the crime, so I could prepare a statement to our State's citizens, as soon as the crime becomes public. Since the FTC has limited resources, they cannot conduct a large-scale investigation and asked me for advice on choosing an organization to help. I naturally told them the Delaware State Police were uniquely qualified because of their work with our State's large number of financial institutions. The FTC accepted my recommendations." The Senator never forgot that the State Police provided contributions and votes in all his elections.

"Margaret, if you hadn't resigned you could work on this case, but you and Paul can still write about it," Lt. Nelson said. "As of today, the FTC informed me Liberty Credit doesn't understand how it occurred. Helen Jenson will be the lead detective."

Margaret and Paul glanced at each other. It seemed the Senator might have solved their problem of the next book's topic.

"How much did they take?" Margaret, the now ex-detective, asked.

"It's over a million two and growing. I'll tell Helen I've authorized her to brief both of you on the crime. I saw her and her husband leave an hour ago. She said something about not wanting to leave her children alone," Lt. Nelson said.

"Glad Helen is the lead. We had a great time working together for three years when she reported to me," Margaret said.

The day after the retirement party, Paul said, "I hope you don't tire of spending all your time with me."

"I won't for at least six months. We have to start the book on the Liberty Credit Card crime and spend a month in Greece on our honeymoon. Boredom seems unlikely. Thanks for the Greek breakfast. I'll cook you a Greek dinner in a few days and call Helen on Monday to ask her when she can brief us on the credit card investigation."

48

On Monday with the phone set to speaker mode. "Helen, it's me and Paul."

"Nelson told me to expect a call from both of you. We took over the case on Friday, so I don't have much to tell you. Give me a week to gather information so a meeting won't waste time," Helen said.

Paul said, "That's fine. Would you like to come over for brunch on Sunday at 9:00 ?"

"Sounds good as long as you serve Margaret's French toast."

Margaret opened the door, and the aroma of bacon and coffee reached Helen.

"Smells great. I'm glad I came," Helen said.

She handed Margaret her coat. "Paul is in the kitchen. I'm going to join him to cook the French toast," Margaret said.

They walked past the table, set with Margaret's finest white bone china. When they entered the kitchen, Margaret said, "How do you like being the boss?"

"The job is different from what I thought it entailed. It has too much paperwork and status report preparation for my boss."

"You'll get used to it. Let your staff do the boring detective work. Do you want to brief us while we eat?" Margaret asked.

"Yes, please give me some coffee first."

While Margaret cooked the French toast, Paul served the coffee to Helen and placed the bacon on the table.

Helen started talking, "The Liberty Credit Card case is the largest financial crime Delaware and perhaps the U.S. has experienced. When I visited the company, they told us twenty-five thousand credit card holders had their cards defrauded. The total value was over one point five million dollars. On Friday, a week later the number of card holder impacted reached seventy-five thousand and the fraud rose to over five million.

"Is the company cooperating with you?" Paul asked.

"Yes, but they'd like our help in stopping the fraud, before solving the crime. I have told them catching the perpetrators is the best way to stop it. However, Liberty's theory of how the crime occurred makes it almost impossible to catch the perpetrators. Their IT Security head, George Belford, has convinced the company's management that the criminals stole credit card IDs over a long period of time and then used them in a short period to defraud the company."

"Did you talk to management?" Margaret asked.

"Yes, I talked to the VP for Finance, Hank Strong. He agrees with Belford, saying their internal security procedures would prevent a hacking of their credit card database. Their CEO, Jim Regan, is not convinced and said, confidentially, he might engage an external IT forensic firm to investigate the events. Please don't mention that to anyone. He doesn't want to alert any employees who might have participated in a fraud that he suspects an alternative explanation for the crime."

"We won't," Paul said, as Margaret nodded her head in agreement.

Helen spent the rest of her visit discussing details of the crime and left ninety minutes after she had arrived. Helen told them Liberty had started replacing the credit cards of the domestic card holders with new card numbers to end the fraud. The company reasoned if the withdrawals stopped, it would show that credit card numbers and passwords had been stolen and there was no hacking of the credit card database.

Helen agreed to tell them everything new about the case. Unfortunately, there wasn't any new information for the next four weeks.

Chapter 9 Planning the Honeymoon

Sunday, January 24, 2010

Paul's friend Professor Kostas Canakis, was a retired Archeology Professor at Binghamton University, where both used to teach. He and his wife Sally called Paul and Margaret on Skype. Margaret answered the call on her PC.

"You both look happy. Marriage must agree with you," Kostas said.

"It does, but we're waiting to hear your recommendations for our month in Greece," Margaret said.

Sally said, "I've just emailed you both a map of Athens, the Cyclades Islands, and a proposed travel itinerary in Greece. Use it to follow Kostas' discussion."

Margaret displayed the map on her PC.

Kostas began, "I recommend you stay in Athens for four days. Since Margaret has been to Athens many times, we'll let you two enjoy the beginning of the honeymoon without me. On day one I advise little touring so you can recover from the seven hour time difference. The second day you should visit the Acropolis, the Parthenon, and the Acropolis museum. You'll both decide what to do on the next two days."

"I can't wait. Always wanted to go to Athens, but I didn't expect to have Margaret as a tour guide," Paul said.

Kostas continued, "Then take a fast ferry at the port of Piraeus to Crete. Stay there for at least a week and begin a tour of the islands, north of Crete with a ferry trip to Santorini. We'll meet you in Mykonos, where you'll stay at our home. After you've seen all you can

Greece

in Mykonos, we'll take our car on a ferry back to Athens and we'll tour northern Greece including Delphi and Mount Olympus. Before you leave Greece, we'll drive through the Peloponnese and visit Corinth and Mycenae, home of Agamemnon, leader of the Greeks in the Trojan War. That's where Prince Paris of Troy seduced Helen, the sister-in-law of Agamemnon. When Helen and Paris fled to Troy, the Trojan War started."

"We have at least ten Greek guide books. We'll study their mythology before we fly to Greece. We don't want to be fooled by a Greek archeology professor," Paul said.

"Don't worry, he'll tell the truth. I'll be there. I feel sympathy for Helen for falling in love with a Greek and being whisked off to Troy, like my Greek took me to Mykonos. But, since I wasn't married at the time of my seduction, I didn't cause a war between the U.S. and Greece," Sally said.

Chapter 10 Discovery of the Body

Friday, February 19, 2010

On a warm day over sixty degrees in February, six weeks after Steve Haven's disappearance, Ken Staples drove his family in a minivan from Falls Church, Virginia to their rural house in Clarksville, Delaware, to begin work on their extensive cold weather vegetable garden.

Ken, his wife, and two teenage sons entered the winterized house looking forward to a gardening weekend. Ken turned on the water, heat, and then asked his sons to build a fire in the living room to chase away the cold damp air. His wife closed the refrigerator door and turned it on. She unpacked the coolers and made a buffet of bread, deli cheeses, meats, and condiments.

The men changed into their overalls and sweaters. They left the house, returned to the minivan, and unloaded the seedlings they had raised at their Falls Church home. The plants included the cold weather and frost resistant types such as arugula, butter lettuce, Romaine lettuce, red leaf lettuce, Brussels sprouts, broccoli, and spinach. The father planned to use their small tractor to turn the ground for planting. The two sons were responsible for removing the dead stalks and cleaning the asparagus patch. They would join their father when they finished.

They walked toward the barn where they stored the farming tools. Ken, surprised, noticed a broken lock on the barn's door. He hoped no one had stolen the tractor and tools. When he opened the door, he saw a car. He glanced around and discovered his tools remained untouched. Ken noticed a motionless head in the front seat. He didn't open the driver's side door repulsed by the stench of the decaying body. He told his kids to stay outside and dialed 911 on his cell phone.

Within thirty minutes, the lead detective Helen Jenson and the Forensics Unit arrived from State Trooper Barrack's 4 in Georgetown.

"I'm Detective Helen Jenson. Did you call 911?" she asked.

"Yes, Ken Staples. I'm the owner."

"Tell me what happened," Jenson said.

Staples told her why they were there and his discovery of the body.

"Did you touch anything in the barn?"

"No I didn't even open the car door. I couldn't stand the stench."

"Good. You can't take anything from the barn, until we've finished investigating the yard, the barn, and removed the corpse."

"Don't worry. We're not going into the barn until you take the body and the odor disappears."

"We'll need your family's fingerprints to eliminate them from others we find. We'll tow the car to our barracks, removing much of the odor," Helen explained. "Forensics will take pictures, recording fingerprints and collect potential evidence. They'll start outside and complete the canvas before entering the barn. When they finish their examination, they'll turn the corpse over to the Chief Medical Examiner. Then the barn is yours."

"How long will it take him?" Ken Staples asked.

"At least four hours."

The forensics staff didn't touch the body. They saw an open bottle of scotch on the passenger seat. They accessed the DMV files and found Steve Haven owned the car.

Detective Jenson addressed the Chief Medical Examiner. "Dr. Hodges, after we complete the forensics investigation, we'll move the car out of the barn so you have room to examine the body."

"I want to see it before you move the car and the body becomes dislodged."

"Go ahead," Detective Jenson said nodding her head.

Dr. Hodges directed his technicians to photograph the body. Upon seeing the bloated decomposed corpse, he decided to bag it and start the autopsy at his lab in Wilmington.

The technicians found a wallet in the corpse's pants pocket. The driver's license confirmed Haven's identity. From the evidence in the barn, Dr. Hodges suspected carbon monoxide poisoning or acute alcohol ingestion as the cause of death.

After examining the body in Wilmington, noting the cherry red skin color, the mucus membranes, internal organs; signs of congestion in the lungs; and hemorrhages in the heart muscle, he concluded carbon monoxide poisoning as the cause of death aided by alcohol. Hodges initially did not state whether the death was accidental or murder.

Detective Jenson noted someone had forcibly opened the barn door and had carefully parked the car. They found none of the tools used for the break-in. She believed a drunk couldn't park the car without hitting something. Thus, she suspected a second person had murdered Haven. She told her theory to Dr. Hodges, after he called her to report the autopsy results. He changed his findings to death by murder.

Saturday, the next day, after finishing a round of golf, Walt Nelson, Senator Downing, and Paul drove to Margaret's home for a late lunch. They decided to talk about recent developments in the Liberty Credit Card case there, rather than on the golf course.

Margaret greeted them at the door and handed them their favorite beverage. She led them to the sunroom where she offered them a buffet. They discussed the golf match and the honeymooner's trip to Greece. When they finished eating, Paul served coffee.

With a cup in his hand Paul said, "Margaret and I are thrilled about writing our next true crime book on the Liberty Credit Card case."

"You made a wise choice and picked a unique crime," Walt said. He then summarized his knowledge of the crime, saying Liberty's Operations Chief briefed him yesterday. He handed Margaret and Paul timelines of the credit card fraud events. "They update this table daily to stay current. There are now over 1.3 million customers complaining of illegal charges of over a hundred million."

"We saw smaller figures on the national news last night," Margaret said. Looking at Paul, "We'll start to outline the book tomorrow."

"That's only part of it," Walt said.

"What do you mean?" Downing asked.

"Detective Jenson received a call to investigate a corpse found in a barn in Clarksville yesterday. It was Steve Haven, the Database Administrator for the credit card database. She and Dr. Hodges ruled his death murder." Walt stared at everyone, his gaze staying with each one for a few seconds.

"Are the Credit Card crime and the murder connected?" Downing asked.

"Jenson didn't know until she questioned the victim's boss, Joann Cummings. She said hearing of his death shocked her. When he didn't return on January 18, 2010, she thought he had gone missing on a January vacation. She stated that the Human Resources department had called his ex-wife, children, and friends, but no one knew what happened to him." Walt stopped talking for a half a minute to let them absorb his words.

"Steve Haven hadn't gone anywhere. Ken Staples found the body in an unheated barn, with the outside temperature averaging near freezing for several weeks. Dr. Hodges couldn't give a time of death," Nelson said.

"Very suspicious," Paul said, jotting down a summary of Nelson's points.

After the golfers left, Paul started filling the dishwasher with the dirty dishes and packing and placing the leftovers in the refrigerator. He told Margaret, "Sit down and relax. You prepared the food, I'll clean up."

"I like our cooking and cleaning rule, but I can't relax, after hearing about Steve Haven's murder. This case could put us in danger, just like in the abandoned homes skeleton case."

"The murder surprised me. I just thought it was a white-collar crime. Anyway I still think we should write our next book about it."

"So do I, but we should take precautions. I've sent a lot of bad guys away. Anyone could decide to assuage their need for revenge by killing you or me. That is why our address and phone numbers are kept private."

"What other types of precautions? We are already careful in our daily life and book tours."

"You should learn how to use a gun to protect yourself and me if I'm incapacitated during an attack."

"I've been thinking the same thing for a while. When do I start?"

"Tomorrow. I'll take you to a gun range in Georgetown."

She trained Paul in using her gun, a Glock 20, and a hunting rifle. After two weeks, Margaret realized he had more skill with the rifle than the handgun.

Paul enjoyed learning how to shoot and care for Margaret's guns. They practiced three times a week for the next three weeks. After just two weeks, Margaret said, "Paul, you're almost as good as I am at using a rifle, and I had all those years of Marine Corps and police practice."

"Haven's murder motivated me. I don't want to be defenseless if we get attached."

"Tomorrow, we'll have you apply for a carry permit for the Glock. It's no use knowing how to shoot if you don't have a gun when you're being shot at."

Saturday, March 6, 2010

At 3:00 p.m. George Belford pulled up in front of Hank's Middletown house and parked in the garage, so no one could see his car on the street.

Hank met George at the door and handed him a glass of ice tea. "Did you enjoy the drive north?"

"It's long. Why do you keep this house?"

"I love it."

Belford gazed at the four acres sounding the house covered with apple, cherry, pear, plum trees and blueberry bushes, and said with approval. "I can see why. You'll have something better in a warmer climate soon."

"You're not trying to guess where I'm going. It's classified."

"No. But I doubt if anyone having as much money as we will would move to a colder area."

"I hear only what the executives tell me about the investigation. What's going on in the trenches?" Hank asked.

George remembered Hank liked that phrase ever since they served together in the early 1970s in Vietnam. Hank, an officer, had befriended George, and helped him in his career. George, who never married, had two sisters: one was Hank's deceased wife and the other who lived in Florida.

George summarized the events. "As of noon, the impacts include nine million customers and claims of six-hundred million. Since the daily customer numbers peaked on February 1, and are steadily declining, the executives believe my analysis that a gang collected IDs and passwords over at least a year and waited for the short Christmas shopping season to use them."

"Good," Hank said.

"I'm sure we won't get caught as long as we don't do it again."

"We won't. Two hundred million should be enough for you."

"It is. Hank, you'll survive on your share, not being stuck in this 'puny little' 5,000 square foot residence."

"Are you worried about anything?" Hank asked.

"Steve Haven and Cummings."

"Yes, it's too bad someone discovered Haven in February. Who plants crops then? I hoped he'd return to the beach in May after the last frost. By then Liberty Credit would have fired us, not for fraud, but for not having strong financial and ID controls. We'd have left the country with no worries of being investigated for Haven's death."

"A detective, Helen Jenson, had been questioning the staff about Haven's connections to the Liberty Credit Card crime."

"What did you tell her?" Hank asked.

"The same as everyone else, including what his boss, Joann Cummings, told Jenson. He drank too much and didn't have the skills or patience to take part in the fraud."

"Did she believe you?"

"Not sure. Jenson doesn't show emotion when she asks questions," George said.

Hank pondered this answer wondering if the State Police were smart enough to solve the case. "Did she ask you who you thought might have killed him?"

"I told her, I didn't know him that well, so I had no idea. But I hope others did."

"Good."

"Hank, you had to murder him. He wouldn't have kept quiet. He'd have bragged about his role in the embezzlement and his wealth to a hooker when he was drunk," George said.

"His discovery might not be all bad. It might intimidate other employees from talking, if they think they could be murdered. How should we handle Joann Cummings?" Hank asked, "I remember her as being smart, personable, and athletic. She plays tennis with other employees, including a few executives."

"While our management, the FTC, and the insurance companies

buy my story, she doesn't. Says we should look into database hacking or internal fraud. I'm concerned that with her executive contacts, she might convince them to look into other areas. If they do, we may get caught. I don't think we can intimidate her."

"Are you still practicing your range skills?"

"Yes," George said, smiling.

"You might have to use them. Not with your gun. I'll find an untraceable one on the dark web."

"How much cleaning up will I have to do before I can access my money?"

"It depends on where the investigation goes, as we agreed. At least take care of them." Hank handed George a piece of paper with an off-shore account and password on it. "I've deposited $2 million. You might need the money to finance your tasks."

Chapter 11 The Liberty Credit Card Debacle

Monday, March 8, 2010

Liberty Credit began in 1985 and flourished with the growth of the credit card industry. It survived the financial crisis of 2007 and 2008. Its 2009 volume exceeded $85 billion, generating $1.4 billion in profit. Total cash and cash equivalent assets equaled $15 billion. Employment totaled 11,000.

The U.S. has five major U.S. credit card companies: VISA, MasterCard, American Express, Discover, and Liberty Credit. Their operations comprise two functions: organizations that issue the credit cards and those that run the computer networks facilitating the transactions between seller and buyer. VISA and MasterCard separate the two functions. They own the transactions networks, while the card issuers, the banks, work directly with the customers. American Express, Discover, and Liberty Credit combine both functions in one organization. Liberty Credit, Inc. had a unique business structure enabling Hank Strong to commit the massive embezzlement. While it's difficult to steal from Liberty Credit, it's impossible from VISA and MasterCard since they do not maintain account balances. The banking customers hold the accounts.

Hank knew his theft would not destroy the company, but put it through difficult times. He didn't care if his Liberty stock became worthless. It was nothing compared to what he had deposited in his foreign accounts.

Hank hired the national accounting firm of Berkley and Jones to begin the audit and analysis of the company's financial health. They started two months after the cardholder Jeanne Baker reported the first fraudulent charge. Normally, Liberty never hired auditors until the fiscal year ended on March 31. However, Hank's boss, CEO Jim Regan wanted them engaged.

At the first meeting, on Monday, March 8, 2010, with Andrew Smithson of Berkley and Jones, Hank described the $768 million credit card fraud which now involved over ten million card holders. He repeated George Belford's explanation that the criminals had amassed at least ten million IDs and passwords and used them over a thirty-day period. Hank said, "We've only counted those who called the help desk. We want your firm to identify every customer who has been defrauded. Many customers pay their bills without looking at them. The case of the first credit card transaction fraud took place on December 4, 2009, while the last reported fraud occurred on January 2, 2010."

"Tomorrow morning you'll meet with Joann Cummings, our Director of the credit card database and applications. She will give you historical transaction data and describe the credit card IT operations. When you are ready to access the data, give her your instructions, and she'll make sure they're implemented."

Andrew Smithson met Joann in her office. "Thanks for coming," Joann said. "We need help in finding out how much they took. I can't imagine how they did it." She noticed his clean-cut handsome look and his three-piece dark gray suit. A typical CPA uniform, she thought, too conservative for me.

"Joann, I can help you with the first item, but according to Hank Strong they're satisfied with Belford the security guy's theory."

"There are other plausible explanations. Like someone hacking our ID and password data, or internal fraud."

"Might be true. But I'm only hired to find out the total

company's loss."

"Too bad," Joann said with disdain.

"Hank Strong told me you'd run a few jobs to help me."

"Correct, what can I do for you?"

Andrew handed her four stapled pages. "If you make these calculations and produce the reports, you'll answer Hank's question." When she reached for the pages, Andrew noticed the beautiful blond haired woman wasn't wearing a wedding ring.

Joann read it, smiling as she absorbed the equations and rationale. "This seems too simple."

"It is. First, add the credit charges against each establishment by all customers from December 4, 2009, to January 2, 2010. Second, find out the revenue Liberty Credit paid each establishment over that period. The difference will tell us the amount of fraud committed against each of them since they never received the money from those transactions. Adding up these differences will tell us how much Liberty lost."

"One of my database programmers will write the SQL code. Come back at 1:00. We will review it together," Joann said. When he shook hands to leave, Joann noticed Andrew's bare ring finger. Joann wondered if she had held his hand too long before he left her office.

Joann ate her chicken salad sandwich and drank bottled water at her desk while reviewing the SQL program. Satisfied, she waited for Andrew, wondering about the attractive accountant. She lamented that in her job, the only young eligible men worked for her and the company had strict rules, which she agreed with, against dating your staff. Joann didn't find her male peers good looking, the right age, or marital status.

Andrew arrived on time. "Do you understand relational databases and SQL code?" Joann asked.

"Yes, I minored in computer science as a college student."

Joann turned on a video screen on the wall connected to her PC. "I'll display the SQL program so you can read it. If I go too fast, let me know."

Andrew had no questions as the text moved on the screen. "Looks good. When will you run it?"

"I'll email the programmer and tell her to run it now. The program should be finished by 7:00 this evening, if you come back then we should be able to see the results."

"Joann, I'm curious regarding your theories of hacking into the customer ID and password tables, and of internal fraud, but I can't talk about them when I'm working, my contract doesn't allow me to. Let's meet for a drink or dinner off the Liberty campus to discuss it."

"Is Gallagher's at 5:30 okay? They have great salads, sandwiches, hamburgers, and local craft draft beer," Joann said. She wondered why men won't ask women a direct question. Perhaps he's only interested in the crime and not me.

Andrew's tense face relaxed. "See you then."

The restaurant built less than five years earlier during the financial boom in Georgetown, in a strip mall, had the interior of a classic 19th century Irish bar. Mahogany stained tables, chairs, and booths adorned the main room. Cocktail hour patrons filled the long bar on the left. Andrew arrived first and sat in a booth where he could see the front door.

He stood up and waved when he saw Joann at the entrance. She had changed from the formal gray business suit she wore at the office to a pink sweater and navy blue slacks that showed off her athletic body. She walked over to him, smiling, "I see you couldn't wait."

"The waitress said I had to order something to sit here. It's a Dogfish Head India Pale Ale."

After she sat opposite Andrew, the waitress appeared, "Can I get you something to drink?"

"Yes, a Berlin Weisse."

In two minutes she placed the beer in front of Joann. "What else can I get you."

Joann ordered a Ruben while Andrew opted for a bacon cheeseburger. Both meals came with fries.

Joann talked first, "Do you always wear a three-piece suit?"

"My company requires it when I'm working."

"Are you working now?"

"No, but I will be at 7:00. I'd prefer jeans or tennis shorts."

"That's my style, but at work I must look presentable and formal. I usually wear pants suits."

"Do you play tennis?" Andrew asked. They both exchanged information about themselves designed to attract each other.

When their food arrived, Andrew said, "We better discuss your theories now before we go back to your office."

Joann said, "Even though the fraud lasted a month consistent with Belford's explanation, it doesn't prove he's correct. The criminals may have realized if they kept it up for a longer time they'd get caught for database hacking or internal fraud."

"True. Makes me suspicious about why they didn't investigate your theories."

"Belford said he looked into database hacking and didn't find any evidence, so he rejected it. He thinks no hacker is smarter than he is and claims he built too many security safeguards into the IT system for someone to commit internal fraud."

"Before I took this assignment, I looked into Liberty Credit. It's well structured and growing. They didn't tell me much about the fraud until I met Hank. I noticed the police classified your DBA, Steven Haven, a murder victim. I didn't think the murder was related to the fraud until you told me your conspiracy theories. Has anyone else expressed the same concern?"

"Not in the company. But a police detective, Helen Jenson, interviewed me and asked questions from which I inferred she thought the fraud might involve Haven's death," Joann said.

"If his death is related to the fraud, I'd be careful. That means someone murdered him so they wouldn't get caught. If they think you're a problem, they'll do the same to you."

Joann's smile turned into pursed lips and the color drained from her face. "Is that why you invited me out? To tell me my life is in danger?"

"No, I'm attracted to you. I thought of the danger later this afternoon. Joann, I hope to see you again."

Now smiling, Joann said, "Thanks for the warning. I want to see you again too. Let's get back to the office."

They split the check.

In her office Joann accessed her PC and printed out the summary report which shocked them both. A total of 13,441,448 credit card holders had their IDs used to steal $1,048,432,987 from the company.

They paged through the special reports. Joann commented, "Still no duplicate users and all charges range between $50 and $100."

When they finished, Andrew asked, "Can you print two copies? I'm scheduled to report this to Hank tomorrow morning."

"Sure. I'll make sure not to tell him the totals if I see him before you," she said printing the copies.

"Do you want to have lunch together, and I'll tell you his reaction?" Andrew said.

"I'd love to but I'm booked for a meeting. Come over to my place later and I'll cook you dinner. You've got me afraid to go out after dark," Joann said, smiling after she made an excuse to invite him to her home. She gave him a personal card with her cell phone number and Georgetown address. "Is 7:00 okay?"

"If I don't see you tomorrow at work, I'll see you then."

They politely kissed each other on the cheek when they parted.

Wednesday, March 10, 2010

When Andrew entered Hank's office at 10:00, he handed him the summary report. Hank looked at the totals. Andrew noticed the large numbers didn't appear to faze him.

"We'll discuss Liberty's reaction and plan to avoid future cyber attacks in our audit," Andrew said.

"Yes, I know. Given our size and growth prospects, we'll write off the billion dollar loss and finance it from our $15 billion cash reserves."

"That handles the initial loss, but what about future attacks? If you don't resolve potential problems, our audit will say so and could impact investors' view of the stock price."

"I'm aware of that. Our stock has fallen thirty percent since the papers reported the fraud. My first step will be to replace George, our IT Security Director. While good, he's backward looking. We need someone who is more forward looking and familiar with emerging security threats. A new hire should boost our stock price."

"That's a good first step. But what about concerns someone hacked Liberty's ID database or that an employee committed fraud?"

"While I don't think that's the case, I have appointments with several IT security firms to do an independent investigation to discover if systematic fraud occurred without our system detecting it. They'll also fix any holes in the system."

"That will help us state in our audit report that Liberty has recovered from their financial losses and have take steps to prevent any future large scale losses."

After Andrew left, Hank believed I've convinced him we're in control. Too bad the IT investigation won't find anything with Steve Haven gone.

Chapter 12 The Romance Begins

Thursday March 11, 2010

When Joann opened her door Andrew kissed her on the cheek and handed her a bottle of Pinot Grigio, and said, "I hope this goes with the food."

"It does. I'm serving salmon baked in butter and dill, plus small roasted potatoes, and asparagus. You look good in jeans and a gray tennis shirt."

"My favorite dinner. Joann, you look great. I like you when you wear your hair down."

"I'll open the wine. Would you like a glass?" After Andrew nodded yes, she said, "How did the meeting with Hank go?" handing Andrew the wine. "But before you tell me, were you aware Liberty fired George Belford? The physical security staff walked him out."

"Yes, Hank told me. He said they want to hire an independent IT fraud investigative firm to look into your concerns."

"Did he mention my name?" Joann now took the threat seriously. She could be in danger.

"No. Neither did I."

They enjoyed themselves, talking about what they wanted the other to hear.

"Thanks for telling me my life might be in danger yesterday. I've decided to change my behavior and be less vulnerable, but I'd still like to keep seeing you."

"So would I," Andrew said, steadily gazing into her eyes.

While washing the dishes after 9:00, they brushed against each other several times. After they had finished loading the dishwasher,

Joann pressed the start button, and they shared a tender kiss.

Their first kiss turned passionate. They put their arms around each other and hugged for several minutes, massaging each others' back, as the kiss continued.

Joann thought, it has been eight months since I held my last boyfriend. He can stop, but I won't.

In the morning, Andrew understood what had happened between them since their mutual attraction was evident at their first meeting. It surprised him since this never occurred at other consulting assignments where all his clients were men in their fifties and sixties. Perhaps he had finally gotten over his last relationship that ended a year ago. This time he would protect himself to keep from getting hurt. He wanted to go slow with an emotional commitment, but would continue to develop their sexual relationship.

Andrew left after an early breakfast.

While Joann entertained Andrew, George pulled into Hank's garage.

"Quite a day. I got fired, escorted by security to the personnel office. The company gave me three months' severance, not that I need it. Made me sign a one year non-disclosure agreement as a condition for the severance," George said.

"I know. I fired you. You're not alone. Our clueless CEO, Jim Regan, praised me for the work I did for the last ten years, but said, 'The Board had to address the $1 billion loss before the stock price vanishes. You have to go.' They gave me a six months' severance and asked me to stay around for three months until we close the books and they find my successor."

"I'll stay in the Wilmington area for a month in case you need me for any special tasks," George said. "I don't think anything will arise calling for additional work after a month."

"Let's hope not, but check with me before you leave."

"Last night I saw Cummings and Smithson being romantic at

dinner at Gallagher's. I'm afraid she's pressuring him to expand the investigation in return for sex."

"George, you have a filthy mind, but we can't take any chances. Act before they fall in love and share too much."

"I don't know if I could resist anything she asked. She's a looker."

"Follow me. I have something to show you," Hank said, as he walked into the garage and handed him a leather gun case. "No one has fired this SOCOM 16. I've removed its serial number. It has a night scope and a silencer. Please dispose of it after you use it."

George looked at his new weapon, knowing it would solve the Joann problem.

"I've known you for thirty-six years. In a month when you leave, don't tell me where you're going. Just access your money in the off-shore account I set up. If we don't know each other's location, if one of us gets caught, they can't say where the other is. If you want to talk before you disappear, call on this throw away secure cell phone and call me at this number. Don't mention our names," Hank said as he handed the number and phone to him.

"Use the cell phone to warn me after you disappear, if you discover we're both in danger."

George nodded and left.

If Hank were George, he would have left the country the next day. He did not want to stay for three months. Hank caught himself, realizing he hasn't paid George, who won't leave until Hank deposits George's share in an overseas' account. While he thought he committed the perfect crime, he knew in the extra three months smart investigators might figure out his relationship to the embezzlement. If he had a false identity and went to a foreign country without an extradition treaty, the U.S. couldn't touch him. Hank had been ready to leave immediately once he had disposed of Steve Haven. Hank had leased a safety deposit box using his false name and stored a passport, driver's license, airline tickets, credit cards, and cash for an instant departure. However, if he left earlier he thought the police would connect him to the crime and spare no resources in finding him. If he waited for three months, the police would not suspect him, and he could enjoy his new overseas life without fear of being arrested.

Friday, March 12, 2010

Early Friday night at dusk, George drove to Joann's house and parked across the street with his driver's side window facing her house. Someone had parked a car in front of the house. After an hour another car pulled into the driveway. Joann and Andrew got out. She carried a tennis racket and held onto Andrew's arm. They started to walk between the car on the street and the front door.

George, not wanting to miss his chance, fired a shot hitting Andrew in the back. His fall dragged Joann to the ground. George could not see her as she screamed while she simultaneously dialed 911. He realized he would have to leave the car to shoot her but fearing the neighbors might react to her scream and see him, he drove away.

On the road he said to himself, "Half way to $200 million."

Chapter 13 Joann Cummings Flees

Friday, March 12, 2010

The 911 operator dispatched an ambulance, Detectives Helen Jenson, Bill Norse, and CSI specialist Ben Johnson to Joann's house.

Detective Jenson arrived and asked the neighbors to leave the Cummings's property. She had a trooper seal off the scene with police tape. The Emergency Medical Technician (EMT) found Andrew had been shot in the back but no vital organs were hit. However, he had lost a lot of blood before the ambulance took him to the emergency room at Beebe Hospital in Lewes, Delaware. During the ride the EMT reported to the emergency room that his vital signs were good, he might need a blood transfusion, but he should survive.

Ben Johnson began searching for evidence, walking over the ground in front of Joann's house and across the street, where the shot could have been fired. He didn't find a shell casing or any other evidence related to the crime.

Jenson walked over to Joann who stood in shock near her front door. "Hi, I'm Detective Helen Jenson in charge of the investigation. We talked earlier about the embezzlement. Who is the victim?"

"Andrew Smithson," Joann whispered.

Jenson asked, "Is he your boyfriend?"

Joann shook her head, and uttered, "No."

"How do you know him?"

"As I told you earlier, I'm in charge of our credit card database and software applications. Smithson works for the Berkley and Jones accounting firm. He was auditing the Liberty Credit Card company.

We're just returning from playing tennis."

Jenson wondered if this shooting had any connections to Steve Haven's murder. "Did he tell you his boss' name?"

"No, ask our Finance VP, Hank Strong who hired him."

"Tell me how the shooting occurred."

"I didn't hear a shot. Andrew fell. Since I held his arm, he pulled me to the ground. At first, I thought he had had a heart attack, but I saw him bleeding from a hole in his jacket. Realizing they might have shot the wrong person, I stayed down and dialed 911."

"Why do you believe it was a mistake? Do they want to kill you?" Jenson asked.

Joann knew her theory of a mistaken killing made sense if she could convince the detective she was a target.

"George Belford, our IT Security Chief, has concluded the criminals executed a massive credit card fraud to steal the money. Liberty Credit's management accepted his theory. They won't even look into the possibility of an employee stealing the money. I concluded someone killed Steve Haven because he discovered the insider who committed the crime."

"That's an interesting theory. I'll look into it. Joann, I need to talk to you tomorrow after I learn more about the attack."

"I'm not staying here tonight. We can meet somewhere tomorrow. Tell me the time and place."

"The State Police Barracks in Georgetown at 1:00 p.m. Do you need directions?"

"No. Can someone move Andrew's car so I can get out?" Joann asked. "I'm going in to pack an overnight bag." While inside, Joann made a reservation at the Breakers Hotel in Rehoboth.

After Joann left, Helen placed a call to Hank Strong. "I'm Detective Helen Jenson of the Delaware State Police. I'm sorry to inform you a consultant of yours, Andrew Smithson, has been shot. While I need to speak to you tomorrow, I need his boss's contact information now."

After he provided James Boyd's information, Strong said, "That's shocking, I talked to him this morning. What time do you want to meet me?"

"Please stop by the Trooper Barracks in Georgetown at 10:00."

Jenson asked Detective Bill Norse on her staff to go with her while they canvassed the neighbors. The police knocked on the doors of twelve homes and found no one had witnessed anything related to the crime; didn't hear any gunshots; see unknown individuals in the neighborhood; or remember cars driving or speeding away.

After Joann registered at the hotel and entered her room, she secured the door, sat on the bed, and called her widowed mother, Alice Cummings.

"Mom, I doubt if they'll televise this in Toledo. A friend and I were returning from playing tennis and while walking to my front door, he fell, dragging me to the ground. He was shot in the back."

"Oh my God. Are you okay?"

"Yes. I'm staying at a hotel." She reclined on the bed and tried not to cry.

"Was it connected to the credit card crime?"

"I'm not sure. But to be safe, I'm disappearing for a while."

"Why don't you come here?"

"If someone's after me, your house is the first place they'll look. I don't want to put you in danger." Joann heard muffled sobbing in the background.

"When will you return?"

"After they solve the murder or until I'm sure I'm not in danger." Frightened, Joann hoped two weeks would be enough time.

At 9:00 a.m. on Saturday, Helen placed a call to Boyd in Manhattan and said, "I'm Detective Helen Jenson of the Delaware State Police. I'm sorry to inform you someone shot one of your employees, Andrew Smithson, last night. He's expected to live."

"I'm not surprised that happened."

"Why?"

"While Andrew had accounting and auditing skills, Liberty Credit's CEO, Jim Regan, hired him to solve the computer crime. He called me several weeks ago and asked to send him their best forensic accountant. Andrew has worked for us for over ten years and solved over a dozen large, $50 million-plus computer crimes. He's responsible for putting away over twenty white-collar criminals. Since he had to testify in court, we didn't hide his identity, and I always worried that one of them would take revenge on him."

"Do you have a list of those who concerned you?"

"Yes, I'll email it to you, and I'll include a summary of their crimes. It will take two hours since I have to drive to the office and compile the list. No one in Liberty Credit knew of Andrew's role, except the company's President. Strong, the Finance VP has no idea. Regan wanted to investigate the crime without involving the Liberty Credit's staff. None of them would have had a motive to kill Andrew."

They talked for another ten minutes, with Jenson getting information on Smithson's history. Jenson accepted that the Smithson shooting was independent of the Haven killing.

Hank Strong knew why Jenson wanted to interview him. She would not expect him to be connected to the crime. She would only see him as the lead financial VP, who would provide her information she could use to solve it. He prepared well.

Jenson began her interview of Hank Strong. "Andrew Smithson is doing well and expected to survive. How well did you know him?"

"Glad to hear he will live. Met him this week. We had three meetings. I asked him to estimate the true loss to the bank of the December credit card fraud." Hank paused thinking carefully of how to answer the question. "Smithson provided the estimate much faster than I expected." He summarized the work Andrew had performed.

"How much did Liberty Credit get taken for?"

"Over a billion."

"Incredible! Has Smithson finished his assignment?" Helen feigned since she knew the answer.

"Not yet, his firm has been contracted to do an external annual audit at the end of our fiscal year on March 31. We have to change procedures to enable Liberty Credit to discover and stop the next credit card attack."

"Did anyone have a problem with him?"

"No. He only worked with Joann Cummings. Talk to her."

"Had he identified anyone at Liberty who could have been involved?"

"No, he wasn't tasked to investigate the crime. I don't think an employee shot him, or had reason to. Only a few of us knew Smithson's assignment."

"The shooting may be connected to the fraud. Give me your view of how it succeeded."

Hank repeated the story Belford had concocted.

At 10:30 Jenson said, "Thanks for your time. If you think of anything else, please call me." She handed him her card.

Joann returned home to pack for her trip to West Virginia. Earlier, before going to the Jenson interview, she had left her cell phone on the kitchen counter after removing the SIM card and erasing the memory so no one could track her or find her contact information.

She took her laptop but decided not to access email. She packed fifteen books, including mystery novels and three histories, hoping they would be enough reading while waiting for the police to solve the crime.

Joann mailed a certified letter to her boss, Ed Davis, asking for a leave of absence, effective immediately, until the police solved the bank fraud. She stated her deputy was qualified to stand in for her. She stressed the attacker might have meant to shoot her. She stopped at her bank and withdrew $5,000 in cash from her savings account. If the thieves stole over $1 billion from Liberty Credit, they certainly had the resources to track her credit card purchases.

Joann had decided to resign if Liberty Credit didn't grant her the leave of absence. She wouldn't learn of Davis' reaction, since she didn't leave a forwarding address, wouldn't access email, or have a cell phone.

Joann arrived at Jenson's office at 1:00. Jenson said, "Andrew Smithson is recovering and will survive."

"Thank God," Joann said. "Even though I've only known him a few days, I really like him."

Detective Jenson started the questioning, "Are you still concerned they meant to hit you?"

"Yes," Joann said, wondering why she asked that question.

"You're in no danger. I talked to the CEO of Berkley and Jones, who said Liberty Credit hired Smithson to investigate the financial losses, not just to do an audit. Keep that information confidential, only the CEO of Liberty Credit and you know. Smithson specialized in computer-related crime investigations. It might have been someone Smithson sent to prison who shot him. His boss gave me a list of potential suspects."

Joann listened to Jenson's soothing voice, but this didn't change her determination to disappear.

"Did Smithson mention his other work?" Jenson asked.

"Yes, prior jobs, but no details of the work."

"Did he discuss his background or mention any of his friends?"

"Yes, he reminisced about his childhood in Albany, college life at Cornell, and a few previous jobs. Andrew never mentioned his friends," Joann said as a tear trickled down her left cheek.

Jenson noticed, and said, "I hope the questions aren't upsetting you. Too bad he didn't name his friends. They would have been useful."

"That's all I know. Is it okay if I leave now?"

"Not yet. Did you become emotionally involved with Smithson?"

"We had several dinners together, and played tennis once. We had a great time."

"Were you dating someone else or did you have a recent breakup?"

"You think one of my old boyfriends shot him?"

"It happens all the time."

"I'm not dating anyone, and my previous boyfriend broke up with me eight months ago. He met someone and fell in love. Now he's engaged. He'd be happy for me if I found someone else."

"Are you sure?"

"He told me," Joann said wearing a perplexed smile.

Joann drove to her uncle's cabin in Canaan Valley, West Virginia after Jenson's interview. The uncle had died five years ago and left it to her. Only one person in the bank and few of her friends knew she owned the cabin. She hoped no one could locate her. The bright sunlit spring day changed her spirits as she drove over the Chesapeake Bay Bridge two hours after she had left Georgetown. The drive to Strasburg, Virginia proceeded without incident since Route 50, the Beltway, Interstate 66 and 81 had light Saturday traffic. Her despair started to lift during these early parts of the trip, and then her outlook changed to excitement and safety as she approached to Canaan Valley over the recently constructed Route 48. She realized she'd be in the mountains she loved for at least two weeks.

Joann arrived at the cabin at 8:00 p.m. after using cash to purchase fried chicken, mashed potatoes, a roll, a bottle of Chardonnay, and groceries at the Country Market in Davis, West Virginia. She watched CNN as she ate. The newscaster did not mention Friday's attack on Andrew. She started reading *The Abandoned Homes Serial Murders*. At eleven, she stopped to watch the network news. Again, no mention of Smithson's shooting.

Since her only activities were cleaning the cabin, shopping, and hiking, she finished the book in two days. As she read about the devious behavior of the criminals, she developed a paranoia that the Liberty Credit crime was so well executed the police might never solve it, and the criminals would continue to finance an extensive search for her until they found her and removed her as a threat to their freedom.

Joann's daydreams about Andrew would intervene periodically as she read. So glad he would survive, she wondered when she would see him again. They couldn't communicate with each other since her move to the cabin. While she had only known him for a short time she spent too many hours dreaming about him and their next meeting.

Andrew Smithson's surgeon at Beebe Hospital called Detective Jenson early Monday morning. "Andrew Smithson is well enough to be interviewed. Can you give me a time when you'll be here?"

"11:00. Where should I go?"

"The front desk."

"Mr. Smithson, I'm Detective Helen Jenson from the Delaware State Police, the lead detective investigating the shooting. Do you know of anyone who would want to kill you, specifically from the Liberty Credit Card Company?"

"No one from Liberty. Only a few people knew why I worked there. Since I had only been at Liberty less than a week, I doubt if anyone feared I had discovered who committed the fraud. However, I have sent others to jail from different companies, who might bear a grudge against me."

"I know. Your boss, James Boyd, also doubted a Liberty Credit employee would have shot you. He sent me a list of eighteen felons you sent to jail." Jenson handed him the list. "Fourteen of the eighteen are still there. While they couldn't have killed you, they could have hired someone. We haven't located the other four, mainly because of time constraints, but we'll work on them this week. Any names on the list you suspect could have fired the shot?"

"Only three. Two are still in jail: Raymond Horton and Ed Bliss. The third, Monty Small, has been free for three years. Both Horton and Bliss, in their sixties at sentencing time, received twenty-year sentences, and they both threatened me since they considered twenty years a life sentence.

"Monty Small had a vicious background. While the court sentenced him to ten years for white collar bank fraud, the police believed he ordered the murder of two bank employees. The police never solved the cases, but did identify Monty Small as the chief suspect. The prison released him after seven years for good behavior," Andrew said.

"We'll look into Small, Horton and Bliss in the next few days."

Andrew said, "I called Joann Cummings this morning on her cell and her office. Her administrative assistant said she wasn't in today, and her cell phone wasn't operating. Do you know how the shooting affected her?"

"She told me she was taking a few days off because of the shock of being so close to the attack. When I see her again, I'll let her know you asked after her." Jenson said, leaving after fifteen more minutes of conversation about Andrew's background.

Once she was gone, Andrew returned to reminiscing about his short time working with and getting to know Joann. He enjoyed the intelligent and insightful analysis she provided at work, and having dinner together had ended a bleak chapter and opened a new emotional horizon. In his last five years, while he had dated beautiful and talented women, he had never fallen in love as fast as he had with Joann.

On Monday morning, when she didn't show up for work, Joann's boss, Ed Davis, called her at home. No one answered, so he left a message, "I understand if you don't come in today or for the next several days after the traumatic shooting at your house. Please call me."

On Tuesday he received the letter from Joann and agreed to a leave of absence and notified her deputy to take over. He called, left a message, and emailed her accepting her request. "I've approved the leave of absence. I'll contact you as soon as the police arrest the attacker."

Joann read and watched TV for the first two weeks of her stay in the cabin. She became despondent as she didn't hear any news related to the case. She did not want to be in constant fear for her life. With her rapid loss of faith in the police, after reading their book, she thought Margaret Hoffman and Paul O'Hare would be ideal detectives. She only had to convince them to take the case. Joann wanted to meet them and propose that the Liberty Credit Card case become the subject of their next book. She felt if she told them the details, known only to her, they might work on it during their honeymoon.

Monday, March 29, 2010

Joann became riveted to the TV when she saw Jenson being interviewed on the 6:30 p.m. news. "Detective Jenson, what's new in the Liberty Credit Card investigation?" the reporter asked.

Jenson gave a partial response, "Originally it appeared to be massive credit card fraud. Through auditing of the computer transactions, we don't know how the fraud occurred. We're unsure whether it was an inside or an outside job. There are two persons of interest, who may help us in the investigation. Joann Cummings is the Head of Credit Card Applications and Database Software for Liberty Credit. She is on leave. George Belford was formerly employed as the IT Security Director. If either individual hears this request please call me, Detective Helen Jenson at 302-555-1890."

Chapter 14 Stalking Joann Cummings

Tuesday, March 30, 2010

Hank Strong answered his disposable cell phone, a few minutes after the NBC newscast ended.

"It's your friend. Did you watch NBC news tonight?" Belford asked, calling from his hotel room in Germantown, Maryland.

"Disturbing."

"I may disappear."

"Before you do, visit with the Cummings woman. Maybe with your help she'll go missing. The cops will think she did it."

"Might take a while."

"Disappear after she's gone. Don't call me."

After Hank hung up, Belford wondered if he would succeed where the State Police failed. In his hotel room, he searched for Joann's name on social media. He found she had Facebook and LinkedIn accounts, and a website. He found no activity since Saturday, March 13.

With no search results, he tried sending her a phishing email. If she opened the email a replica of the Olive Garden's email format offering a $20 discount on her next meal for two would appear. If she selected the offer an email would be sent to Belford verifying he could access her laptop. Next, the Olive Garden's webpage containing the coupon would appear on her screen so she'd be unaware of the email sent to Belford.

He would then access her laptop to find her geographic location by reading her emails. Belford wanted to kill her as soon as he could.

As insurance he activated his Relay cell phone ease-dropping software and entered the number of the cell phone she left at home. All calls made or received would be identified and recorded. Conversations heard by the phone's microphone would start the app. The phone would record non-phone conversations for later playback.

Belford woke early, made coffee and turned on his PC. Nothing. She had not opened the phishing email. Disappointed, he remembered she liked her cell phone and assumed that he'd locate her after he turned on the Relay system. Again nothing. Belford knew she had brains and successfully managed complex projects, but he had underestimated her security skills. She remained hidden. He had to try another approach to find her.

Belford did not like the risk he would take to plant sound-activated sensing devices throughout her house. If the police had the home under surveillance, they'd arrest him. Suppose Cummings didn't live alone, he couldn't plant the devices with other people in the house. He wouldn't enter her house if he found it protected by a burglar alarm.

After driving three hours from Germantown, Maryland, he arrived at Joann's house near noon. Belford parked his car two blocks away and walked to her house, hoping the dark black wig, blue tinted contact lenses, plus two-inch elevator shoes would fool any witnesses. He wore casual clothes. As he walked by the house, he looked at the front and both sides and did not find signs indicating the house had an alarm. He saw no cars. Others living in the house remained his last concern.

Then Belford drove to his home in Milford, Delaware, checked to see if the police had it under surveillance. Finding they didn't, he took five listening devices from a small safe in his bedroom and placed them in a plastic bag. After removing his disguise, he took a nap and set the alarm in his cell phone for 4:00 p.m.

His security training when he worked as an undercover cop paid off well. As darkness descended, he left dressed in a blond wig, blue eyes, a gray business suit, with normal shoes and holding a cane. He limped noticeably to any onlooker.

Belford drove around Joann's residence at 7:00 p.m. and noticed a few lights on. When he stopped, he didn't see any movement of shadows near the lights nor any cars parked close to the house. He focused a high-powered listening device on several of the windows, hearing no sound. After spending less than five minutes, he drove away and returned two hours later and repeated listening to the windows. They were quiet. The lights still illuminated the inside of the house. Belford returned at 11:00 p.m. and found the lights off and the house quiet.

After parking a few blocks away, Belford took off his suit jacket, put on a black hoodie and latex gloves, stuffed the listening devices in his hoodie pocket, and walked to Joann's. He picked the lock on the back door and hid devices in the living room, kitchen, bathroom, study, and one of the two bedrooms.

Leaving quickly, he drove to Rehoboth Beach and registered in an inexpensive motel on Route 1, still wearing the disguise and using a false identity. He stayed in the motel, except for quick trips to the supermarket to purchase food and beverages. He would leave only if he heard the listening devices.

Joann's fear rose after learning of the police's interest in her. She couldn't return to Delaware to talk to Hoffman and O'Hare. She was concerned the police might detain her, so she decided to stay in West Virginia. Joann suspected police protection might not be effective against the embezzlers with their one billion dollar bankroll.

Now that a direct meeting with Hoffman and O'Hare wasn't feasible, she spent the rest of the evening analyzing alternatives for recruiting them. Communicating by mail or email could reveal her location. Joann considered using third party intermediaries to send messages to Margaret and Paul but soon realized she trusted no one well enough.

After a sleepless night, she bought a new computer at Walmart in Maryland and a disposable cell phone at Wawa. While at the Country Market waiting in the checkout line, she glanced at People Magazine and saw Margaret Hoffman and Paul O'Hare on the cover. The headline stated, "Writing Couple Honeymooning in Greece, Ten Months after their Marriage." She placed the magazine in her cart.

Joann returned to the cabin, put the groceries away, and read the article outlining the trip's itinerary. The authors had reservations to fly out of Philadelphia on a direct flight on April 15, 2010 and land in Athens the following day. The couple was scheduled to stay for a few days in Athens at the Central Athens Hotel and then go on an extended tour of Greece starting at Crete.

A perfect solution, she'd meet them in Greece.

She changed her mind about not leaving the cabin since she realized she had to pick up her passport in her desk at home. She wanted to meet Detective Jenson without being identified. She only had to convince Jenson to help her.

Joann called Jenson on her untraceable cell phone, "Detective Helen Jenson, may I help you?"

"This is Joann Cummings. I watched the news last night. Why do you want to talk?"

"Hi, how are you? You're very hard to find. We need to discuss your theory of the Liberty Credit Card embezzlement."

"Shall I bring a lawyer?"

"No, we've ruled you out as a suspect."

Joann said, "I'll meet you at my house at 2:00 p.m. on Friday if you come alone, and the police don't make it public that I've talked to you. I don't want anyone to discover my location."

"I'll agree not to make it public. But I need to bring a colleague, Detective Bill Norse, a computer expert who concluded it was embezzlement and not computer fraud. You couldn't have done it."

"Then I want to meet him."

"Good, he'll ask most of the questions."

Joann arrived at her house before 1:30. She went to the study, opened her main desk drawer, picked up the passport, and put it in her purse. She walked into her bathroom and took seven contact lens cases with different colored lenses. Finally, she opened her bedroom closet and took an overnight bag with three different colored wigs she had used in an amateur acting group, and placed everything in the trunk of her car.

Belford received a signal. The listening devices detected Joann walking around her house. When he arrived, he saw Joann's car in the driveway and a Delaware State Trooper's car parked in front. He turned left before he reached the police car and parked one hundred yards out of sight. Putting on earphones, he listened as Joann explained why she thought it wasn't credit card fraud.

Both detectives arrived a few minutes before 2:00 p.m. and introduced themselves.

Joann asked them to sit at the kitchen table. "I'm thirsty and hungry. The drive took seven hours." The conversation began after Joann placed a cheese plate at the center and plastic bottles of water in front of everyone.

"Joann, since you're taking extreme precautions from being discovered, can I assume you still feel threatened?" Detective Jenson asked.

"Yes, especially since the discovery of Steve Haven's body and learning the State Police think it's embezzlement, not credit card fraud."

"The police can provide you protection," Jenson said, and picked up a piece of cheese.

"No, I'll protect myself," Joann said as she opened the bottle and sipped water.

"Why did you suspect internal embezzlement rather than credit card fraud?" Jenson asked.

"Fraud seemed too complex. Too many individuals had to be involved to steal that many credit cards numbers and passwords and stage the fraud over a one month period." Joann almost grinned seeing the detectives nod their heads. "I wondered why Liberty Credit management accepted it."

"Insurance. Insurance covers credit card fraud but not embezzlement," Norse said.

"That makes sense. Massive credit card fraud could never succeed. Something had to go wrong, even assuming they built a database of stolen information and automated the credit card fraudulent transactions. Too many moving parts," Joann said.

"I agree. Card cancellation is another reason to reject credit card fraud. Over thirteen million card holders had their accounts accessed in a one month period. Usually at least one-hundred thousand individuals cards would be canceled by their owners or by Liberty Credit. We examined the audit trail and didn't find one canceled transaction because the account had been closed. The probability of no closed accounts is so low, we concluded embezzlement and not fraud caused the financial losses," Norse said. He drank some water, but avoided the cheese hoping to keep his weight down.

Joann's look changed into a smug smile, now they believe me after Andrew's shooting.

"Why did you conclude I didn't take part in the crime?" Joann asked.

"You're a manager of the credit card database and its IT applications, not a DBA, or a programmer. The historical login database told us you accessed the application programs, but rarely touched the real database. To test the applications, you used a testing database with phony data. Sad to say, you didn't have the skills to steal using the database," Norse said.

"Saved by ignorance," Joann said relaxing back into her chair. "While you don't want us to tell anyone you're here, the police from the eastern states will be on notice to detain you. Are you sure you can evade those cops?" Detective Jenson asked.

"No, but I'll try."

"We noticed you liked to speed. Three tickets in the last five years," Norse said.

"In my youth, I'd smile and get a warning."

"Don't speed. If you get caught, the cop will have to detain you," Jenson said.

Joann wondered, are they trying to help me? "I won't. Thanks for the warnings. Have the airports been alerted?"

"Yes," Detective Jenson replied.

"Is it possible to have the TSA alerts rescinded?"

"Yes. Are you going overseas?" Jenson asked.

"Perhaps. It should be safer."

"Give us twenty-four hours."

"It'll be several days before I decide what to do," Joann said as she finished her water.

"Were you suspicious of anyone?" Jenson asked.

"Not initially, anyone with access to the database might have done it. I suspected Steve Haven, when he didn't return from his vacation on January 18. But when I learned of his murder, I realized it couldn't be him. The criminals might have killed him because he had discovered the embezzlers," Joann said. "That's why I was so scared. They might kill me because they were worried Haven told me what he discovered. I'd look at everyone on Haven's staff."

"We'll need a list," Jenson said.

Joann retrieved Jenson's business card from her purse, read her phone number and email address out loud, and said, "I'll email you an organization chart of my entire group."

"What about other employees?" Norse asked. "George Belford first."

"Like me, he doesn't have the skills to access the database. However, as head of IT security he might coach the embezzlement programmers about the constraints of the software. If he is part of the group, he's capable of manipulating the security system so it wouldn't trigger alerts when they ran illegal transactions."

Belford's interest turned from curiosity to fear, when he heard Joann explain his role in the operation. He had to kill Joann. After the police leave, I'll take care of her. Then leave the U.S. as soon as possible, my only hope of not being caught and receiving the $200 million.

"What about Ed Davis and Hank Strong?" Norse asked.

"Like me, they don't have skills or access to the database. They're probably not involved."

"Are you staying here?" Jenson asked.

"No I want to follow your car for a mile or so. That should stop anyone from trailing me."

"How do we contact you if I have more questions?" Jenson asked.

"You don't. I'll call you periodically."

As Joann and the two detectives walked to their cars, Helen said, "I almost forgot. I've been talking to Andrew Smithson. He asked about you. I told him you had decided to go disappear to avoid being attacked."

"Has he recovered from the shot?"

"Yes. He is still working on the case, but not at your company."

In her car Jenson said, "She's scared. I'll call TSA when we get back to Georgetown."

"It appears Smithson might be ahead of us in the investigation. We should talk to him and see if he can help us," Norse said.

"I'll set up a meeting," Helen said.

Following Jenson's car, Joann lamented she couldn't talk directly to Andrew, especially since she had experienced emotional ups and downs over the last two weeks, completely happy remembering their time together or depressed wondering if their companionship resulted from male sexual desire and not from a yearning for an emotional partner.

"Christ," Belford swore in his car, watching Joann leave. If I can't finish the job tonight, she'll disappear again. I'll have to enter Jenson's phone into the Relay system. Not a bad idea. It will help me track the investigator and learn Joann's cell phone number. No need to get caught following two cars. Belford drove away.

At the Georgetown Barracks, Helen called Andrew Smithson's cell phone on her land line. She received a message, "This number has been disconnected."

Helen realized Smithson's cell phone had been changed to protect him. That's strange, she thought, I talked to him over a week ago to update him on his case. She called his boss, James Boyd, "Detective Helen Jenson from Delaware. I need to talk to Andrew Smithson, but his cell phone is disconnected. How can I get in touch with him?"

"We've placed him in a safe house, since we don't know if whoever shot him will try again. I'll have him call you."

Five minutes later Helen's land line phone rang, "It's Andrew Smithson. You want to talk to me."

"Yes, two items. We discovered someone shot and killed Monty Small, so you don't have to worry about him again. We also need to ask you a few questions about the Credit Card case."

"I'd rather not discuss it over the phone. Can we meet in your office, tomorrow afternoon at 2:00?"

"Have you recovered enough to drive?"

"I'll have someone drive me."

Andrew's driver parked in the barracks parking lot after a five-hour drive from the safe house. Helen escorted him to an interview room.

"I'd like you to meet Detective Bill Norse. He is assigned to the Credit Card case. He will work with you and Berkley and Jones, to help Liberty Credit figure out how they lost over a billion dollars."

Andrew gave his perspective. "We believe internal employees embezzled the funds, rather than outside criminals who committed credit card fraud. I was moved to a safe house since Steve Haven's murder and my shooting might be connected to the crime."

"Detective Norse is a computer expert and came to the same conclusion," said Helen. "I suggest we combine our IT sources to help identify the employees involved. Bill will work with you in that area. In return, the Delaware State Police will use our resources to find and arrest the criminals."

"My boss suggested the same arrangement. Please contact me on this secure cell phone." Andrew wrote the number on two business cards and handed it to them. "Bill is welcome to work at our secure location or we can communicate by secure email."

"For now, let's use email. If needed we can help you at the safe house. No need to tell us where it is until we set up logistics for Bill or other staff to join you."

Bill and Andrew spent the next half hour briefing each other on how they determined embezzlement and not credit card fraud was used in the crime, their investigative strategy, and how to contact each other during the investigation.

Before Andrew left, Helen said, "Joann has also left the area and should be safe."

"Is she under your protection?"

"No she refused our offer."

Andrew commented, "That fits her personality."

On her drive back to West Virginia, Joann felt relieved she wasn't a suspect and was surprised at the progress made by the Delaware State Police. But she still wanted to recruit Hoffman and O'Hare to solve the crime.

While Joann had decided to travel to Greece and meet the authors, she realized after reading many technical crime novels, she needed electronic help to locate them. She stopped at a surveillance store in Washington DC where private detectives, jealous spouses, or curious individuals could purchase listening and tracking devices, concealed cameras, and other tools to clandestinely learn about an individual's behavior.

Joann asked the clerk, "I have a young daughter who has just started to drive. Do you have a device to track the car?"

"Of course. Let me show you several models."

Joann chose the battery-operated version that only worked when the car moved. A magnetic cover allowed her to attach it to the car's metal where no one would notice it.

"Anything else?"

"I'm a single mother and my daughter spends time at home when not in school and when I'm at work. She has a boyfriend, and I don't want her alone with him. What kind of system do you have for something like that?"

"Audio listening devices."

Joann selected a battery operated pen. The clerk told her, "It operates as a real pen. You have to plug it into a USB laptop for charging and listening." He handed her its connector.

On Monday, Joann stopped at a public library, and made reservations to fly from Philadelphia to Athens on April 14, 2010, the day before Hoffman and O'Hare planned to arrive. The People article had sketched their itinerary, and stated they would stay at the Central Athens Hotel for several days before departing for Crete. So as not to lose them after their arrival in Greece, she made reservations for five days at the hotel.

Joann did not want to meet them in crowded Athens. She preferred an isolated location where they would not be able to alert the Greek police that the Delaware police were looking for her, before she could convince them of her innocence.

Joann always enjoyed the leisurely drive down Route 32 on the way from Davis to her cabin. After stopping at her rural delivery mail box, she broke into a cold sweat. She discovered a letter accompanying the normal advertisements. Retrieving the letter, she noticed the return address of Joe Reynolds, one of her staff. The tension left her as she put the envelope on the passenger seat without opening it and drove to the cabin. She assumed Reynolds wanted to make arrangements to rent the cabin in July as he had done for the last five years.

> Dear Joann,
>
> Hope you are well and this letter reaches you at your WV cabin. The IT staff are both scared and depressed, with the murder of Steve Haven, and your and George Belford's disappearance. Many think both of you are dead because of the credit card crime. While I am more optimistic about your survival, I have recently become nervous after examining the computer system performance data for December. The data show interesting variations that may be associated with the crime. I want to meet and discuss it with you at your earliest convenience. Please call me on my cell phone 302-555-7214.
> Yours truly,
> Joe Reynolds

When she finished reading she exclaimed to her empty cabin, "Christ that's not what I'd thought he'd write." The letter reminded her of the cause of her exile. She realized he might have data to help solve the crime.

Joann called him on her new cell phone. "Hi Joe, I received your letter and I'm alive. Can you meet me tomorrow?"

"What time? Do you want me to drive to the cabin?"

"Let's meet at 2:00 p.m. at the Water Street Restaurant in Friendsville. It's near Deep Creek Lake in western Maryland. Please tell no one I'm here or my cell phone number. I am alive and I'd like to remain that way. I'm still concerned someone wants to murder me. If the bastards find out where I'm staying and you're talking to me, we may both be in danger."

"Meet you at 2:00," Joe replied. His optimistic concern turned to panic, his stomach became queasy, and his pulse raced when he heard Joann say he might be in danger.

The restaurant had few other diners in the mid-afternoon. Joann took a seat in the back away from other customers. Five minutes later Joe walked in carrying a briefcase.

"Thanks for coming," Joann said. "I'm hungry. If we both order we won't look suspicious."

"Good, I'm famished."

After ordering, Joann asked, "What did you find?"

"During a regular sequence of five minutes, several computer applications had an increase in their computer time for two minutes. Then the system metrics returned to normal. When I added up the individual computer time used by these applications and all the other applications running, the totals equaled the system total for the three minutes when the resource use was normal. But it differed by 0.02 percent when resource time increased. I couldn't find a reason for the difference, leading me to conclude someone had executed another program on a scheduled basis and erased metrics of its running from the IT system logs."

"Can you prove it?" Joann asked, thankful that the older experienced system programmer retained his youthful curiosity not found in the modern application programming whizzes.

"Yes, the data's in my briefcase. The waitress is coming. Let's wait until she serves us, before I start."

"Chef Salad, with oil and vinegar?"

"Mine," Joe said.

"Yours must be the meatloaf and mashed potatoes," the waitress said as she placed it in front of Joann.

After the waitress left, Joe asked, "What happened to your diet?"

"It hasn't changed. At work I eat light, but since I exercise I enjoy my evening meal. The meatloaf here is the best I've ever tasted."

After Joe ate several forkfuls of turkey, cheese, and lettuce to assuage his hunger, he opened his briefcase, took out a folder containing computer log information, and explained his earlier statements. They talked for a half hour until Joann was convinced he had tracked the illegal operations. "Have you talked to the police?"

"Not yet, I want to identify who ran the program first. I'm concerned if word gets out, the hacker will do something to the data, to mask my discovery."

"Be careful. Don't let anyone know what you're doing, the bastards are ruthless."

"I know. A copy of this data is on a thumb drive in my safe deposit box. Tell the cops, if something happens to me," he said frowning.

"I will." Joann shuddered to think Joe might be in danger.

"I'll call you when I find anything."

"Buy a disposable cell phone to contact me. We don't know if the bastards are listening in to the IT staff's calls. Call me as soon as you get the new number. I use a disposal phone," Joann said.

"I'll get one at a 7-Eleven on the way home."

"I've set up a new email account. You can send me email messages. The first should be your new email account address, new cell phone number, and nothing else." She wrote her email address on a napkin and handed it to Joe.

They parted and three hours later, Joe called and gave Joann the information she requested.

"Joe thanks, but rather than you calling me, I'll call you, so I can protect my location." She knew her current disposable phone couldn't work in Greece. "Do you have a passport?"

"Yes. Why?"

"I'm going overseas, and it might be safer if our next meeting isn't in the U.S. Can you get away?"

"Yes, but now my wife's safety concerns me."

"Can you send her to visit one of your children away from Washington for a while?"

"Since she knows what's going on, it will be easy to convince her. I'll send her to our daughter Eve. She can use her mother's help with three young children, and she lives San Diego."

Thursday, April 8, 2010

After Belford left Joann's house he checked out of his Rehoboth Beach motel and returned to his Germantown home. He spent a week planning his escape from the U.S. He had the fake passport, driver's license, and social security card provided by Hank Strong. He wanted to settle in a safe country, without a U.S. extradition treaty, where he could live undetected and enjoy his wealth.

Belford used the internet and beamed as he noted the alphabetical list of eighty-nine countries without U.S. extradition treaties. The results initially elated him, until he realized most of them were African countries where except for former English colonies, he didn't speak their languages, former Communist nations, or small islands in remote locations. Belford rejected most since they were countries where he had no cultural or linguistic commonality.

It took a full day to examine twenty of the acceptable countries. He began a methodical review, storing their favorable and unfavorable attributes on a spreadsheet.

The countries formed by the breakup of Yugoslavia, in the Balkan Peninsula appeared the most appealing. Several of his friends returning from a sailing trip to Croatia had touted its landscape, climate, beautiful women, and Italian food. The next day he reviewed each region and town within Croatia and decided to locate near the walled city of Dubrovnik on the Adriatic Sea.

Belford researched Dubrovnik and its suburbs and made hotel reservations in a quiet district of the city. Belford spent the rest of the evening watching internet shorts and tourist videos of his future home.

The next day he became impatient after not having intercepted a call between Joann and Detective Jenson for a week. Belford decided he had to learn more about Joann, so he opened Facebook under a fake name, and accessed her webpage. He used the Facebook About Page to discover her friends and relatives, enabling him to tap more cell phones. Clicking on the Friends button showed a list of forty-three friends, and he scrolled the page to view each friend's picture and name. He hit the print screen button and saved each image, adding a new list of Joann's friends to his PC.

The Facebook effort took most of the day. Belford discovered Joann's mother's page, but she didn't list her cell phone number. He opened the Spokeo.com cell phone search app and entered her name. Within minutes, and after paying the nominal fee, he had her cell phone number, which he entered into his phone tracking system. He performed the same operation for ten other individuals he deemed to be relatives or close friends. In the late afternoon he drove to Barnes & Noble where he purchased six books on the geography and history of Croatia.

That evening he took two hours to review the phone calls of Detective Jenson, Joann's mother, and the other ten individuals. Only one phone call interested him. The one between Joann and her mother that day.

"Hi Mom. It's Joann. I'm going away for several weeks."

"Joann, I'm worried. The police are looking for you. Are you okay?"

"Yes, I'm fine. I talked to the police. They wanted information on Liberty Credit and don't think I'm guilty of anything."

"Then why don't you quit hiding."

"I have my reasons. Remember not to tell anyone I called and what I said."

"Not even your brother?"

"Especially him. He'll post it on Facebook."

"You're probably right. I won't say a thing."

Belford worried it might take hours to review the Facebook posts for Joann and her friends, keeping him awake until late into the morning. Skimming through Joann's posts he realized she was a private person. She mainly posted on political and cultural topics, and seldom on her personal, working, or family life. This effort only took Belford a half hour. Belford thought he still had time to find her. The work paid off when he searched her relationship posts, especially those of her ex-boyfriend. Joann liked to travel to her mother's home, to Florida to scuba dive, to California and Colorado to hike, and to West Virginia to relax.

Belford realized she wasn't at her mother's since they had just talked on the phone the previous day. Joann could not be in California and Colorado since she had to be near DC to talk to the police. That left West Virginia. Since it was a big state, Belford continued searching, mostly opening her ex-boyfriend's posts.

One narrative of their vacation in Canaan Valley in the fall of 2008 where they viewed and took pictures of the scenery and hiked in the mountains solved the problem of where Joann might be hiding. The ex-boyfriend had posted pictures of her cabin located on a side road and one of the road with its name displayed on a sign, as it intersected Route 32 running through the valley. Belford then used personal search software to discover Joann's history including any property she owned. After paying his small fee for detailed information, the screen displayed the address. Concerned the cabin might not be on a search engine map, he accessed MapQuest.com. That program calculated a route for him to follow, estimating a travel time of three and a half hours between Germantown and the cabin. He set the alarm for 6:30 a.m. and wanted to leave for the cabin by 7:30.

Joann woke up in a relaxed mood at 8:00 that morning and continued her packing. She hoped to leave by noon for the seven hour drive to Philly and stay in a hotel before boarding the flight the next day. After breaking to cook sausage patties and scrambled eggs, she watched the morning news and weather.

Belford left the house at 8:00 and drove north on Interstate 270. By 8:15 he was headed west on Interstate 70 on the way to West Virginia.

Joann finished packing at 10:00. She gathered her ticket information, passport, and put them in her purse.

Belford exited Interstate 70 at Hancock, Maryland and drove west on Interstate 68. He turned south on Route 220 at Cumberland, Maryland and headed into West Virginia eventually reaching Route 50. At a red light, he opened his glove compartment and retrieved his Glock 20 automatic hand-gun and loaded the clip. He put it back into the glove compartment and continued driving. At 10:45 he reached Davis, West Virginia, the northern entrance to Canaan Valley. The GPS guidance system reported he was twenty minutes from her cabin. His pulse quickened in anticipation of eliminating the last link between Liberty Credit, himself, and his new wealth.

Joann had packed the car by 10:45 and returned to the cabin to clean it and throw her sheets and table cloth into the hamper. She paused at her bedroom bookcase and realized she had nothing to read on the plane. After ten minutes of searching, she took the Hoffman's and O'Hare's book and three mysteries, one each by David Baldacci, Patricia Cornwell, and John Grisham. After getting in her car and turning the engine on, she remembered she had not turned off the water.

Five minutes later Belford passed the Country Market and his pulse raced. Only fifteen minutes left. He could taste the $200 million. He wondered if he lusted for the kill too much. Not caring whether he had a maniac personality or was doing it to get rich and save himself, he drove on. He never exceeded the speed limit since he didn't want a rural cop to pull him over which would send him to jail for the rest of his life. Belford glanced at the GPS every few minutes, smiling as the travel time fell below three minutes. He turned left onto a tree-covered hill. After driving two minutes on a bumpy asphalt road, the GPS in a woman's voice said, "The destination is less than a quarter of a mile on your left."

Belford pulled off the now dirt road and parked one hundred yards from the cabin. He assumed she had a gun as he imagined all West Virginia residents did. The mountains had bears, coyotes, and many said mountain lions that could devour the unwary. As a city-raised man, he looked apprehensively around as he walked off the road often brushing the trees toward Joann's fate. At fifty yards, he still did not see the cabin behind a curve in the road, but savored their coming meeting.

As he reached the bend he heard an engine start and the sound of a car coming toward him. Joann had left the cabin with the gas pedal pressed to the floor. The wheels kicked up dust from the road. She rounded the curve, not seeing Belford as he jumped into the woods to avoid being hit, while at the same time reaching for his gun.

The car sped past him before he could aim. Belford cursed and coughed as the dry dust engulfed him. Standing still, he thought of chasing her. He realized if he didn't catch her he'd never find out her destination. Still cursing to himself, he held his gun out and walked toward the cabin, hoping a new boyfriend or relative drove the car.

When he was only ten yards from the cabin, Belford didn't see another car. He walked softly minimizing noise until he reached the locked front door. He walked around the back of the cabin and looked in the windows not finding anyone else inside. Since she had locked the windows, he broke one.

Belford wore gloves and climbed through the window putting his hands on her desk. As he gazed inside the cabin, he realized she was as meticulous here as at work. He always appreciated her organizational skills. Whenever he had asked her a question or emailed, she always responded within minutes from memory or from information in her desk or filing cabinet.

While the cabin didn't have filing cabinets, he hoped the desk held Joann's plans. Belford took only a minute to find an inch thick file in the lower left-hand draw labeled Liberty Credit Fraud Investigation. She left it since she didn't think anyone would find her. He removed the file and placed in on the desk surface. Scanning the file's pages, it wasn't till he reached the last stapled items informing him she had reservations to fly to Greece, the next day. Even with this knowledge, he knew he couldn't catch her in the U.S. since once he left the U.S. he wouldn't return. He'd try and find her in Greece.

Unaware of the near-death encounter, Joann reached the Philadelphia International Airport and registered in her hotel, ordered room service, and had a relaxing sleep. She arrived at the airport at 3:00 p.m. the next day in time for her 5:30 departure.

Chapter 15 The Honeymooners Arrive in Athens

Thursday, April 15, 2010

As befitted their new-found wealth, Margaret and Paul enjoyed a first-class flight. Both ate and slept well on the plane and awoke Friday morning viewing Europe on the left side of the plane. Around eight in the morning, they flew over Greece. They clearly saw the mountains of northern Greece, the Gulf of Corinth separating the mainland from the Peloponnese, and finally the city of Athens surrounded by mountains and water as they approached the Athens International Airport. After a rapid passage through Customs, compared to American airports, they took a cab to the Central Athens Hotel.

Since they had to wait until the afternoon to move into their room, Margaret, an experienced Greek traveler from her Marine days, when she was stationed at Souda Bay in Crete, decided to show Athens to Paul. The hotel agreed to look after their luggage. Turning left when they left the hotel, they entered Plaka, the wonderful maze-like retail section. It contained block after block in any direction of small stores selling art, books, clothes, food, meals, perfume, and jewelry. After purchasing two tee-shirts to wear sailing and as proof of their Greek adventure, they entered a restaurant for Paul's first experience eating an Athenian meal. They ordered a glass of local red wine, at a third the price of wine in an American restaurant that tasted twice as good. Paul ordered a second to accompany the stewed lamb with potatoes.

When they checked into the hotel and Paul started to open the door, Margaret said, "Hotels here differ from those in the States."

"How?"

"You'll see."

After they entered the room, Paul flicked the nearest light switch. Nothing happened. "What's wrong?"

"Nothing." Margaret said. She took the key holder and placed it into a slot near the door and the lights came on.

Paul laughed.

"The power only comes on if we insert the key," Margaret said.

"They should use this in the U.S. The hotels would save a lot of energy. Why aren't we as smart?" Paul said.

"Greek civilization is over two thousand years older than ours."

After they brought their luggage into the room, Paul explored. He entered the bathroom and looked for the light switch.

"It's outside the bathroom," Margaret said as she switched on the light.

Surprised, Paul said, "That's an improvement. No more stepping on towels, soap, bottles, and water on the floor and falling. Can we change the wiring in your house?"

"Our switch is near the door so we can turn it on before we enter. We don't need to move the switch, but they should use this system in new homes with kids."

Paul looked around and saw the sign written in English, Greek and several other languages. *Please do not flush toilet paper or other objects.* "It's the same as on our sailboats."

"It keeps the sea clean and visibility clear. You'll see when we take the ferry to Crete."

At 6:00 p.m. Margaret and Paul wandered into the bar at the top floor of the hotel with their cameras to view the scenic vistas. They sat down and both ordered a local white wine, and felt the settled relaxation after walking for four hours. It was still light, so they had a perfect view of the Acropolis, a mesa-like hill rising out of the city plain, west of the restaurant.

After drinking the wine and reminiscing about their day, Margaret said, "Let's go take pictures of the Parthenon."

"Don't we get to relax?"

"No, Marines and their spouses never tire, besides if we wait the sun will be too low in the sky and will blind us and the camera. It's our only chance."

Knowing he couldn't change her mind, he led the way outside the bar. When he reached the balcony and its four foot high brick wall, he said, "Thanks, I didn't realize the beauty of the Acropolis with the hill being crowned by ruins."

"Paul, if you like that view you'll love the next three days. Tomorrow, we'll walk to the Acropolis, tour the Parthenon and the other building on its summit. Then we'll spend the afternoon in the Acropolis Museum. I'll probably have to drag you away."

"Probably," Paul responded. He had been reading tourist guides about Athens and had anticipated the trip for months.

"On our second day, we'll visit the ancient Agora, the market place and political center of Athens from 600 B.C. After lunch we'll visit the Museum of Cycladic Art, and you'll learn about the islands we'll visit after our stay in Crete. The next day we'll tour the National Archaeological Museum that displays artifacts from the stone-age, ancient Greece, and through the Byzantine period."

"I'm beginning to feel tired without taking the tour," Paul said smiling.

"If we have time, we'll go to the National Historical Museum which covers events from the Byzantine to modern Greece. Since these sites aren't located close together, we'll take the Greek subway and bus systems."

As they stood facing west taking multiple pictures, Joann Cummings walked into the bar. She spotted the couple and left before they had a chance to turn around and recognize her.

Satisfied with the twenty-five pictures each took, they returned to their table and ordered. "Paul, I have another photo surprise for you after dinner. Flood lights bathe the whole Acropolis, an eerie display but it makes for great pictures."

Joann assumed the honeymooners would visit the Acropolis, which she had decided to visit on Saturday. She didn't want them to recognize her before she could sell them on her proposal, so she wore a disguise of a brown wig and brown eyes. She held a small digital camera and wore brown slacks and a dark brown sweater to meld with her darker hair and eyes. This image contrasted with the blond blue-eyed face and blue sweater the reporter presented on TV.

While the Acropolis looked high from the hotel bar, Joann found the walk to the ticket booths at its entrance easy. She strolled through Plaka in the early morning. The chill invigorated her. Approaching the Acropolis, she followed the signs and walked around the mount gaining altitude at a slow steady pace. Joann entered and posted herself near the Beule gate where Margaret and Paul had to pass to enter the temple area. While waiting, so as not to appear like a statue, she milled around taking pictures of the temples and the surrounding areas.

After a wait of less than an hour, the couple walked past her and gazed around with the look of awe worn on most tourists' faces. They both glanced at her for a second and showed no sign of recognition. Feeling safe Joann decided to enjoy herself and explore for the rest of the day.

The next morning, still wearing the brown wig and contact lenses, with a change to black slacks and a gray blouse, Joann entered the breakfast room carrying a Greek tour guide. She spotted Margaret and Paul sitting at a table near the back of the room. After filling her tray, she decided to learn more about their Crete departure, and sat next to them and listened.

After a few minutes hearing them reminisce about yesterday's events, Margaret said, "We have two more days before we leave on the fast ferry to Crete. We can rest on the boat since we might need it after walking all over Athens."

"We did okay yesterday. Walking or playing tennis almost every day at home has kept us in shape," Paul said.

"True, but Crete has a mountainous terrain, and it's different from walking in flat Delaware," Margaret said.

Joann thought they're over twenty years older than me and look as trim and attractive as Olympic track stars.

Margaret and Paul talked about their schedule for the next two days.

Joann looked up at a middle age man who walked up to her table and said, "May I join you?"

"Ten years ago you could, but I'm married now, so I have to say no."

As the man ambled away, Margaret leaned over and said to Joann, "That was smooth. We've been married less than a year. I'll have to remember that. Is your husband here?"

"No, I'm not married and wasn't interested. We split up three years ago."

Paul laughed.

"It's my first trip to Greece, and I want to enjoy it alone," Joann said.

"How long are you staying?" Paul asked.

"I haven't decided."

"Don't you work?" Margaret asked.

"No, I had a great and amicable settlement from the ex. I'm looking for a place in Europe to buy a vacation home. I'll visit southern France when I leave Greece."

They introduced themselves. Joann used a first name of Mary and told them she now lived in Washington, DC. She used her maiden last name of DiMaggio. "Where are you going?" Joann asked.

"Two more days here. Then we take a high-speed ferry to Crete and stay for ten days. I spent a year at the NATO naval base at Souda Bay in western Crete thirty years ago as a Marine. I can't wait to see how it's changed," Margaret said.

"Wouldn't it be faster to fly?" Joann asked.

"Yes, but our overnight trip to Crete is a continuation of our honeymoon," Paul said.

Joann thought about Andrew and wondered how it would be to go on a romantic trip with him to Crete one day.

Margaret looked forward to the romance of making love in a port-side cabin as the ferry gently rocked.

"After I leave Athens, I'm going to rent a car. Can you give me any advice?"

"Yes, don't rent a stick shift even if you drive one in the U.S. The cars are underpowered here and with the hilly terrain, you're bound to pop the clutch and roll down a hill. Americans need automatics." Margaret said, as she opened her purse, took out a receipt, and handed it to Joann. "We're renting from Greek National Rental Cars when we're in Crete. They're a dependable company."

Joann wrote the contact information on the inside of her tour book.

"Can you recommend a good hotel in Crete?" Joann asked.

"It depends where you go. Most of the ferries and planes arrive in Irakio. We're staying at the Hotel Olympic Irakio. Your guide book should describe other good hotels," Paul said.

"Are you going to visit Souda Bay?" Joann asked.

"Yes, we'll spend two days in Irakio, so we can visit the museums and the Knossos ruins, then on to Souda. After that, we'll drive west along the coast, stopping along the way at various sites until we arrive at Elafonisi on the southwest coast, my favorite Crete beach."

Joann had the information she needed, so she politely listened to them describe the rest of their itinerary, before she excused herself. "Thanks. So nice to meet you. Enjoy the rest of your honeymoon."

Belford received no information from his cell phone listening system after he returned from Joann's cabin. He decided to leave the U.S. and move to Croatia to avoid capture.

He called Hank, "Just missed my target. Found out she has decided to go to Greece. I am going to follow to complete my task."

"Hope you're more successful this time. As soon as I hear I'll deposit your money. I'll take care of Smithson, assuming he's in the U.S. and doesn't follow Joann. Two more Liberty Credit Card employees' dead should dissuade others from talking about us to the police."

Since Belford intended to find Joann and did not want to be identified during the search, he packed a set of disguises to wear when stalking her. He took a blond and a red wig to cover his gray hair, several mustaches, a full blond beard to hide his face, and a green sweatshirt with a built in pillow to increase his apparent weight by twenty pounds.

The first leg of his flight left the Philadelphia International Airport at 4:30 p.m. on April 16 and arrived in Athens at 9:30 a.m. the next day. The connecting flight left Athens at 11:30 and arrived in Dubrovnik a short time later. He took a cab to the hotel where he had reservations. He had decided to look for a small condo where he could arrange for a month to month lease.

Although he had no idea of Joann's ultimate location, he hoped she had stayed in Greece. He reasoned if she was elsewhere in Europe, Dubrovnik would be convenient after he learned her address. Once in the European Union, he was not subject to a customs inspection for traveling to other European countries.

Belford knew he could bring a gun on a plane leaving the U.S. if he declared it and carried it in his luggage. But he left his gun behind so wouldn't alert the TSA since under his new identity, he didn't have a legal permit to carry it. An avid bow hunter, he needed to buy a bow and arrows in Croatia when he arrived.

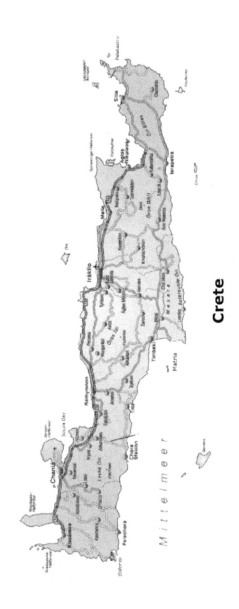

Chapter 16 Ferry to Crete

Sunday, April 18, 2010

After breakfast, Joann returned to her room, accessed the internet, and booked a flight on Athens Air for the fifty-minute flight to Crete that afternoon. She followed Margaret's advice and made reservations to rent a small automatic Fiat. Not wanting to stay at the same hotel as the authors, she accessed trivago.com. Joann selected the Capsis Astoria Irakio a few blocks away and across the street from the Archeological Museum. Joann wanted to meet them in an isolated location, afraid if they met in the same hotel, the ex-cop would reflexively turn her over to the Greek police.

The short flight thrilled Joann, since she had a window seat and compared the Greek landmarks and islands with a map. She had read Crete had mountains over six thousand feet high. Nevertheless, as the plane approached the island, her view of the snow-covered peaks astounded her. As an avid skier, she felt disappointment not having brought her skis. She wondered if they skied on Crete and if the ski areas were open in mid-April.

Joann checked in at her hotel at 6:00 p.m. and immediately walked downtown to find a restaurant. The crowded downtown filled with shops and restaurants impressed her, as she had not realized Irakio was the fifth largest city in Greece. While she ate, she developed the next day's moves. Since Margaret and Paul would not arrive until six on Tuesday morning, she had a full free day. Joann hoped to find locations near their hotel where she could see them entering and leaving the front doors without being observed. After finding six spots, she walked back to the hotel. For the rest of the morning, she decided to visit the ruins at Knossos, something she had read about as a child, and then spend the rest of the day in the Archeological Museum.

On Tuesday after learning the temperature would be above normal in the high seventies, she left the hotel dressed in a third disguise: light blue shorts, a white blouse, white sneakers, green contacts, and red hair. While the honeymooners had arrived at 6:00 in the morning, she did not think they would have rented a car before 9:00, at which time she walked to their hotel to spend the day stalking them. She hoped to find their car and install the tracking device, so she could approach them in a less populated area to ensure privacy as she made her proposition.

Monday, April 19, 2010

Margaret and Paul checked out of the Central Athens Hotel early in the morning and left their bags there while they shopped at the Plaka. They took a taxi to the port of Piraeus at 4:00 p.m. where they boarded the Anek, a Superfast Ferry. Margaret had reserved an outside port cabin so they could see any visible islands on the voyage. After sunset, they ate Greek seafood accompanied by white wine. Returning to their cabin at nine, they took advantage of the romantic setting, retired early, made love, and set the alarm for 5:00 a.m. for the boat's 6:00 a.m. disembarkation.

Before they went to sleep, Paul hugged and kissed her and said, "That was great. We'll have to take more ferries."

"It is romantic."

After gathering their luggage, they took a cab to the Greek National Rental Cars' office. Since they could not check into the Hotel Olympic Irakio until the afternoon, they asked the rental car attendant for a good restaurant and directions to Knossos. Both had an inquisitive trait, expected in an ex-detective and a former professor. They spent the rest of the day reading every sign describing the ruins or restorations they examined. The exhausted couple arrived at their hotel and took a well-earned nap. They continued the honeymoon after they

112

woke up and enjoyed a shower together.

While drying himself, Paul said, "I'll never tire of looking at you."

Margaret embraced him. "I get excited looking at you." She took his hand and led him to the bed. "Let's give each other fond memories of Crete."

"Fond and long," Paul said.

Joann, in disguise, stood watching the surrounding streets and the entrance to the hotel after 9:00 a.m. and walked around for two hours changing locations. She returned to her hotel to rest, resuming her stalking after 1:00. Still not sighting them after several hours, she walked toward the waterfront, to enjoy the scenery.

At 7:00 p.m., while sitting in a cafe, Joann saw them leave the hotel over the rim of her wine glass. They walked toward her and entered a restaurant. Joann was relieved that at least they hadn't changed hotels, which she had begun to fear. Ninety minutes later Margaret and Paul walked back to their hotel and stopped at a blue Ford Fiesta.

Satisfaction oozed throughout Joann's body as they went in the hotel. She wrote the car's make, color, and license plate number in her address book, then she walked to their car and attached the tracking device to the inside of the front passenger side wheel guard. She walked gingerly as she returned to her hotel.

Chapter 17 Meeting Joann Cummings on Crete

Thursday, April 22, 2010

Joann remembered from the conversation in the Athens hotel bar that Margaret and Paul wanted to drive to Souda Bay. They didn't say how long they'd stay there. That location didn't interest Joann. She decided to remain at the Irakio hotel until Margaret and Paul left for Souda. She slept deeply and woke up to her alarm at 6:00 a.m. She turned on her laptop and activated the automobile tracking software. It showed no movement.

After showering and getting dressed without a disguise, she enjoyed the hotel buffet. Still, no car movement by 7:30. Joann waited, watching the English language BBC on TV. Finally two hours later, her laptop beeped. She followed the image of the car on the map. It drove west to Souda. Joann made reservations for a hotel in Chania and checked out of her Irakio hotel and followed Margaret's car.

After Joann arrived in her new hotel, she accessed the tracking system verifying they had stopped in Souda. She opened her guidebook and selected sites to visit.

Two days later, Joann checked the tracking software at 10:00 a.m. and watched Margaret drive west toward Chania. She followed the blue Ford Fiesta. Not knowing their destination, she kept the laptop on and plugged into the cigarette lighter outlet. They stopped at Kissamos for a few hours. Joann parked outside of the town and waited. Then Margaret and Paul continued the drive along a mountainous, narrow road with hairpin turns, south following the western Crete coast. This frightened Joann who was used to the wide limited-access highways in the U.S. So she slowed down and the gap between her car and theirs widened. When they stopped a half-hour later, she found the blue Ford Fiesta in a parking lot at the Meltemi Restaurant.

When she noticed the restaurant sign and their car, Joann's appetite revived. She thought this spot - on a deserted highway at least a thousand feet above the Mediterranean - satisfied the privacy requirements she had for meeting with the authors.

She saw Margaret sitting at a table and Paul standing outside taking pictures of the scenic coast and sea. Approaching the table, Joann said, "Excuse me. May I join you?"

Margaret turned toward her, "You sound like Mary DiMaggio."

Paul hearing the conversation returned and sat at the table.

"I've just finished reading your book about the skeleton murders. Your faces match those on the back cover, Margaret Hoffman and Paul O'Hare. I loved the book. Are you familiar with the Liberty Credit Card case?"

"Yes, we know about the case, as does everyone in the U.S. who watches the six o'clock news," Paul said.

Margaret stared at Joann. "But you're not Mary. You're Joann Cummings," she said, while looking at Paul.

"I wore a disguise so you or anyone else in Greece couldn't recognize me."

"How did you get here? The Delaware State Police are looking for you," Paul asked.

"Flew in to Athens from Philly and followed you here. I know the Delaware and possibly the Greek police would like to find me, but I have a proposition for you. If you like it, you won't contact them," Joann said.

"Sit down so we can talk without straining our necks," Paul said.

"We're hungry. Please join us." Margaret said, eager to learn information they could use in the book.

Joann sat down.

Margaret said, "I'm a retired Delaware state trooper. Tell me why I shouldn't notify them."

Joann understood Margaret hadn't been told the State Police cleared her since Detective Jenson told her this information would be kept secret. She said, "If you turn me in, I'll be killed and the case will never be solved. I didn't participate in the crime, but I might be murdered because I can help solve it. Since someone shot Andrew Smithson, I've terrified of being shot next. I'll tell you why I can help solve the crime during my proposal. If you agree, you'll also help me avoid getting accused of being a participant in the crime."

The waiter asked, "What would you like?"

The waiter took their orders and left.

"I propose for your next book you write about the Liberty Credit Card Embezzlement." Joann noticed they looked at each other. "You must get a million similar proposals."

"None since we arrived in Greece. Go ahead," Margaret said.

"Since I'm part of the story, you'll learn more about it than the police ever can."

A minute into her discussion Paul interrupted her, and said, "Do you mind if we record this?"

"No."

Margaret, surprised at Paul's suggestion, placed her cell phone on the table between them.

Joann began. She spent the next thirty minutes discussing what had happened, including why she thought it was inside embezzlement and not credit card fraud.

Paul, using the techniques he learned in the Del Tech interview course, occasionally interrupted Joann to learn more details about a point she made. Margaret quietly listened to the two, happy that Paul had progressed from reading old documents for his historical research to questioning live individuals. She concluded the tuition for the course was well spent, and knew Paul's new interview skills would be useful in completing their second novel.

"Do you accept private detective jobs?" Joann asked.

"We've never considered a private detective assignment. We're authors," Paul said, knowing what they could earn as private detectives would be miniscule compared to income for another best seller.

Joann shared her fears, "For supplying you with information for the book I want you to solve the crime. If you don't catch the criminals, I won't survive to tell you my story."

"Detective Jenson and her staff are very capable. I don't know what we can add," Margaret said.

"She seems competent, but both of you have skills she doesn't have and you aren't bound by constraints of the legal system. I liked the way Paul zeroed in to get more details, when I wasn't specific enough. You'll also be gathering material for the book. If you solve the case, the new book will outsell your first book."

"If we accept your proposition, we won't do anything illegal," Paul said. He tried not to gloat as he thought her statement on future book sales might be correct.

"Paul and I'll discuss your offer. Do you have an international capable cell phone we can call? We'll get back with you later today. In the meantime enjoy Crete."

"I will. Please, don't give this to anyone. It could threaten my life if you do." Joann wrote her cell phone number on a napkin and left. Before driving back to Chania, she took a last look at the beautiful mountain scenery melding with the bright blue sea,.

Paul said, "It was hard not to tell her we had already decided on writing about Liberty."

"I know, but I need to talk to Helen Jenson before we work with her. You have interview skills I didn't know you had." Margaret said. She leaned over to kiss his cheek.

Paul beamed. "I studied hard, like I did in graduate school. It's 2:30 p.m. here, and 5:30 a.m. in Delaware. Let's wait a few hours before we call."

"Good idea, let's drive to the beach at Elafonisi. I'll call her at 4:30

Greek time," Margaret said.

After a leisurely, scenic drive, they arrived at the beach and spent an hour swimming in the clear blue water gazing at the coral below them. Then they changed clothes, walked to their car, and made the call.

"Helen, it's Paul and Margaret. We're on speaker phone."

"What are you doing calling me? You're retired and on your honeymoon. Where are you?"

"On a little beach in southwestern Crete. How is the Liberty Credit Card case coming?"

"Better than the newspapers report. But I don't want to talk about it over the phone."

"I'll try to be general. The BBC on TV said you're looking for two individuals, Joann Cummings and George Belford."

"That's correct, but we haven't found them. Have you seen them?" Helen said laughing.

"We talked to Joann Cummings in a restaurant on the top of a mountain overlooking the blue Mediterranean a few hours ago."

Margaret and Paul heard the noise of plastic bouncing off a desk, "Sorry, I dropped my phone. Could you repeat what you said?"

"We had lunch with Joann Cummings. She proposed that we write up the Liberty Credit Card crime as our next book," Margaret said.

"But you had decided to do that anyway."

"Joann Cummings didn't know that," Paul said.

"If she's a suspect how did she get past TSA at the Philly airport?" Margaret asked.

"She's not a suspect. We didn't ask TSA to stop her. She said she'd feel safer out of the country than here with police protection, so we let her go. We've talked to her and she has cooperated with us. We're confident she'll return when asked to testify."

"Hard to believe. Did you send her to us?" Paul asked.

"No. We don't know where she is. Don't tell anyone she is not a suspect. It's part of our strategy to catch the perpetrators," Helen said.

Paul and Margaret looked at each other nodding their heads yes.

"We won't," Margaret said.

Margaret and Paul drove north over a less exciting route through Elos and Topolia east of the coast. They stopped often to take pictures of the White Mountains and gorges on the way to Chania where they had hotel reservations for the night.

When they settled in their hotel room, before going out to eat, Margaret placed a call to Joann. When she answered, Margaret said, "It's Paul and Margaret. We've talked to Detective Jenson, and she verified your innocence. We want to continue our discussion."

"I'm at the Casa Veneta in Chania," Joann replied, trying to keep her voice businesslike and hoping they would never learn, she knew their GPS location.

"We're also in Chania at the Amphora hotel." Margaret replied.

"Let's meet, after breakfast." Paul said.

"What time and where?" Joann interrupted, trying not to reveal her glee.

"Don't know yet," Margaret said. "We're going out for dinner, and we'll find a restaurant. I'll call you in the morning after 8:00."

"Enjoy your meal. I'll look forward to your call."

George Belford had toured the sights of Dubrovnik for several days. He checked his cell phone listening device as least five times a day. He had just finished walking on the wall of the enclosed old part of the city, returning home hot and sweaty. Before taking a shower, he tried the listening system. It registered a conversation between Joann and the honeymooners, whose phone numbers he had. Belford listened to Margaret's and Joann's phone conversation later in the evening, verifying they would join the case. When he learned of her proposal, he knew he had to kill her, since Margaret and Paul, with Joann's help, might be more successful than the Delaware State Police.

He added Margaret's phone number to the listening system.

Chapter 18 Traveling in Crete

Sunday, April 25, 2010

Margaret called Joann. "Hi, we'll be eating at our hotel. Can you join us here at 9:00?"

"Yes. Did you enjoy the beach yesterday?" Joann asked, thinking of something to do in the afternoon.

"We did."

After morning greetings, Margaret said, "The buffet is at the back. Let's fill our plates."

When they returned to the table, Paul said, "Let's talk about the case after we finish eating."

"Tell me about your visit to the beach," Joann said.

"The drive to the beach was the worst roller coaster ride I've ever experienced. Up and down the mountains on a narrow road with blind hairpin turns. In the small villages, the roads were so narrow only one car could pass. The Greeks are courteous drivers, always stopping to let us by," Paul said.

"Since the year I lived in Crete, I forgot the first impression the mountain roads have on the tourists," Margaret said.

"However, the drive back wasn't as scary," Paul said. "We took a different route with wider roads and fewer sharp turns."

Paul and Margaret's description of the beach and surrounding area excited Joann.

After they finished eating, Margaret placed her cell phone on the table and explained, "As before, we'll record our conversation to collect data for the book and perhaps to help us solve the crime."

"Yesterday, I talked in generalities, today I'll provide detailed information on my staff and others who may be related to the crimes," Joann said handing them a piece of paper with handwritten names, positions, a summary of their responsibilities, and her suspicion of their potential role in the embezzlement.

Impressed, Paul said, "A great start."

Margaret questioned her about each individual on topics related to the crime. After twenty minutes of reviewing each name, Margaret said, "We're interested in George Belford, as are the Delaware Police. The company fired him. He has disappeared."

Joann explained, "Belford could have helped the programmer avoid the security checks when they stole from the company. But he didn't have the skills to write the programs."

"Who were his friends in the company?"

"He didn't have that many, that I know of, except for Hank Strong, the Finance VP, and the murdered Steve Haven, our Database Administrator. Strong and Belford are brothers-in-law. Both fought in Vietnam together. Strong recommended the company hire Belford."

"Doesn't Liberty Credit have nepotism rules?" Paul asked.

"Yes, but since he reported to my boss, Ed Davis, the Operations VP, and not Strong, the rules didn't apply to him."

"What was his relationship with Steve Haven?" Margaret asked.

"They worked closely together to build security into the system and were drinking buddies."

"Could Haven have written the embezzlement program?" Paul asked.

"Yes, that was my first suspicion when he went missing. However, when they found him dead, I assumed he discovered the crime and someone killed him before he could tell me or the police," Joann said.

"Could he be the leader of the embezzlement gang?" Paul asked.

"I doubt it, I never thought of him as an organizational genius."

"Could Haven have been killed to prevent him from telling the police who paid him to write the embezzlement program?" Margaret asked.

"I don't know," Joann said, shocked at her own naïveté about investigations and more frightened than before about the cold-blooded behavior of the criminals.

Margaret said, "That's enough for us to start our investigation. We can talk in a few days after we validate our new theory."

"How long will you stay in Crete?" Joann asked.

"For another week. Then we travel to Santorini for two days and go to Naxos. What are your plans?" Margaret said.

"Nothing specific."

"For the next two days we'll stay here and visit the museums and the old mountain villages. Then we will hike down the Imbros Gorge. Perhaps you'd like to join us. We might have more information by then," Paul said.

"I'd love hiking in the mountains, I'll meet you there. I'm thinking of driving to Elafonisi today."

"Take the less stressful central route," Paul said. "We'll meet you at the head of the Imbros Gorge at 10:00 a.m. on Tuesday. Then, we'll drive to the bottom of the gorge, leave one car and drive back to the entrance and start hiking." He showed Joann the location in his guide book.

"If you learn anything new, please call us," Margaret said.

Joann decided to wait until after the hike to propose the authors meet Joe Reynolds in Naxos. He might have discovered more by then.

That morning at 8:00 in his Dubrovnik hotel, Belford turned on his PC and activated the Relay program and waited. He heard both the initial phone call and the breakfast conversation. Belford learned their destinations for the next three days. He made airline and hotel reservations for Irakio, Crete. He packed a suitcase with clothes for five days and a backpack with his disassembled bow. Before leaving, he extended his reservation in the Dubrovnik hotel for another week.

Belford arrived in Irakio Monday afternoon the day before the scheduled hike. After renting a car at the airport, he drove to the gorge.

He examined a map of the trail for potential ambush spots. To ascertain their desirability, he walked down the gorge and settled for a site two miles from the trail's start. At the bottom of the trail, he took a bus back to the top to retrieve his car and drive to his hotel.

On the day of the hike, Belford wore a disguise of a red wig and a twenty pound enhanced stomach. He carried the disassembled bow in a backpack and walked to the ambush site.

Margaret, Paul, and Joann left Chania in two cars and drove southeast to the turnoff at Vamoa and continued south to the gorge. The drive had different but spectacular scenery. The road wandered through a pass in a high valley in Crete's White Mountains. As they approached the Imbros Gorge, steep gray cliffs rose near the road. Isolated trees clung to the cliffs.

After passing through a tunnel cut into a cliff, Margaret saw the restaurant and parking spaces to the left marking the beginning of the path down the gorge. She pulled in and stopped by Joann's car. So Joann and Paul could appreciate the hike, Margaret showed them the descending five-mile small dirt path they would walk on for the rest of the morning and into the afternoon.

Then the authors, followed by Joann, drove to the bottom of the gorge where she left her car. At the beginning of the return trip, Margaret said, "We talked to Detective Jenson. She said they had been examining a potential connection between Haven and Belford. They had been friends and drinking buddies, but they found nothing more. The police examined their phone records, both personal and business and didn't find an unusual pattern around the time of the embezzlement. The emails were all business, or a few had suggestions they met for a drink after work."

"That's too bad," Joann said. "I hoped my theory might have solved the case."

"It doesn't mean Belford learned of Haven's research, just that Jenson's team hasn't found any evidence he knew," Paul said.

Joann wondered if Andrew would appreciate the country as she did. While she had only known him for five emotionally intense days before his shooting, she assumed he would enjoy the same things she did. Joann thought it would be nicer to take this hike with Andrew just enjoying the scenery and the aura of a new love, rather than being worried about being killed and scheming to stay alive.

After they returned to the top of the gorge, they started to walk. Each carried two bottles of water to avoid being thirsty on the two-and-a-half hour hike. Margaret watched Joann's pace as she periodically stopped to wait for them, noting Joann was younger and in better shape. She said, "Why don't you go ahead since we can't keep up with you."

Joann reached the ambush location fifteen minutes ahead of the authors. Without other tourists near her, she turned the corner of the rocks into the kill zone. At a distance of thirty yards, she presented a perfect target for Belford. As he placed the arrow in the bow, aimed, and shot, she bent down to look at a beautiful group of violet five-petal mountain flowers with green leaves growing out of the rocks. She didn't hear the arrow whistle by.

The arrow flew over her head and down the gorge for another fifty yards before glancing off a rock and falling to the ground in an area covered with bushes.

Belford thought, Christ, that woman won't die. Before he could shoot another arrow, an older couple wandered into the clearing and started talking with Joann. Belford realized further attempts at killing Joann in the gorge were too dangerous. Another missed opportunity for the $200 million. He'd have to follow her in Greece until he completed his task. He waited until Margaret and Paul passed, reentered the path, repacked his bow, walked up the mountain to his car, and returned to Irakio.

Joann reached the end of the trail thirty minutes ahead of the authors. The three tourists spent the rest of the day examining Chora Sfakion, the town at the bottom of the gorge. They ate dinner together in a small restaurant overlooking the sea and the ferry port.

Paul said, "Tomorrow, we'll be taking a ferry to a small town, Ayil Roumeli, at the base of the Samaria Gorge, which is even more spectacular than the Imbros Gorge. There are no roads into the town. It can only be accessed by sea. We might hike part way up the gorge. You're welcome to join us."

"Thanks, but I'm returning to Chania."

"We should share our travel schedule, so we can stay in touch." Margaret said, as she handed Joann a copy of their itinerary for the rest of their time in Crete. "We are going to drive east stopping at Matala and Lerapetra on the south coast before heading northeast and visiting the ruins north of Palekastro and spending the night in those towns. Then we'll drive west to Agios Nikolaos for an overnight stay, returning to Irakio for dinner on May 1 before taking the morning ferry to Santorini."

Joann said, "I'll join you in Santorini and Naxos. What is your destination after Naxos? I don't want to stalk you, but I'll make hotel reservations so we can be in the same area."

"We're going to Mykonos to stay with our friends, Sally and Kostas Canakis." Paul said. "Kostas was a professor of Archeology at Binghamton University in upstate New York, when I taught there."

The three spent the rest of the meal discussing Paul's past. When they finished eating, Paul said, "We've started an outline of the Liberty Credit Card Embezzlement case. We want you to read it."

"When?"

"In Santorini. We're still working on it," Margaret said.

"I might have something to add. One of my staff has been examining the computer systems data and discovered discrepancies, related to the fraud. He's concerned about his safety as I am. He's flying to Naxos to brief me," Joann said.

"Good - getting him out of the country might be the safest move."

Belford listened to the recording of the conversation later that evening at his hotel in Irakio. He cringed when he heard one of Joann's staff had discovered problems related to the embezzlement. It had to be a systems programmer. Since Joann had four on her staff, he didn't know their name.

Belford hoped to meet the programmer in Naxos and had to add him to the list of those he had to eliminate. He decided to take a plane from Crete to Athens and enjoy the sights of the ancient city. He didn't want any Naxos residents to recognize him by staying there four days before Joann and the system's programmer arrived.

Safe in her hotel in Chania, Joann received an email from Joe.

Joann,
Significant progress in our project. Request guidance.
Joe

Joann emailed back:

Joe,
Good news. Put details in safe deposit box. Fly to Naxos, Greece by Monday, May 3 and tell me in person. Email me the date and time of arrival and hotel in Naxos city where you will be staying.
Joann,

Joe replied.

Joann,
Have stored the data. Tell you the arrival date and location later.
Joe

Santorini

Chapter 19 Santorini

Sunday, May 2, 2010

The three tourists boarded a high speed Seajets ferry for departure at 8:40 a.m. and arrived at Santorini mid-morning. Joann looked in awe at the sheer cliffs of the crescent-shaped island rising from the blue waters of the caldera, and said, "I hope we don't have to climb that cliff."

Margaret laughed. Paul looked at the crowded ferry port filled with people, ticket offices, restaurants, buses, and taxis, and said, "Let's get a cab." Joann and Margaret followed him to the cab stand. The cab drove on the tight-switched road located on the side of the cliff, and reached the top a few miles south of the island's main town, Fira.

Observing the white buildings with blue window sills and doors spread over the town's hilly terrain, Paul said, "The view of the town made the ferry trip worthwhile."

Margaret and Joann agreed.

Joann's hotel was only a short two-block walk from the authors' hotel, along the main road of the town. Since they could not check in to their hotels, they left their luggage there and walked a block toward the shops and restaurants sitting on the top of the cliff overlooking the sea to the west of the island. As they passed the expensive clothes and jewelry stores, Margaret commented, "These shops are ten times more expensive than those in the Plaka district. I'll restrict my shopping to Athens before I go home," Margaret said.

"While we can afford these stores, I'm glad you aren't tempted by them," Paul said. But he wondered if he could find something affordable and special for her.

They found a restaurant with a view of the sea and the other islands in the caldera waters. Paul gazed south pointing at an outline of the peaks of Crete, visible in the clear sky. Joann asked, "Are all parts of Greece beautiful with perfect vistas?"

"I reached that conclusion long ago during my one-year stay," Margaret said.

In the afternoon they returned to their hotels, checked in, rested, and agreed to meet at the same restaurant at 6:00 and to review the new outline of the book.

After they ordered dinner drinks, Paul sat on the east side of the table to avoid the glare on his PC screen from the bright low sun in the west and showed Joann the outline. The chapters followed the chronological order of the crime, but did not include their interactions on Crete. Since the crime had not been solved, the outline was incomplete. Paul had divided many of the chapters into scenes.

"Joann, please read the outline and make suggestions to improve it," Paul said.

"Why didn't you include the shooting of Andrew Smithson and his investigation?" Joann asked.

"We understood from Detective Jenson that his shooting wasn't related to the credit card crime," Margaret said.

"I went underground because I thought one of the embezzlers attacked me and missed, but hit Andrew. At least that part should be in the book."

"You're correct, he did motivate you," Paul said as he added a scene to the outline, "But we didn't know if his attack was related to the crime."

"Andrew is still working on the case but not at Liberty Credit. He is at a secret location to avoid a repeat of the attack. I guess you weren't aware of that. Please keep it a secret, but I suggest discussing his role in the analysis of the crime."

"We will," Paul said as he made corrections to the outline.

"The last time I talked to Detective Jenson, she said they still hadn't located George Belford. Do you suggest we increase his coverage?" Margaret asked.

"Yes, add to his background and include a chapter on the police search for him."

Joann recalled the scenes in *The Abandoned Homes Serial Murders* where the bad guys used a computer to listen to cell phone conversations and pick up the sounds from normal conversations. She thought Belford, a security expert, might know these techniques.

The three agreed to travel to Naxos together and meet Joe Reynolds at Margaret's hotel on Tuesday May 4, 2010.

They decided to take a bus in the morning to the restored 1700 B.C. Minoan ruins of Thira, near the town of Akrotini, on the southern end of the island. Then after eating they would tour the Red and White beaches west of Thira.

In the privacy of her hotel room, Joann removed the battery cell phone battery as a precaution, and decided to only use email to communicate with Joe.

The excavated ruins at Thira had a temporary roof over them protecting the ancient buildings, archeologists, and tourists from the sun and rain. The ruins amazed them. Thira had been destroyed by an earthquake and volcanic explosion in the caldera around 1650. Yet the partially excavated city showed an arrangement of buildings and streets that would be recognized by all modern tourists.

Margaret and Paul took copious pictures of the restored area. They had decided to write a tour guide of Greece for retired Americans. Joann took a few pictures and wondered if Andrew might enjoy visiting archeological ruins as much as she did. This uncertainty made her realize how little she knew of him.

The boat tour of the Red and White beaches relaxed them since they didn't talk or think about the embezzlement case. They stared at the spectacular site of the black sand on the beaches, surrounded by the sheer red and white cliffs surrounding the beaches. All three took pictures.

Joann opened a new email from Joe at her hotel.

Joann,

In Naxos, and staying at the Apollon Hotel near the bus station and the Mitropoulos Museum in the main town. This island is fabulous compared to Delaware. I'm going to see the town on foot and the rest of the island using buses. I have reserved the hotel room for four days. Let me know when and I'll meet you at the ferry.

Joe

Joann replied:

Joe,

Blue Star Ferry at 10:10 a.m. on Tuesday, May 4. I'll book a room in your hotel.

Joann

Belford listened to the tourists' plans to arrive in Naxos on the morning of May 4, 2010 on the Blue Star line. He became concerned when the Relay system stopped recording Joann's cell phone and regular conversations in the morning. Unless Margaret used her phone he could not hear their conversations.

Later that day, he flew to the island, registered in a luxury hotel, the Nissaki Beach, and woke after a good night hoping to learn the identity of the programmer.

Naxos

Chapter 20 Naxos

Tuesday May 4, 2010

Joe left his hotel and walked to the ferry jetty section of the port arriving fifteen minutes before the boat's scheduled docking. In the warm May weather, he wore a blue tee shirt with Naxos embroidered across his chest, white shorts, and leather boat shoes. Joe went hatless displaying his bald crown surrounded by white hair. He sat on a bench in front of the ferry passenger boarding area and read a Greek tourist guide, deciding what he should visit in Naxos before returning home.

Belford left his hotel ten minutes earlier than Joe for the longer walk to the ferry port. Not wanting either Joann or Joe to recognize him, he did not go onto the jetty, but sat at a restaurant across the water drinking coffee. He used his binoculars to scan the waiting zone on the jetty. After a minute, he noticed a bald, white-haired man, who he knew as Joe Reynolds. He relaxed. He would eliminate one of his problems.

The ferry arrived ten minutes late. Belford scanned the front where passengers disembarked. He saw Joann walk down the gangplank conversing with a couple who he assumed to be Margaret Hoffman and Paul O'Hare

Earlier cell phone recordings between Joann and the authors had given Belford the name of Joann's hotel which he had located on a tourist map. Fearful Reynolds might recognize him, Belford stayed away. If he intended to stalk them without being seen, he had to change his appearance. He congratulated himself on packing the disguises.

After the four met in the breakfast room of the Apollon hotel, Paul asked, "Joe, do you mind if we go to your room and record you? It's easier than taking notes. You can review the transcript for accuracy after we finish."

Joe agreed and in his room Margaret placed her cell phone on a coffee table between them and turned on its recording app.

"Margaret and I have few skills in information technology," Paul said. "Joann, please ask if you think Joe should provide more details in the IT area. Margaret and I will do the same for the specifics of his findings related to the crime."

Joe repeated the briefing he had given Joann in western Maryland to the two authors, lengthened by their questions and his answers."

When he finished reciting what he had told Joann earlier, Joe said, "Joann, listen carefully, this is something new."

"Okay," she said. Her stoic look changed to anticipation as she smiled and her eyes focused on Joe.

"I examined the users who accessed the database during December. Only two used an IP address where they routed their connections through a sequence of IP addresses to hide their identity. One user could have accessed the system both times. The first occurred at the start of the embezzlement and the second when the embezzlement ended. My theory is the first started the embezzlement while the second tried to remove all traces of the crime. Since the initial hacker could not remove the User ID from the system logs, someone else had to in the second operation. The configuration of our security procedures only allows the Security Chief, George Belford, to remove a user so they don't leave a trace on the activity logs."

"Christ, you've solved part of the crime," Paul said. "Do the State Police know this?"

"No, I haven't told them."

"Is this documented?" Joann asked.

"Yes, it's on a thumb drive in my safe deposit box and on this one." Joe handed the drive to Joann. "I'm sure it's safe with my boss."

"We need to tell the police," Joann said. Both Margaret and Paul agreed and nodded their heads.

"Go ahead. I didn't think I had the authority to release the company's information," Joe said.

"Well, I do. I'll email it to Helen Jenson as soon as I can get to a computer," Joann said.

"You can use my laptop," Joe said.

"I'd need to call her after we email her. We can all join the call. Joe you have to explain in more detail to Detective Bill Norse, a computer expert, what you've found," Joann said.

"I guess I'll have to redo the book's outline tonight," Paul said.

Joe turned on his laptop. "Joann it's yours."

She opened the email app and composed a secure message to Helen Jenson.

Helen,

Have new information. Access attached file. Margaret will call at 8:00 a.m. your time.

Joann

"Joe, please give me the USB drive." Joann inserted the drive into the PC and attached its contents to the email.

After Joann emailed Helen, Margaret said, "It's 7:30 a.m. in Delaware. Helen will be in her office in thirty minutes."

"I've never been to Greece, but compared to Delaware this island impresses me with its mountains, beaches, architecture, ruins, and vistas. My flight reservation home is open-ended so I can explore the country. Has anyone been to Naxos before?" Joe asked.

"Yes, I have," Margaret said. "This town has plenty to see and so I suggest that after we make the call, we walk across the causeway to Portara Island and visit the unfinished Temple of Apollo. It's a great site for taking pictures of the sea and the city. On our return, we should walk up the hill to the Kastro, the original walled city. It has several interesting museums."

The three agreed to join Joe on a bus tour of the island. They talked about the relative merits of visiting other islands and the mainland until Margaret placed the call.

"Helen, Joann Cummings sent an email with an analysis of credit card transactions during December and January."

"Yes, I've received it, but haven't opened it," Helen said.

"One of Joann's staff, Joe Reynolds, has joined us in Naxos. He compiled the information and will explain it."

Joe spent the next fifteen minutes discussing the data and answering questions from Helen and Bill Norse.

"Your analysis confirms our theory about Belford. But we have made little progress since we talked ten days ago. This data should help."

"Any new information on Belford's location?" Paul asked.

"No, he's disappeared and might have left the country."

"What about his brother-in-law, Hank Strong?" Paul asked.

"He is still working, turning over his responsibilities to his successor. He has five weeks before he leaves the bank. We haven't been able to discover evidence involving him," Helen said.

Belford had returned to his hotel after the four entered the Apollon Hotel and listened to the conversation that activated Margaret's cell phone and relayed it to his. He also listened to the call from Margaret's cell phone to Helen Jenson. It worried him to realize he had not eliminated Joe Reynolds early enough to protect himself. Now Detective Jenson and the Delaware State Police suspected him and thought Hank Strong was connected to the crime. Before it unraveled, he needed to contact Hank on his secure cell phone and warn him. Since he didn't want to risk reaching him at work, he decided to call him early the next day. He knew Hank would say anything to avoid prison, including implicating him.

Belford heard Joe say he wanted to listen to the local bands before retiring for the evening. No one said they would join him. This time he'd use a knife since it would be impossible to fire an arrow in the dark in the night club district of a crowded downtown. He had to get close to Joe.

In the early evening Belford, dressed in his disguise, ate early near his hotel. He walked north and sat outside of Joe's hotel and waited, hoping to track him as he left alone to visit the bars of Naxos.

Joe appeared in the early evening and walked toward the ferry slips. Then he turned south on the Paralia toward the nightclubs in the Pigadakiah section. He stopped at a small restaurant and ordered lamb and macaroni. An hour and several glasses of local red wine later, he walked south again and visited several bars. He enjoyed the different musical genres in each bar including jazz, European rock, and Greek songs.

At 11:00, he decided to return to his hotel, retracing his steps on the Paralia on a dark moonless evening. Joe missed the turn at the Ring Road to return to his hotel and continued toward the causeway to the Temple of Apollo.

A sober Belford followed the teetering Joe. Belford walked rapidly to reduce the distance between them. He closed in when he saw Joe walk behind a line of shrubs on the causeway, ten yards from the ferry jetty. Without making a noise, Belford reached Joe in the deserted area. When he was less than a foot behind him, he placed his left hand on Joe's forehead and pulled it back. Belford ran his razor sharp six-inch knife across Joe's neck, severing the carotid arteries. Before Joe could fall, Belford held and dragged him west to the rocks lining the causeway and pushed him in the sea. Joe's body sank in a few feet of water. Belford's heart hammered in his chest, the percussion a mix of panic and exhilaration.

Belford threw his knife into the sea and examined his clothes, but didn't see any traces of blood. He walked south on the quiet streets, grinning since he knew he was closer to his $200 million, till he reached his hotel room near midnight. To celebrate, he uncorked a bottle of Ouzo he had purchased earlier in the day and poured several ounces of the clear liquid over ice cubes in a small glass. He watched the liquid turn cloudy as it mixed with the melted water. This transformation fascinated him so he repeated it four times before he crashed into a deep but restless sleep.

At 6:30 in the morning, a Greek man in his early twenties ran along the Paralia from the south looking at the morning sea. He loved running in the cool of the morning before the heat of the day made it too exhausting. When he approached the causeway to the Temple of Apollo, he turned left and headed for the island. Twenty yards on the causeway, he stopped, startled by the sight of a body half floating in the water with the head and torso impaled on the rocks. He called the police on his cell phone. They instructed him not to touch the body, and to stay near it.

Two policemen arrived, a patrolman and a detective, who examined the body. Upon turning the corpse's head, the patrolman noticed the extensive cut on the throat which the lapping water had washed clean and told the detective, "He's been murdered."

The detective called the Central Police Headquarters on Syros, the capital of the Cyclades Islands, since only the headquarters homicide squad could conduct a murder investigation. The two local policemen secured the crime scene by closing the causeway to the island. A police boat arrived from Syros two hours later with six passengers: a homicide detective, two criminal scene investigators, a member of the coroner's office, and two officers.

The homicide detective, Eaton Nikas, searched the pants' pockets retrieving a passport, wallet, and a room key to the Apollon Hotel. Since the wallet contained over two hundred Euros and four credit cards, the detective concluded robbery was not the motive.

Wednesday, May 5, 2010

Belford waited until 2:00 p.m. local time or 7:00 a.m. Delaware time to call Hank Strong, hoping he had not left home for work.

"It's your friend with bad and good news," Belford said.

"What?" Hank still half asleep replied.

"The police know how the embezzlement occurred. A detailed examination of the computer system logs revealed our operation. They think I'm involved, and they're looking at you."

"Christ, I've five weeks to go. If I disappear now, they'll conclude I'm part of the crime."

"Stay home. Our main concern has increased from Cummings to Joe Reynolds, the systems programmer, and two authors, Margaret Hoffman and Paul O'Hare. Hoffman is an ex-Delaware State Police detective. They've agreed to work with Cummings to catch us and write a book about it."

"I read their first book, which showed Hoffman as a great detective who led the effort to solve the Vietnam serial murders. She might be able to figure out who committed the credit card crime. I should leave while I still have a chance."

"Don't. Reynolds can't talk anymore. Hoffman, O'Hare, and Cummings are in Naxos, Greece, as am I. If everything works out in the next two days, I'll have solved our problems. Check the newspapers. If I run into trouble, I'll call and tell you to leave, deposit my $200 million, and you won't hear from me again."

Hank was at his Middletown home. He broke into a cold sweat during the conversation. He never thought the police would connect him to the crime. After he hung up, he understood his vulnerabilities. The call destroyed his confident demeanor. While he kept his phony identity documents in a safe deposit box registered in another name, he had stored enough incriminating information at his two homes for the police to arrest him.

He gathered the potentially damning foreign travel plans, a special laptop that stored programs to break into the company's IT systems, files on Belford, Steve Haven, and a plan of the embezzlement. He threw the travel material into his fire place and lit it. As it burned, he deleted the files on the laptop and USB drives, reformatted and wrote random data on them. After the fire cooled, he shoveled the ashes into a bucket and flushed them down a toilet.

Not happy with the laptop, he took it apart and removed the drive disk from its housing. He used a hammer to bang the disk to destroy it. Hank smashed the USB drives beyond recognition. When finished, he placed the debris in a white trash bag.

Afraid to risk another minute to welcome a police team, he called in sick. After a tasteless meal, he left the house and drove south on Route 1 to his Bethany Beach house.

Still in panic mode, he used the fireplace to burn any more damaging material. He repeated destruction of the electronics holding incriminating files and placed them in a trash bag. When satisfied the police would find nothing to connect him to the crime if they searched either home, he returned to Middletown, disposing the destroyed hardware trash bag in the Rehoboth-Lewes Canal on the way.

Joann entered the breakfast room at 9:00 to meet Joe before joining the two authors at the bus terminal an hour later. Not seeing Joe, she thought he must have had too much to drink last night.

A hotel staff member walked over to her table accompanied by Eaton Nikas. After being introduced as a Greek detective, he asked, "Do you know Joe Reynolds?"

"Yes, I had arranged to meet him here. Is anything wrong?"

"Yes, he's been murdered. I need you to come with me to identify the body."

The fear, absent since her arrival in Greece, returned. Nausea bubbled in her stomach, her breathing became rapid, and her head ached. She wondered how they tracked Joe and killed him. Joann stood up shaking, and said, "I'll follow you."

After she identified the body, Nikas asked, "Why would someone kill Joe?"

"I don't know. We work at the same company. We're friends were going to tour Naxos." Joann didn't mention the connection to the Liberty Credit Card embezzlement case.

Nikas described how they found Reynolds, stating he wasn't murdered for his money.

After he finished questioning Joann, he transferred Joe's body to Syros for an autopsy.

Paul and Margaret arrived at the bus terminal and waited. Both looked toward the causeway and saw the police activity and wondered what had happened. They became concerned when neither Joann nor Joe had arrived by 9:30. They walked five minutes to the Apollon Hotel and Paul asked the desk attendant, "Please ring Joann's Cummings's room."

"She's not here. The police came and she left with them."

"Do you know where they took her?"

"To the police station. It's a short walk." The desk attendant handed them a map with a markup of how to walk there.

When they arrived at the station lobby, Paul asked, "We heard Joann Cummings is here. Can we talk to her?"

"As soon as the detective finishes," the desk attendant said.

Fifteen minutes later, Joann walked into the lobby, saw Margaret and Paul, and said, "I have bad news. Let's get out of here."

After they left the station, Joann said, "Someone murdered Joe. It wasn't robbery. His wallet and passport weren't taken. Since arriving in Greece, I felt safe. Now, I'm frightened again." She started crying. After wiping her tears, she said, "The criminals have found me. I'm responsible for luring Joe Reynolds to his death. The killer might have seen us with Joe. We could be next."

Margaret, said, "The killer must have been part of the embezzlement gang. But how did they find his location?"

"The same way Ralph Cohen told you about in North Carolina that we mentioned in our book. Someone hacked our cell phones," Paul said. He thought living with Margaret might be too exciting. Does this always happen around her? Now that I've been trained in firearms, I can't get a gun when I might need one.

"They listened to our conversations and our calls," Margaret said, as she took her cell phone from her purse and removed the SIM card and turned off the phone. Paul did the same.

Joann said, "Being paranoid, I killed my cell phone a few days ago. I'm scared, more so than earlier in West Virginia. We have to leave. The killers might now be after you both."

"What did you tell the police about Joe?" Paul asked.

"Only that we're friends, worked together, and planned to tour Naxos for the next two days. I didn't mention the embezzlement, or you, afraid I'd be detained."

"Good, that would only complicate matters, especially since we have no proof it's connected to the embezzlement," Paul said.

They entered the hotel and went to Joann's room. "Joann's correct. We have to leave," Margaret said.

"How?" Joann asked.

"Fly to Mykonos. We need to get new cell phones and can't use our laptops to make reservations," Margaret said.

"The hotel has a business center. We can use their PCs," Joann said.

"I'll email Helen telling her I'll call her at 8:00 Delaware time on her land line and not to use her cell phone."

Paul Googled air transportation information between Naxos and Mykonos on the hotel's PC. He said, "Unfortunately, there are no direct scheduled flights between the islands. All flights go through Athens. Today's only connection took off at 8:50 a.m."

Margaret, not wanting to stay on the island another day, said, "Can we charter a flight?"

Paul realized their wealth could rescue them, and contacted a private charter airline arranging to leave at 4:00 p.m.

"For safety, we should stay together. Joann please check out, and the three of us can get a cab to our hotel," Margaret said.

After they arrived, Paul said, "Let's get new cell phones and an early lunch." As they left the hotel, Margaret scanned the area to see if someone had followed them. They ate in a small restaurant near the hotel and returned a few minutes after noon.

Margaret called Helen Jenson's land line on her new cell phone, "Remember in the skeleton case someone tapped our phones to learn what we are doing?"

"Yes," Jenson said, thinking that's why she's not calling me on my cell. "How do you know?"

"The police found Joe Reynolds, the programmer you talked with yesterday, with his throat slit. The killer didn't take his wallet or passport, so the police said it wasn't a robbery. We're leaving Naxos. Get your staff's cell phones changed. I'll call you in a few days," Margaret said. She told Jenson each of their new cell phone numbers.

"Did you tell the Greek police about the possible connection between his murder and the Liberty Credit Card embezzlement?" Helen asked, wondering if she should contact them.

"No, too risky. We wanted to leave, since we thought someone had been watching us. If we told the police, it would complicate matters. Joann would have to stay in Naxos and become an easy target. Since the murderer tapped our phones as well, Joann convinced us we could be in danger."

"Then I won't call the Greek police," Helen said.

"Send Belford's picture to my cell phone. If he's the killer, we want to avoid him."

Next Paul called Kostas, "We're arriving a day earlier on a private plane at 4:30. Can you pick us up?"

"Of course. But why?"

"It's complicated. I'll tell you when I see you. We're bringing a friend," Paul said.

Kostas realized he had to leave his wife home because his small car only held four.

Before they boarded the plane, Margaret scanned the airport and didn't notice anyone suspicious.

Belford slept late, waking up after 11:00. The hangover kept him in bed for several minutes until he knew he needed liquids and aspirin.

He turned on the TV hoping to watch reports of the murder. At noon, during the Greek segment of the BBC news, a thin, middle-aged, attractive female announced the Naxos police had found a body on the causeway. She provided no other detailed information. She included the typical request for viewers who saw or had any information to call the police.

The bottled water and medicine stopped his shaking, but his stomach told him he needed food. After he ate, he returned to his room and listened to the recordings of his targets' conversations and cell phone calls on his laptop. Belford enjoyed the conversation between Margaret and Paul at the bus station while they waited for Joann and Joe. His satisfaction continued as he followed the two at the police station. When they met Joann and learned of Joe's death, he congratulated himself on his well-executed murder.

Upon hearing Paul say, "...someone might have hacked our cell phones," followed by complete silence he cried, "No!" to an empty room.

AEGEAN SEA

Mykonos

Chapter 21 Escape to Mykonos

Wednesday Afternoon May 5, 2010

As they settled in their seats on the plane, Joann relaxed for the first time since the police spoke with her that morning.

Margaret said, "We're safe now."

Paul replied, "Yes, but we should stay at Kostas's for a while, in case Belford or whoever killed Joe comes to Mykonos."

The authors held hands and looked out the Lear Jet's window surprised at the beauty of Naxos and how close the Cyclades Islands were to each other. Mykonos was only twenty-four miles north of Naxos. The pilot, with an expansive personality, described Mykonos as they approached it. He recited the history of the island and gave his passengers an aerial tour. The pilot's travelogue almost made Joann forget why they had fled Naxos.

Kostas met them at the airport, and on the drive to his house they told him the story of the embezzlement and Joe's murder.

Kostas horrified said, "Sally and I live in the north-western part of the island, in the hills with a stunning view of the ocean, several islands, and Mykonos town. We'll drive until we get north of Mykonos town and head up the road to Cape Armenistis. You'll love the view, hills covered in desert brown soil and vegetation to our right and a cliff to our left overlooking the sea several hundred feet below. My house is two miles from the cape and has a six-foot alarmed wall surrounding it, so if you stay here, you'll be protected."

"We don't want to get you and Sally involved. We'll only stay a few days until we can arrange a flight back to the U.S.," Paul said.

"Nonsense. From what Margaret said, you'd be safer here than going back to the U.S.," Kostas said smiling, thankful he could help an old friend and also excited to assist the famous authors in the investigation. "We have four bedrooms so we won't be crowded."

When they reached Kostas's house, he opened the driveway gate by pressing a button on the opener attached to the visor. Once inside the compound, the three passengers gaped in astonishment at the colorful and abundant garden in the front yard. One olive tree, two orange trees full of fruit, and a green vine covered part of the ground, while the rest had no covering because of the lack of rainfall in the summer. They noticed cats and chickens coexisted in the yard.

Kostas saw them staring and said, "The cats keep the mice away, and the chickens give us an unlimited supply of eggs, and an occasional main entrée. If the cats get too near the baby chicks, the threat of being pecked by the mother hens makes them retreat."

Kostas's wife, Sally, greeted Margaret and Paul with a kiss on both cheeks and said, "Please come inside. Can I get you a glass of cold lemonade?" She looked at Joann and extended her hand, "Joann, welcome to our house."

"Thank you. It's gorgeous."

As they drank ice-cold drinks, Paul summarized the escape tale for Sally. When he finished, she said, "How can we help?"

"Hide us here," Joann said.

"We can do that. Kostas has drawn up a tour of the island, but I guess we'll have to postpone it until you're out of danger," Sally said.

"I have a picture on my cell phone of someone we suspect may have followed us. Please print it, carry it, and look for the man in the picture. Tell us if you find him, then Delaware State Police could extradite him," Margaret said.

"Is she deputizing us?" Kostas said.

"I want to, but I can't. I'm a civilian in a foreign country," Margaret said.

"We'll do it, if you promise to mention us in your next book," Sally said.

Kostas saw Joann looking through a window at the white capped covered sea. "Let's go outside, and I'll show you interesting sites from our back yard."

They followed Kostas and Sally. Margaret and Paul held hands as they enjoyed the rugged desert hills and the blue sea waves crashing against the beach. Joann said, "Staying here with you for a week will be like living in heaven."

"Now, I know why you both retired here. Upstate New York has its mountains, rivers, and lakes, but that's nothing compared to this view," Paul said.

"Yes, we wake up every morning feeling thankful. Tomorrow, we'll have breakfast in the glass-enclosed deck," Sally said.

Looking at the waves crashing on the shore, Joann asked, "Is the wind always this ferocious?"

"No, the Greeks call this north wind the Meltemi. It's early this year and is blowing at thirty knots," Kostas said, pointing to his weather station a few feet away. "By regulation, if it gets over forty knots, boat traffic between the islands will cease. The wind averages twenty knots."

"See the two southwest islands?" Sally said pointing, "They're Delos and Rinia. When you're not in danger, we'll take you to Delos. It contains one of the most complete ancient Greek ruins and was a religious site. We'll spend the whole day roaming the old city. We have to leave on the last ferry since no one is allowed to stay overnight. Kostas naturally loves the site," Sally said.

"Unfortunately, we won't know how long that will take. I'm in contact with my old staff at the Delaware State Police. If they catch Belford or solve the crime, they'll tell us. Then we can enjoy the island," Margaret said, leaving her hand on Paul's thigh, eager to get on with their honeymoon.

"Let's print Belford's picture," Kostas said.

"Stay as long as you want," Sally said.

Joann thought, while Margaret and Paul are rich and retired, I'll soon run out of money if I don't get back to work. She had calculated her cash would last three more weeks at her rate of spending. Fortunately, since Kostas would not charge for her stay at his house, the money would last longer.

Kostas went to the ferry dock daily for a week, to check on arriving passengers from Naxos. Sally drove to the airport and waited near the baggage claim in the morning when the Athens plane arrived.

Joann watched the BBC and the German networks hoping to catch news of the embezzlement case. Since it involved the U.S. and not Europe, neither network reported much related to the crime. She listened in on Margaret's calls to Helen Jenson, every other day, but the Delaware Police reported no progress in the investigation.

The first night Margaret and Paul slept together in one of Kostas's bedrooms, Paul expressed his concern, "Margaret, this is our second criminal case together, and someone might be trying to murder us. Does this happen all the time?"

"No. Criminals usually leave cops alone since in many states murdering one can get them the death penalty. I'm just as surprised as you are."

"While you had a gun and the Delaware State Police behind you and could protect us in Delaware, here we have no resources."

"Since you've been trained, I wish both of us had a gun, but they have to find us before they can harm us. If we keep hidden we'll stay safe."

Margaret and Paul spent the rest of the time at Kostas's home, besides sleeping late and enjoying their honeymoon, annotating the new book's chapters. They wrote drafts of their Greek trip starting after they had met Joann, and included Joe's murder, and the escape to Mykonos.

After Joann, Margaret, and Paul flew to Mykonos, Belford thought of calling Hank, but decided not to. He didn't know where they were, whether they had decided to stay on Naxos or leave, for an unknown destination.

In the afternoon, Belford went to Apollon Hotel's reception desk, "Hi, I'm looking for an old friend, Joann Cummings, who said she was staying here."

"I'll check the registration. She's not here now, checked out yesterday."

"Did she say where she was going?"

"No."

In the afternoon, Belford searched the streets without success. That evening Belford reviewed his stored hacked conversations and cell calls. He first heard Margaret and Paul's had decided to visit Mykonos on April 26, during a conversation they had with Joann the day of his unsuccessful attempt on her life. They mentioned they would stay with Sally and Kostas Canakis. Belford, not wanting to risk using his laptop to search for the Canakis couple, used the hotel guest PC and Googled them. Belford found an extensive academic history and a magazine article describing Kostas house with several pictures of the white and blue trimmed building and a street name. He printed the pictures.

Belford left the next day on a high-speed ferry arriving in Mykonos after dark. Since Joann might recognize him, he wore a disguise.

After the Greek police returned to Syros and completed the autopsy, Detective Eaton Nikas contacted the U.S. Embassy in Athens. "I'm calling to inform the Embassy that Joe Reynolds, a U.S. citizen has been murdered on Naxos."

The Embassy staff asked for passport information that Nikas supplied. "How did Reynolds die?"

Nikas summarized what they had discovered. Since it wasn't a robbery or bar fight he asked, "We'd be interested in any information concerning Mr. Reynolds, to help us solve the crime. The local Naxos police have collected his property and will send it to you."

"I'll contact the FBI and relay your request."

"Should we send the body to the Embassy?"

"We'll advise you after we contact next of kin."

The American Embassy staff followed standard procedure and tried to contact Joe Reynolds' wife to arrange for shipment of his body to the U.S. Since Joe had sent her to stay with Eve, his daughter, they could not reach her by phone. The Embassy connected with Eve in San Diego the next day.

"I'm with the U.S. Embassy in Athens, Greece. How can I reach Mrs. Reynolds, your mother? We've called her at her Delaware home and no one answered, and she didn't return our calls."

"My mother's here helping me take care of my children. Why do you want to talk to her?"

"I'd rather talk to your mother."

Eve, knowing her mother couldn't hear since she went to the pool to watch the kids, said, "My mother has a heart condition. My father is in Greece. If anything happened to him, it would devastate her if you told her."

After a brief silence, the official said, "Someone murdered your father on the Greek Island of Naxos. I'm calling to inform you and to make arrangements for shipment of his body home."

Eve cried out, "No. No. No. I warned him!"

"What do you mean?"

"Dad works at the Liberty Credit Card Company as a systems programmer. He discovered evidence related to embezzlement. I told him to tell the police. He refused, and told me he's working with his boss and had decided to visit her in Greece. There have been several murders and disappearances associated with the crime. I begged him, but he didn't listen."

"The Greek police asked us to inquire if Mr. Reynolds had any enemies, which was my next question. Thanks for answering it."

"I'll have to get back to you on shipping Dad home, after I talk to the rest of the family and tell my mother." Only after she hung up and began to sob did she write down the call's return phone number.

The Embassy staff contacted the Dover, Delaware FBI field office to relay the information requested by the Greek police concerning the potential connection between the death of Joe Reynolds and the Liberty Credit Card embezzlement.

"Helen, we heard from the staff of the U.S. Greek Embassy. Someone murdered Joe Reynolds in Greece. He worked at the Liberty Credit Card Company. Are you aware of his death? Do you think there could be a possible connection with it and the embezzlement?" Agent Roger Stannis asked after he had opened the FBI's electronic file on the case.

"Yes, my old boss, Margaret Hoffman, told me about it. She was vacationing in Greece, on Naxos Island, where the murder occurred. Reynolds, a systems programmer, had analyzed the computer system logs and discovered one individual ran a program that transferred money from the company to other locations. We haven't identified the hacker."

Stannis thought Reynolds being on the same island as Hoffman interesting and not innocent. "Why did Reynolds go to Greece? How did you learn about his analysis?"

"Fear of being murdered, like Steve Haven or those missing and potentially killed or involved with the crime, including Joann Cummings and George Belford. Reynolds met with Hoffman who encouraged him to send us the data. He did the day he was killed." Helen didn't mention Joann's role to protect her location, afraid she might be next.

As Stannis keyed this information into the case file he asked, "Did Reynolds identify any potential participants in the crime?"

"Yes, he thought George Belford, the IT security lead, had to be involved to doctor the log files to remove any traces of who executed the embezzlement program."

"We're still searching for him. Do you think he's involved with

THE BILLION DOLLAR EMBEZZLEMENT MURDERS

Reynolds's death?" Stannis asked.

"He either murdered Reynolds or had someone do it. We believe it's an attempt to silence those who might be aware of the crime."

"The Greek police have asked for help in solving his murder. What should I tell them?"

"Ask them to look for Belford, but don't reveal Reynolds's analysis of the credit card data."

Stannis updated the report, included Belford's physical description and photo, and addressed it to the Greek police. He then forwarded it to his superiors for approval before emailing it to the American Embassy in Greece.

Monday evening 8:00 Greek time, May 11, 2018

"I hope I'm not interrupting dinner," Helen asked.

"No, we're in Greece. We haven't started," Margaret said.

"Roger Stannis, of the FBI Dover office, called me in response to a request by the Greek police to send information regarding the Joe Reynolds murder."

"Do you mind if I put you on speaker phone? I'm with Paul, Joann, Kostas, and Sally."

"No." Then Helen summarized the conversation for them.

"So you didn't mention Joann had joined us."

"Roger didn't ask."

"I'm worried. Belford may have had an accomplice. Kostas and Sally have met every ferry and plane over the last week and found no sign of him entering Mykonos."

"The Greek police are looking for him. That should help. If we learn something, I'll call."

After Eaton Nikas received the Stannis' report, he read it and remembered Joann worked at the same company as Joe Reynolds. He thought perhaps she knew more about his relationship to the embezzlement then she volunteered during her interview. Nikas called her hotel on Naxos, but she had checked out and left no forwarding address.

Nikas posted an alert for Belford, indicating the American police suspected him in the murder of Joe Reynolds and as a participant in the Liberty Credit Card embezzlement. The alert directed the police to detain Belford and then contact him. Being involved in a major international crime excited Nikas.

Belford arrived in Mykonos two days after Joann, Margaret, and Paul, having decided the only way to find them would be to go to the island and search for them.

Belford knew he couldn't register at the Leto Hotel nor rent a car in his disguise. He took a cab to his hotel in the central part of the town. Before he checked in, he entered a stall in the men's room of the restaurant, removed the disguise, and stored it in a backpack.

Belford had arranged to rent a four-wheel-drive Jeep Wrangler when he booked the hotel on the internet. He wanted a powerful car that could climb the steep hills without overheating. That night he reviewed a map and charted a course for the road to Cape Amemistis where he hoped to find Kostas's house.

The rental company delivered the Jeep the next morning. Belford took the backpack to the car. Before driving he put on the wig and sunglasses. Since he wanted to stay in the car, he felt a full disguise unnecessary.

With pictures of Kostas's house on the passenger seat, he drove higher into the hills and glanced back and forth between the pictures and the homes facing the sea. Belford found three possible matches and continued driving until he had to turn around at the road's end at the Cape Amemistis lighthouse. The higher vantage point of the return trip helped him eliminate two of the buildings. Belford drove at ten miles per hour past Kostas's house noticing that the walls surrounding the compound made it impossible to see anyone on the grounds. He realized he couldn't park outside the house to watch people entering or leaving so he returned to his hotel.

Since he didn't locate them for four days, driving past Kostas's house or searching for them in Mykonos, he concluded they might not be on the island. Belford didn't know where they had gone, but kept seeing Kostas hanging around the ferry terminal. He wondered if Kostas waited for the threesome to arrive. Belford didn't leave Mykonos.

After Belford's call, Hank became more panicked and fearful the Delaware State Police might be close to solving the case. At first, he decided to leave the U.S., but changed his mind repeatedly. How did the police and the IT system programmer discover so much when he had designed the perfect crime?

Wednesday, May 13, 2010

"We've spent a week looking for Belford and haven't found him," Kostas said to his wife as they met in a waterfront-harbor bar after their last surveillance.

"Perhaps he's not here, or another person murdered Joe Reynolds. We should tell our guests, so they can enjoy Delos island," Sally said.

"Let's take them to Delos tomorrow, and get them a rental car," Kostas said.

Kostas outlined their proposal. "Staying here and only seeing Mykonos from the deck using the telescopic lens on your camera must bore you."

Joann still traumatized by Reynolds murder, fearing she'd be next, said, "I don't mind."

"We're making steady progress on the book," Margaret said.

"You have a great house, wine, and food, but I'm getting cabin fever," Paul said.

"Kostas and I have been looking for a week and haven't seen Belford. Mykonos is a small town. If he were here, we'd have spotted him," Sally said.

"You're probably right. We have no hard evidence he killed Reynolds," Margaret said.

"Tomorrow, we want to take you to Delos and show you the ancient ruins. On the way back, Margaret can rent a car so you can enjoy driving on the island."

"I'm ready for Delos. I've read a few hundred pages on the history of the island since we arrived," Paul said.

"If we stay together, we should be okay, even if someone besides Belford is looking for us," Margaret said.

Joann didn't respond. The two couples looked at her.

Margaret said, "I know the island. We'll visit the best areas outside Mykonos town. If someone is searching for us, it will most likely be in town. The three of us can spend a week touring Mykonos without going downtown again. After we visit Delos, we can drive to Elia on the south coast, it has a great beach, view, and restaurant."

Joann still hesitated, thinking of the shooting of Andrew Smithson, the murders of Reynolds and Haven, and her own fear. She wondered if Andrew thought of her as much as she did him, sad that she couldn't know since she didn't know how to contact him. She looked at the confident Margaret, the ex-cop, and said to the hosts, "I'll go. I can't imprison myself in your home for life."

They arrived at the Delos ferry jetty, and Sally handed each a bottle of water. "We'll need this. There is no shade on the tour." They boarded the passenger ferry for the thirty-minute trip.

The wind roared over the water whipping up waves and causing an exciting passage. Kostas briefed them on the history of the island as they bounced in their seats. "It has been a religious center since 1000 BCE. The ancient Greeks dug up the dead and removed the skeletons to purify the island and insure its sacred nature. Every visitor must leave at night. The park management doesn't allow anyone to live or die here." He talked for twenty minutes.

Paul whispered to his wife when he finished talking, "I've never heard Kostas lecture. He's great. No wonder his students loved him."

They landed on the island, happy to leave the rocking ferry for solid ground. After walking a short distance to the entrance to the park, Kostas said, "We turn left here to visit the Greek ruins." He resumed his descriptions of the ruins in his booming lecture voice as they walked through the site. His enthusiasm for the ancient buildings, statues, and roads attracted a following as other tourists listened to him. A small crowd of twenty clapped after he finished his description of Apollo's birth in a pond in the middle of the ruins.

At noon, exhausted and sweating from the tour in the warm May morning sun, Sally said, "Let's eat."

They left the Greek ruins and walked south up a slight hill to a small informal restaurant. They ordered water before reading the menu. Because of the heat, everyone ordered Greek Salads and Tzatziki, made from yogurt, cucumbers, lemon and dill. No one ordered wine.

After they ate, they started out walking west toward the Roman ruins of the island. Paul noticed the steep incline of hill and thought, I'm glad Margaret and I exercise. He glanced at Joann and seeing her confident look, realized she would have no problems.

Kostas started a new lecture on the Roman ruins, impressing Margaret, who said, "Kostas, you know so much about this island. You should write a book."

"I have. Yesterday, I had to finish reviewing the publisher's proofs. My descriptions paraphrase what's in the book."

"Why didn't you tell us?" Margaret asked.

"I didn't want to give you exalted expectations of my description of the ruins before we visited the sacred island."

Kostas continued talking until they left the island. On the ferry, Sally said, "No need to eat out tonight. Since it's hot and we're tired, I will serve cold Tzatziki, Fish soup, and Aubergine salad." Paul thought with that diet Kostas will live forever.

After the return ferry ride, Kostas drove them to the airport, Mykonos Car Rental's location, where Margaret chose a four-wheel drive automatic Fiat 500.

After she signed for the car, Kostas said, "You're now free to explore the island."

"Tomorrow we'll drive to Elia," Margaret said.

Chapter 22 Touring Mykonos

Thursday, May 14, 2010

Margaret and Paul sat in the front seat while Joann relaxed in the back seat. They began the trip to Ano Mera, the second largest town in Mykonos. Margaret drove down the hill toward Mykonos town, but turned east on a secondary road on the way to Lake Marathi. They wanted to avoid being identified in Mykonos.

Margaret made frequent stops so they could appreciate the scenery. Paul and Joann marveled at the brown, rock-covered hills, with stone fences and the large lake on the small island. Margaret would never tell Paul, she had taken the same drive with Josh, her deceased first husband, over thirty years ago. She intended to relive their experiences privately, while developing new memories with Paul.

The trio reached Ano Mera at noon. During the drive, Margaret had not detected anyone suspicious, so she suggested they park, stroll through the town, find a restaurant, and then drive south to the beaches at Elia.

When they started the steep descent from the hills between Ano Mera and Elia, Joann exclaimed, "How enchanting, the brown hills with a few grazing animals, so different from flat Delaware."

"I'll never tire of this drive even though I've done it many times." Margaret said. "With the clear air we can see the blue sea, the sparse farm land on the hill sides, and an outline of Naxos to the south. We're headed to the Myconian Imperial Hotel on the beach."

When they arrived, Margaret parked next to the hotel. "Is anyone going to join me?" She took off her blouse and shorts, revealing a trim figure in a solid blue one-piece bathing suit.

No one said yes. "Go to the open bar. I'm going for a fifteen minute swim."

Sitting at a table, they had a great view of the sea and the steep hills to the east and west, extending out to border the half-circle cove. Their eyes followed Margaret as she dove into the water and swam fifty yards out and turned to swim parallel to the coast. Several large sail boats moored near the beach impressed them. Paul said, "Elia has the longest sand beach in Mykonos. I hope she doesn't swim it all."

Joann said, "Paul, you have an energetic wife. She has great stamina."

Paul smiled. "Margaret swims daily in an Olympic size pool." He thanked his luck every day since he met her for being so perfect for him. "The beach is empty now. Margaret told me in summer, tourists, beach chairs, and umbrellas cover the sand to the water's edge."

They ordered a glass of local wine, including a white wine for Margaret. They sipped as they waited for her return. On his first swallow, Paul heard Margaret's cell phone ring.

"Aren't you going to answer?" Joann said.

"No, I learned early in our relationship a call might mean police work. They'll leave a message."

They discussed Joann's work at the credit card company, and her theory of the embezzlement, citing Belford and Hank Strong as the likely ringleaders. Paul started on Margaret's wine, which had lost its chill and ordered her another. Margaret returned just as the waitress placed the new glass in front of her seat.

Joann said, "You're a great swimmer. Isn't the water freezing?"

"Not that cold, it's in the mid-sixties. But I warmed up once I started swimming."

"You had a call," Paul said.

Margaret retrieved her phone from her beach bag. "Helen Jenson called," she said to the group.

She returned the call and placed her phone on speaker mode. "Helen, you phoned."

"Yes, a few developments might interest you. The Greek police informed us they haven't located Belford. Andrew Smithson's company has volunteered his services since they learned of the murder of Joe Reynolds. Andrew will call Joann at 7:00 p.m. your time to learn more details of the computer system. I gave him Joann's phone number.

Joann, who half listened to the conversation, while looking at the continuous hypnotic small waves breaking on the shore, became alert, and breathed more rapidly with her adrenalin pumping. "I'll wait for his call."

Helen continued talking, "We're spending more time on Hank Strong. Yesterday we received a list of his calls: cells, land line, and business. He had talked to Belford as we expected. We hoped he had connected with Steve Haven, but he hadn't. Joann, can you tell me about their relationship. Did their jobs give them a reason to communicate?"

"I never noticed them talking to each other. They had no need since Haven reported to me and Strong had to go through me if he wanted to use Haven."

Paul listened with rapt attention to the phone conversation, hoping it would help solve the crime and assist them in writing the book. The conversation ended with Helen's question about Haven.

Paul said, "It's time we get back."

The trio returned to Kostas's house after six. Sally and Kostas greeted them at the door.

"Your expressions tell me you enjoyed the drive," Sally said.

"I'm glad we went. I'll never tire of the scenery. Especially, when I saw an occasional goat or sheep graze on the hills. If I didn't have to earn a living, I'd stay here," Joann said.

"Quite a compliment to our small island and you've only taken two trips," Kostas said. "If you love this island, you'll be addicted to Greece when you visit the other islands and the mainland."

"Tomorrow, we'll take a short trip north up the hill to the Cape

Armenistis lighthouse and then drive to the coast to tour the northwestern part of Mykonos," Margaret said. "The lighthouse drive to the coast is more spectacular than the road to Elia."

"I look forward to the ride," Joann said.

"I'll be right back," Kostas said. He returned with a carafe of local Mykonos white wine and poured each a glass.

"To celebrate your safe return, I've prepared a special meal of roasted boneless lamb with gravy and Greek potatoes. We stopped at I Scream in town. We'll have chocolate and pistachio ice cream for dessert," Sally said.

At dinner, Paul said, "The wine tastes great. I wonder if we over-estimated Belford's threat. How would he know we're in Mykonos?"

"We can't tell how long he bugged our cell phones and conversations, and if he heard us discuss Mykonos," Margaret said.

"I read about your scheduled honeymoon in Greece, including Mykonos in People Magazine. Millions did and know." Joann said.

"True, but I hope I'm right," Paul said.

Joann's phone rang at 7:00. Since she remembered Andrew had said he would call, she excused herself and walked to her bedroom.

"Andrew, how are you? I miss you."

"Fine, I miss you too. My company has put me under total seclusion. They only let me call after Joe Reynold's murder, and Detective Jenson asked me to help."

"What can I tell you about the IT system?"

"Not much, I used that as a ploy to talk to you."

Joann beamed. "Thanks, you make me feel good. How are you helping?"

"Reviewing the data Joe Reynolds sent, but I haven't found anything yet. Helen agreed with my suggestion to examine the emails and internet searches not only of Hank Strong's but everyone in the Liberty Credit Card Company who could access the credit card database. They haven't told me what they found."

They spent the next five minutes discussing her adventures in Greece and the murder of Joe Reynolds.

"We've been in hiding in Kostas's home for the last week. Since neither Kostas nor his wife spotted Belford, we toured the island staying out of the town where we thought he'd most likely be." She described the delights of the trip to Delos and Elia. "Tomorrow we'll visit the Cape Armenistis lighthouse on the northwestern tip of the island."

"I'll get a map of Greece so I can follow your travels. I'll call you every day."

Joann ended the conversation feeling better than she had since Joe's murder.

Chapter 23 A Fatal Mistake

Friday, May 15, 2010

Frustrated and wanting to see if they had stayed in the house or left, Belford parked his Jeep Wrangler on Kostas's road halfway between his house and the Cape Armenistis lighthouse. Since Margaret drove a different car than Kostas, unknown to Belford, he didn't see them leave or return.

To spy on Kostas's house, he left his car dressed in his full disguise and carried a camera with a telescopic lens. He focused the camera on Kostas's courtyard. Besides Kostas's car, he saw the Fiat and wondered if his prey used that car. Belford thought, no wonder I didn't find them yesterday.

A car drove toward Belford. He raised the camera to his eye and faked taking pictures of the exotic scenery of the brown hills, ferry ports, and turquoise sea. Belford changed his parking place four times and resumed his watch. Finally, he saw the trio get into the Fiat.

Margaret acted as a tour guide identifying landmarks and vistas as she leisurely drove toward the lighthouse.

Joann commented, "Another steep road."

"Wait till we drive toward the coast if you want steep," Margaret said.

As they passed the photographer, he stood with his back toward the road and his camera against his eye. Margaret noted the car, but said nothing as she passed it and proceeded to the brownish dirt parking lot.

When they drove by, he turned and watched them progress toward the lighthouse. Belford scanned the island southwest of his location and discovered a steep road hugging the hillside descending toward the sea between him and the lighthouse. Not wanting to miss them, he moved his car above that road and resumed his picture-taking guise.

As they left the car Paul said, "This wind feels as strong as a hurricane. I'm glad I have a sweater." He reached in the back seat and grabbed his blue woolen turtle neck.

"While it's cold, the view is beautiful. What's the large island past the light house?" Joann asked.

"Tinos," Margaret replied.

Joann didn't respond, but like the others, stared at the white one-story building surrounded by a stone wall with the lighthouse tower emerging from the middle of the structure. The trio walked over the undulating dirt road on the ridge of a hill leading to the lighthouse. Signs forbidding entrance to the operating lighthouse disappointed them. Then they realized the extra altitude gained from climbing the nineteen-meter-high lighthouse stairs would not have improved the view of the scenery.

They walked to the edge of the hill and looked at the Aegean Sea six hundred feet below crashing into the beach and rocks. "Now I see why they needed a lighthouse," Joann said.

Margaret pointing down toward the western side of the island. "That's the road we'll use to drive to the beach."

Joann gasped, then said, "Well at least it's not as steep as that road on Santorini from the ferry."

After taking pictures, they returned to the warmth of the car and Margaret started the drive toward the coast. When she passed the photographer's car, she noticed he sat in the driver's seat.

Belford thought if she takes the steep road, I can run them over the cliff since I have a bigger and stronger car. He waited until they were several hundred feet ahead before pulling out onto the road. "Yes!" he shouted as she made her fatal turn. Belford sped up to catch and kill them, knowing he'd earn his $200 million and live out his days in Croatia.

Margaret drove slower than fifteen miles per hour to avoid the dangers of the hairpin turns. She checked the rear-view mirror and watched the Wrangler speeding toward them. Her adrenalin kicked in and she floored the gas pedal remembering the defensive driving techniques she had learned as a cop and Marine. "Joann is your seatbelt on?" Her tone did not reveal the threat that pursued the group.

"Yes. Why are you driving so fast? Are you trying to scare me?" Joann asked.

Paul had looked back to check Joann when he saw the vehicle barreling toward them. "I'm scared, but not by my wife's driving. That car looks as if it's trying to rear end us and knock us off the road," he said. "I wish I had a gun."

Margaret braked to slow down and drove in the left lane hugging the cliff for a switchback turn. As she reached the new straightaway, she accelerated and returned to the right lane. The road's loose stones peppered the underside of the car.

"Christ, I'm losing her," Belford screamed. He floored the accelerator, realizing if he didn't catch her, she'd go to the police. At the next turn, he didn't apply the brakes, and his car skidded but held the road. Belford saw her almost a full straightaway ahead, and he pressed the pedal harder reaching over fifty miles an hour.

Margaret checked the rear-view mirror and relaxed as she saw the growing distance between them and his recent acceleration. She braked at the next turn, pulled into the left lane, and stopped, hidden from her pursuer's view. "I'm hoping he drives by us. Then we'll turn around and return the way we came and find a cop," she said, confident they would soon lose the Wrangler.

Belford panicked as he barely slowed for the turn. He felt he had too much speed. He hit the brakes hard. The car skidded and almost came to a stop at the apex of the turn. He ground his teeth as if that could slow the wheels. He tried to turn the car, but the wheels locked. The car slowed. Belford realized it wouldn't stop in time. As it skidded off the road and flew over the cliff, Belford yelled, "No!"

Belford watched the passing cliff as gravity took over. His body lifted but held tight to the seatbelt. The shock of the car hitting a rocky outcropping jarred him. Belford waited to die.

When the car hit the rocky beach, it burst into flames. The airbags saved him from expiring on impact, but not from the fire's scorching heat. The hot air almost suffocated him making him wheeze and cough. He struggled to release his seatbelt, but it was impossible because black gasoline smoke blinded him and burned his lungs. Pain intensified as the heat and flames moved closer, first engulfing his legs. He spasmed until the fire burned through the nerve layer of skin. Shock ended his conscious thoughts.

After Margaret stopped, they looked back up the road as they heard the screeching of the brakes. The sudden silence told them the skidding car had left the road. Then they heard the Wrangler crash against the rocks as they left the car and rushed to the other side of the road and watched the flaming wreck below, fascinated as the fire eliminated one threat to their lives.

Paul said, "Margaret, you can drive whenever you want. If I drove, we'd be at the bottom of the cliff."

"God, that happened so fast, I didn't have time to get scared. Margaret, I'm glad you were a cop," Joann said.

"It's not over. We need to tell the police what happened and learn who tried to kill us," Margaret declared.

She drove at fifteen miles per hour to the coast and toward the still smoldering car. They waited until the Greek police reached the scene a few minutes later.

The policeman ordered the gathering crowed to stay away from the car. He asked in Greek and English. "Did anyone see what happened?"

Before Margaret could respond, an Englishman spoke, "My wife and I first heard and then watched the chase. We looked up at the mountain and saw this car chasing the Fiat parked over there." He pointed at Margaret's car.

The cop walked over, "Is he correct?"

Margaret, thankful they had a witness, replied, "Yes, we want to know who chased us."

"So do I. I need you to stay here. I'll call for a detective. The body might be burned beyond recognition." The policeman noticed it was a rental car and gave the license plate number to a detective at the police station. After he found out Jerome Watkins had rented the car, the detective left the station to join the first policeman.

When the detective arrived, he asked the trio to identify themselves and if they knew Watkins. They said no, and told him their names.

"Who drove the car?

"I did," Margaret said.

"Why did he chase you?"

"It might be related to the Naxos murder of Joe Reynolds. Both he and Joann Cummings worked at the Liberty Credit Card Company where someone embezzled billions. They were investigating the crime and may have gotten too close to discovering the criminals," Margaret said as she sighed, recalling the events on Naxos. "There have been two murders and one shooting related to the crime. Joe and Joann came to Greece to avoid being the next victims. But it didn't help Joe. Apparently someone followed him. After Reynolds's murder, we fled Naxos to avoid being killed."

The detective called the homicide police on Syros, repeated Margaret's story to Eaton Nikas, who responded, "I'll bring a crew.

Don't move the body, and tell your witnesses to meet me at the police station in three hours."

They returned to Kostas's home. Sally, working in the garden greeted them, "You're back early?" Noticing their grim faces, she asked, "What's wrong?"

"We want to tell you and Kostas together," Margaret said.

"Follow me, he's inside writing."

Kostas, stunned by the somber faces of the group said, "What happened?"

Paul summarized the events, praising his wife. Kostas and Sally realized their efforts to have them tour Mykonos could have killed them. Their sheltered academic world in Binghamton, New York didn't expose them to murder. To Kostas, embezzlement was a white collar crime.

"Is it over now?" Sally asked.

"We're not sure," Margaret said. "We'll stay behind here until we know."

Kostas drove them to the police station.

The medical examiner hoped the extent of the burns would not make identification too difficult. Fire destroyed the wallet and the passport. Nikas got the passport number from the rental car agency and called the U.S. Embassy to inform them of the death of Jerome Watkins.

The Embassy called back an hour later, "We contacted Watkins next of kin and found he died eight months ago. The deceased must have used a fake passport. Please call if you find his real name."

Nikas ask the Mykonos police officer to go to the car rental agency to pick up a copy of the fake Watkins driver's license so they had a picture of the renter's face.

When Detective Nikas met the trio, he showed them the photo, "It's a picture of the deceased. Do you know him?"

Joann, astonished, yelled, "It's George Belford! That proves he was part of the Liberty Credit Card embezzlement."

"I know. We have been searching for him throughout Greece. I wanted to watch your reaction to his picture. Tell me about your relationship with him."

Joann, talking with a sense of relief, summarized what she knew about Belford, described her position in the company, Andrew Smithson's shooting, her fear and flight to Greece, meeting Margaret and Paul, the Joe Reynolds tragedy, and staying with Kostas in Mykonos.

"Will Belford's death free you from fear?" Nikas asked.

"I hope so," Joann said.

"We don't know if he had an accomplice," Margaret said.

"My next job is to trace Belford's movements in Greece to learn if he acted alone. You can help. We can protect you if you tell us where you are staying, when you will leave Mykonos, and your next destination."

"We will," Paul said.

Kostas gave Nikas his business card. "They are staying with me."

"Margaret, introduce me to the detectives in the U.S. please. I will tell them Belford's fate and answer any questions they have."

Margaret called Helen Jenson, "George Belford tried to kill us, but he's dead now." She described the chase.

Helen asked, "Did he have an accomplice?"

"We don't know, but I want you to speak to Detective Eaton Nikas."

"Detective Jenson, we will email you the fake passport information Belford used to leave the U.S. and enter Greece. We need to track his movements since leaving the U.S. and if he purchased a cell phone under his false identity. Once we have this information, we should be able to trace his movements in Europe and determine if he acted alone or met an accomplice."

"Detective, tell me your email address, and I'll send you whatever information I find."

After the phone call, Nikas turned toward Kostas. "Please keep them in your home until we discover if Belford acted alone. The police will post a twenty-four hour guard."

"Don't worry, we're not going anywhere. We had enough excitement today," Paul said.

Chapter 24 Enjoying Mykonos

Friday evening May 15, 2010

Nikas called the American Embassy. "Detective Nikas here, we have identified the corpse with the false identity of Jerome Watkins. He is George Belford of Milford, Delaware." Nikas read his passport number. "The Delaware Police wanted him for questioning related to the embezzlement at the Liberty Credit Card Company. The Greek Police have been searching for him for days."

"Thanks, I'll locate his next of kin and call you with directions for shipping Mr. Belford's body back to the States. I'll notify the FBI and the local Delaware Police."

Belford's sister, Beverly in Tampa, Florida agreed to accept the body.

Not wanting to wait for Andrew's call, Joann called him after they finished eating. "Hi, Andrew, you don't know how much I miss you."

"Miss you, too."

"Andrew, you won't believe what happened today." Joann described the chase scene, Margaret's driving stunts, Belford's crash, and the investigation by the Greek police. Andrew listened without interrupting her.

When she finished, he said, "Wow, you've had quite a day. I wish I was there with you. Are you all right?"

"It happened so fast I didn't have time to get scared."

"How long before the Greek police decide if Belford worked alone?"

"Don't know, but we're staying at Kostas's home until they tell us.

If he didn't have an accomplice, I'll return to Delaware. Can I see you then?"

"I'll check with my company. Just because Belford didn't have a partner in Mykonos, doesn't mean there aren't others in the U.S. willing to murder you. I'd be careful about returning." Joann frowned at his response, expecting him to be pleased.

That evening, Belford's sister called Hank Strong. "Hank, since you were one of my brother George's best friends, I'm sorry to tell you the State Department called me earlier. George died in a car accident on Mykonos Island in Greece." Beverly paused.

Hank remained silent. He would never speak to his best friend of forty years and a comrade in war and crime

"Are you there?" she asked.

Hank's mind went blank. George couldn't rescue him. He didn't speak. Sweat erupted on his forehead. While his breathing slowed, his heart raced. After a few seconds, he answered Beverly's question, "Yes, I'm here, just shocked. I didn't know he had gone to Greece."

"James M. Lowell Funeral Home has made arrangements to ship the body here. I'm having him cremated. We'll hold a memorial service on Wednesday at 11:00 a.m. You're welcome to come."

Hank's panic subsided, and he responded with a steady voice. "Thank you, I can't go. I'm leaving the company in two weeks, and I'm training my replacement. Do you know what caused the accident?"

"The call was brief. They didn't describe what happened."

Hank wondered if Belford's connection to the embezzlement would stay hidden. While having no direct evidence, he assumed Joann caused his death. He decided to finish George's task, now driven by revenge, not just hoping to intimidate others from testifying against him.

Local Mykonos newspapers reported Belford's death which Reuters then circulated to its international customers. Delaware TV stations included it in the Saturday evening news. The broadcaster speculated about a possible connection between the murders of Steve Haven and Joe Reynolds, the death of Belford, and the Liberty Credit Card scandal. He noted the Delaware crime authors, Margaret Hoffman and Paul O'Hare, had been involved in a high-speed chase by Belford which resulted in his death in the car accident. The announcer speculated whether the credit card embezzlement would be the topic of their next book.

Strong's panic returned. He felt his heart race. Fearing heart failure, he remembered to lie down, relax, and take deep breaths to slow it down. A severe headache followed. Fearing for the immediate future, he thought he should leave. After a half-hour, he realized again that he couldn't leave with only two weeks left without causing suspicions. Hank felt helpless without his protector. He decided to look for a replacement for Belford from his underworld contacts. He could not satisfy his need for revenge unless he located Joann.

While waiting for Nikas' report, sheltered inside Kostas's home, Margaret and Paul wrote of Belford's attack on Saturday morning, while it was still fresh in their memory. They finished the first draft within several hours and asked Joann to read it and share what she remembered, including her emotions, during the car chase.

Joann added several sentences describing the harrowing ride.

After chronicling their attempted murder, the authors sketched an outline of the trip to Naxos, Reynolds's murder, and their stay on Mykonos. They finished these drafts in two days, including incorporation of Joann's suggested factual revisions.

Helen Jenson received TSA's reply. Jerome Watkins had boarded a Philadelphia flight bound for Athens, with a connection to Dubrovnik, Croatia on Saturday, April 16, 2010. Helen's review of the security camera recordings showed he traveled alone.

The Croatia police found no evidence he had an accomplice. The

Greek police's review of the Athens airport cameras didn't show him contacting anyone.

Nikas back-tracked the past locations of "Jerome Watkins" from his death through his second landing in Athens and flight to Naxos. The airlines provided Nikas with the flight numbers and arrival times, noting he traveled alone. Nikas remembered the rental car agency staff on Mykonos had said Watkins stayed at the Leto Hotel.

Nikas returned to Mykonos and interviewed the staff at the rental car agency and the hotel. No one at either organization had ever seen Watkins with anyone.

One hotel staff member said, "I noticed something strange about Watkins. After he left the hotel, he did not drive away, until he put on a blond wig."

"How many times did that happen?" Nikas asked.

"Maybe five times, but it could have been more. I am not on duty all day, and I am off two days a week."

"Did you see him leave the hotel last Friday?"

"Yes, and he wore his blond wig when he drove away."

"I need to see his room and luggage," Detective Nikas said.

The hotel staff let Nikas into Belford's room. The detective searched his closet and backpack and found the complete disguise. Nikas thought no wonder we never identified him: Belford never looked the same as the photos the Delaware Police sent.

Nikas incorporated his findings in a report concluding Belford acted alone in Greece. He called Margaret Hoffman and sent the report to her, to Helen Jenson in Delaware, and to the US. Embassy.

Margaret assembled her husband, Joann, Kostas, and Sally in the living room Monday night and relayed Nikas' conclusions to the group. They listened intently. After she finished, everyone clapped.

Paul said, "We can now walk around Mykonos Town without fear. Tomorrow night, Margaret and I'll take everyone to dinner at the best restaurant overlooking the harbor. Kostas and Sally will choose."

"Since you've only been to three locations, Delos, Elia, and the Lighthouse, I recommend you visit Panormos Bay on the north coast, Ayia Anna in the east, and spend at least three days wandering around Mykonos Town," Kostas said. He took out a large map and explained what they'd find at each location. They agreed with his suggestions.

Kostas said he had to work on a document.

"What's the topic? Paul asked.

"Delos. The publisher asked a few more questions."

Sally offered to provide guide service on Tuesday. They left in her car and parked in the lot east of the windmills facing the harbor.

Sally said, "Paul, I hope you enjoy the tour. Joann and Margaret will. We're headed to the shopping section of the town."

"I'm sure I'll survive." Paul welcomed the destination, since he wanted to buy gifts for his wife, as well as children, and grandchildren.

Sally led them past the restaurants facing the harbor in the maze of narrow winding streets bordered by white and blue trimmed buildings. Joann noticed a chic dress shop. "Can we go in here?"

Sally answered, "Of course."

Joann purchased a white skirt and blue blouse.

Paul declined to follow the women and went off on his own to find a jewelry store. He noticed the prices in Mykonos were fifty percent lower than in Santorini. He purchased a ruby necklace and a silver bracelet for his wife, hiding the purchase in the pocket of his shorts.

After stopping in innumerable dress shops and jewelry stores, Joann and Margaret ran into Paul. They spotted a book store. "Let's see if they're selling our book," said Margaret.

Paul noticed a sign identifying English-language books and examined the titles, but could not find their book.

Joann said, "Don't worry, they'll carry the next one since you have set several chapters in Mykonos, and two murders in Greece." She noticed a section of English-language cook books of Greek cuisine and purchased one.

Paul brought two for his children. Margaret selected one to take home to Delaware as a reminder of their honeymoon.

Margaret passed a gaudy tee-shirt shop and said, "Paul, we should get something for our grandchildren."

After entering the store, Paul picked out the gift shirts and also looked for a few suitable for tennis. He found several blue and white shirts with Greece and Mykonos text or outlines of the island embroidered on them.

The foursome became weary after shopping for two hours. Joann, tired and hungry said, "Let's eat. My treat."

Sally led them to a restaurant facing the harbor. They sat outside in the shade under a canopy facing the harbor in front of the restaurant.

When they finished, Sally said, "We have done enough shopping. This afternoon you'll learn about the history and culture of Mykonos." Sally took them to three museums: the Archeological, the Maritime, and the Folklore. Exhausted by the end of the afternoon, they met Kostas at another harbor restaurant.

After receiving a hug and a kiss from his wife, Kostas asked, "Joann, how did you like Mykonos?"

"What I appreciated most is the absence of fear as we walked," Joann said. Margaret and Paul endorsed her comment.

After they finished, Paul paid the bill.

Kostas took them on a detour to the fabulous I Scream homemade ice cream cafe. "I'll get dessert."

They ogled at the more than fifty trays of freshly made ice cream displayed behind a glass case. They savored dishes of chocolate, strawberry, and pistachio.

Kostas said, "The dessert will give you strength for tomorrow."

The next two days, the trio traveled over the Mykonos country side, enjoying the views of the hills and ocean, visiting Panormos Bay on the north coast, and Ayia Anna in the east. This time Joann and Paul joined Margaret swimming in the transparent blue water.

On Thursday, they returned to Mykonos Town. Paul accompanied

Kostas in his car. Margaret drove the two women, who walked and shopped together. Kostas and Paul returned to the house after three hours, while the women stayed. This allowed Paul to purchase additional gifts for Margaret, including a green sweater and rolled-up prints of the town, island, and the lighthouse north of Kostas's house. He hid them in his suitcase before she returned.

While Andrew and Joann talked every night, Joann would never forget the call on Thursday evening May 20, 2010. The earlier calls with Andrew were social.

On this call, she described her adventures on Mykonos, and he told her of progress on the investigation. "I've seen almost everything on the island, and with Belford dead, I'm ready to return."

"Be careful, the embezzlement group might have other killers."

"I'm homesick and miss you." The tone of her voice revealed the extent of her loneliness.

"My boss has solved both problems. Joann, you can come and stay with me and help us in the investigation. We'll get you tickets from Mykonos to Athens, and to Norfolk, Virginia for Saturday. I'll send a car to drive you back here."

A wave of euphoria spread through her Joann's body. "I can't wait."

"You can tell your friends you're leaving, but don't tell them your destination. I'll buy the tickets and tell you the flight number. You can pick them up at the airport."

During dinner on Friday, Joann announced, "I'm returning home tomorrow. Can I get a ride to the airport for a 7:00 a.m. Mykonos to Athens flight?"

"We'll take you. Will you'll be safe? Even though Belford is dead, there may be others," Paul said, worried the return was premature.

"That's why I'm not telling anyone where I'm going." Joann grinned visualizing Andrew face.

"How can we contact you so your input can improve our draft chapters?" Margaret asked, concerned their rapid progress on the book might end.

"I'll send you a new email address."

While returning from the Mykonos airport after dropping off Joann, Paul said, "Things will be quiet without Belford chasing Joann."

"I agree. While I've enjoyed Greece so far, we've been here five weeks. Our original schedule called for a month-long honeymoon. Because of the credit card embezzlement, we haven't toured the mainland. I miss home and the investigation," Margaret said. "And I'd like a real honeymoon."

"Let's return next year to finish our honeymoon," Paul proposed. They kissed and embraced each other. "Since I've known Kostas for decades, I'll talk to him. He'll understand."

When they parked the car in the driveway, Kostas greeted them, "I'm sad to see Joann is returning home. Hope she's okay."

"Joann seemed confident. While she loved Greece, she missed Washington, DC and her friends," Margaret said.

"Both of you have been here a week longer than you planned. Are you homesick?" Kostas asked.

"Yes," Paul said, thinking Kostas like a true friend has given us the option we wanted. "We need to return to Delaware to work on the case, the book, and protect Joann if she needs us. We will visit next year to continue our Greek honeymoon."

"You're always welcome. When do you need to leave?" Kostas asked.

"Tuesday, so I can eat the ice cream at I Scream downtown a few more times," Margaret answered.

"Hope you're hungry now. Sally has prepared a Greek breakfast."

Chapter 25 Return to Delaware

Saturday, May 22, 2010

After Joann landed in Athens, she passed through customs and security and entered the international waiting area. The departure gate sign showed her plane would take off at 11:45 a.m. Greek time, and arrive at the Philadelphia International Airport at 3:55 p.m. EST.

Joann called Andrew between planes in Philadelphia while she waited for her 4:50 departure to Norfolk. "Andrew, I'm in the U.S. I'll see you in less than three hours."

Andrew told her, "Add two hours, since I'm staying at the Outer Banks and not Norfolk. Al Saunders, six feet tall, thin, with gray hair and a clear completion will pick you up at the airport. Saunders will be driving a white 2007 Chevy Malibu, and will wear a gray summer suit. Ask for his identification before you leave with him. If he doesn't show it to you, or the car is different go to the nearest cop or TSA official, explain your concerns, and call me." Andrew said in a business-like manner.

Joann thought, he must not be alone. "Will do."

"You'll be tired when you arrive. We can work on the investigation tomorrow."

Now she was reassured, knowing they'd work on something else this evening.

Al Saunders met the plane Saturday evening armed with a picture of Joann. He did not display a sign with her name to preserve their anonymity. He knew he'd find the stunning five-foot six-inch blond. When he saw her, he walked up to her and asked, "Joann Cummings?"

"Yes. You are?"

180

"Al Saunders, I work with Andrew Smithson."

"Show me identification."

Al handed her his driving license and a folded piece of paper. Joann opened the paper and emotionally melted as she read the handwritten note, "Welcome home. You'll love the beach house. Andrew."

Joann enjoyed the two-hour ride to the Outer Banks of North Carolina. The difference between the North Carolina coast studded with barrier islands and the mountainous terrain of Greece reminded her how flat most of the East Coast was.

Al, a good conversationalist, talked about his company, several investigations involving him, but did not discuss Andrew's situation or ask about her relationship with Andrew. She mentally thanked him for his discretion.

He drove on Route 158 straight to the Wright Memorial Bridge separating the mainland from Bodie Island and turned north toward Duck on Route 12. They turned left before Duck's small commercial area. After a few hundred yards, Al entered a gated development and parked the car under the large three-story, cedar-shingled house.

Saunders carried her luggage and inserted a key card into the front door lock. He opened a second door to enter the foyer. When they went in, it surprised Joann to see a guard sitting at a desk.

Joann beamed when she saw Andrew standing behind the desk.

"Hi, Joann, you look great even though you have had a long day, leaving Mykonos before sunrise, flying, and driving for twenty hours. You must be tired. Let me show you your bedroom."

"It's good to see you again. I'll follow you," Joann said. Andrew picked up her luggage.

Andrew entered an elevator and pressed the button for three. After the elevator door closed, he said, "You still look beautiful. I'm glad you're here."

"Thanks, I slept on the plane so I'm not so tired. I'm glad to see you. But I'd like to see my bedroom."

He opened her bedroom door with a key card and handed it to her, "My bedroom's next door in case you need anything."

"I need a shower."

Andrew placed her luggage next to a white love seat decorated with blue pictures of shellfish.

After her shower, Joann noticed the queen-size bed covered with a partially pulled down blue comforter and four white pillows. She wanted him to join her.

He came in and after he closed the door, Joann flew into his arms and whispered, "I missed you holding me." They kissed and caressed for minutes without talking.

Finally, he said, "I'm glad we can be together again. I've been thinking of you since the shooting and my exile here."

Joann kissed him again. "I don't want to talk." They fell into bed. The hours melted away while they rekindled their love.

Joann awoke content the next morning. She rolled over to see the lovely morning light. She stayed cuddled in Andrew's arms quietly until he stirred.

Andrew said, "Good morning," and pulled her closer.

"Sorry, I crashed last night. We didn't talk much," Joann said.

"You were tired, but thankfully not too tired. We can spend all day talking about our discoveries analyzing the Liberty Credit's computer logs. I'm going to my room to shower and dress, I'll be back in twenty minutes. Then breakfast."

Andrew took her to the kitchen on the second floor at the back of the house. "Is bacon, scrambled eggs, and toast, okay?" he asked.

While Andrew cooked, Joann asked, "How safe is this house, if Strong discovers our location? We assumed no one would find us in Greece but they did."

"It's designed as a safe house, with over six thousand square feet of livable and workable space. If Strong shows up, our visual and motion detectors monitor the grounds twenty-four hours every day, and would detect him or anyone else before they entered our property."

Andrew left the stove and pointed at the windows, "These are bullet proof and could withstand automatic weapons fire." Returning to the stove he turned the bacon over and pointed at the walls. "They include two inch steel plates that will also stop automatic weapon fire.

"That's reassuring," Joann said.

"There's more. All the rooms have an automatic fire extinguisher system. If an explosion occurs inside the house the flames would be doused within seconds. We feel impregnable."

"It's just my paranoia. I sure Strong will never locate us," Joann said. "What is the view beyond the closed curtains?"

"They're always closed for security, but go and look out for a second."

She did, "The ocean waves are beautiful. I didn't realize the house sits on a small hill." She pulled the curtain closed.

"Another security feature."

After they finished eating, Andrew showed her the computer room on the first floor above the ground floor parking area, filled with IBM rack servers and Cisco Systems networking servers.

"That's a powerful system for this house," Joann said.

"Yes, we need it for forensic IT work," Andrew said.

They entered Andrew's second floor office, which included two gray metal desks facing a blue sofa fronted by a walnut coffee table. Light beige wall-to-wall carpeting covered the floor. Two windows with venetian blinds provided the room with privacy from outside eyes. A ceiling fan light illuminated the room with its off-white walls. "The room has lead sheets next to the steel in the walls to prevent electronic eaves-dropping. You'll sit at the left desk, next to mine. When you disappeared, Liberty Credit put your IT account on hold. We'll get it activated this morning."

"I guess my vacation has ended." Joann sighed, wondering how broke she was for not working for ten weeks. She had not checked on her bank account since Crete.

"The company told me you were on administrative leave with

pay."

A wave of financial relief flooded over her. She said, "I work for a great company."

Andrew handed Joann three folders. "I'll summarized the findings of each study, but be sure to read and comment on each one."

Joann felt the thickness of the files. "Andrew, you've done a lot of work while I was in Greece."

"Yes, without you around, I could focus. The first file contains results from reports Helen Jenson asked me to run. She wanted to find out if any executives had used the Liberty computers for abnormal or non-business-related activities."

"That's against the rules, but many use it for personnel email to fellow employees and friends."

"We examined the one thousand, one hundred and nine staff at the director level or above. Nine hundred and fourteen used the computer for non-work related items. Emails were the highest illegal activity. Several ran fantasy football teams. Five VPs had suspicious emails. Six VPs, three male and three female were engaged in adulterous affairs. We supposed they used the company emails so their spouses wouldn't know."

Joann wondered who they were, but decided not to ask, "Interesting, I guess that behavior is normal for a company our size."

Andrew continued, "One VP and one director proved more interesting, Hank Strong and George Belford. They first exchanged strange emails in November of last year. The report has fifty-three non-business related emails on sports."

"George hated sports. He told me."

"We found out and told Helen last week, she seemed most interested and thanked us. The emails appear coded. A retired National Security Agency employee is trying to find the key to deciphering them. Please read them today to see if they make sense."

"I assumed George and Hank had more brains than to communicate on the company's email accounts. Did you tell the company of your findings?" Joann said.

"No. It wasn't our job."

"Good, but it is mine." Joann read the reports smiling at the findings on adultery. She suspected several of the wayward employees and was pleased to have it confirmed. Joann thought she shouldn't intervene on their harmless social life and decided to refer only specific cases violating company rules to Human Resources, where the couple had a supervisor/staff relationship.

Andrew received an email from the Liberty IT account manager saying Joann now had total access. She drafted an email to the staff on the list regarding use of the systems for non-company business, warning them to stop or face termination. Joann's boss, Ed Davis, VP for Operations, told her not to send the email until after the police solved the embezzlement case, since those affected could be involved in the crime. Davis wanted them to remain employed during the investigation.

At noon, they went to the kitchen and made sandwiches.

On Sunday morning, Paul and Margaret sat at the table on the deck and wrote their investigation plan of what they hoped to complete in the next two weeks. It included updating the current draft, writing drafts on sections they had left blank and setting up interview schedules for when they returned to the U.S. They wanted to talk to Helen Jenson, Andrew Smithson, Hank Strong, and other Liberty executives.

When they finished, they saved it, the draft novel, and their research notes onto a USB drive. They emailed them to themselves as a final security measure.

In the afternoon, they drove to town and spent a few hours walking and shopping. Margaret and Paul purchased several paintings. Paul chose a water color of the famous windmills, an unofficial symbol of the island. Margaret picked a street view that included the I Scream store.

Paul said, "These paintings will always remind me of our trip."

They took Kostas and Sally to the Olla Mykonos restaurant in the Little Venice area of Mykonos Town. They stopped for ice cream on the way back to their car.

On Monday, Paul and Margaret drove south to the Ornos Beach for their last swim in the Aegean. Margaret spent an hour swimming in the blue waters of the horseshoe-shaped beach, while Paul left the water after a half-hour. He then worked on editing the draft.

In the afternoon, around 4:00 p.m. Greek time or 9:00 a.m. EST, they started to schedule interviews in Delaware.

Helen Jenson answered their first call.

"It's Paul and me. We're returning on Tuesday and want to meet you on Wednesday to update our draft book."

"I'll be busy until Thursday. Can we meet then? I want both of you to brief me on everything that occurred with Belford in Greece."

"Can you meet at our house after work? We'll get a pizza," Paul said.

"I'll be there at 6:00. Do you mind if we make it formal and record your interview?" Helen asked.

"No. Can we can get a copy?" Margaret said.

"Yes, when we close the case."

"That's understandable," Paul said.

"What else do you want to do this week?" Helen asked.

"Interview others associated with the crime and work on improving our draft," Margaret said.

"Is Hank Strong one of them?"

"Yes," Margaret answered.

"Don't contact him until Thursday. Don't ask why. We'd appreciate your cooperation," Helen said.

"Of course," Margaret said. The three discussed the trip home and ended the conversation a few minutes later.

"I guess I should have prepared myself for her request. It's hard to accept how quickly my leverage with the State Police has declined," Margaret said, looking at Paul who smiled back.

"Helen has taken charge, and she is all business. You trained her well. It's what you'd have done. Of course, we'll do what she asks to keep our relationship with the police. What do you suppose Helen and her staff will do between now and Thursday?" Paul asked.

"If I were in charge, my team would execute search warrants on the Liberty executives. There's still plenty for us to do on Wednesday back home like cleaning up the garden."

The authors spent the rest of the day reviewing and updating the draft on the adventure in Greece, so they would be ready for the interviews. At 3:00, Paul looked at Margaret, and said, "I'm tired. Would you like to join me for a nap?"

Margaret, holding his hand, led the way to the bedroom.

Forty-five minutes later Paul said. "Isn't it great we can't keep our hands off each other."

That night Sally cooked them a special dinner of squid with rice and red peppers. The four stayed up till 11:00 drinking ouzo. Kostas and Paul entertained the group recalling and embellishing their academic experiences and successes.

The next morning, Margaret and Paul woke up with headaches. They drove their car to return it to the rental car company at the airport in time to board the 7:00 flight to Athens.

Hank Strong met Fred Livermore, Hank's replacement for George Belford, on Monday morning at 7:00 in Trap Pond State Park situated in the midst of chicken and grain farms in rural Laurel, Delaware.

Fred had served with George and Hank in Vietnam. After he left the Army, he joined the Philadelphia Police Department. Fred started out as a patrol cop and after ten years made detective. He became a private detective after he took a partial pension. Ten years later, the District Attorney's Office revoked his license because of unethical practices in several divorce cases. He then marketed himself as a discrete "friend" to his previous clients.

Hank had originally hired Fred to investigate the background of a beautiful blonde woman whom he had considered marrying. Fred discovered she had been married three times and had won hefty divorce settlements that made her a rich woman. Hank ended the relationship, and became indebted to Fred.

Hank wanted to obtain Army weapons on the Internet and asked Fred if it was possible. Fred gave Hank a short course about the dark web and taught him how to purchase illegal guns.

Fred parked his 2008 blue Ford Windstar in the lot near the Bald Cypress Center. Hank parked fifty yards away. Carrying a coffee mug, he walked to Fred's minivan, and slid in the front seat.

"Too bad George had an accident in Greece," Fred said.

"Yes, he was a good friend. I miss him." Hank frowned. "I need you to find an employee who's disappeared."

"The price is much higher if I have to do more than provide false passports and driver's licenses."

"Understood. How much higher?" Hank said, thinking no matter what it costs, I'll kill him after he gives me what I want so he can't testify against me.

"$10,000."

"That's steep," Hank said, holding back a smile since he had envisioned a much higher fee.

"It's risky working for you. Too many people die."

"No one will die. I want you to find Joann Cummings. I'll pay that amount plus expenses. Half now and the rest when you find her." Hank handed Livermore a manila folder containing her personal and contact information. "Start with her mother, Alice Cummings and Joann's boyfriend, Andrew Smithson. Alice Cummings lives in Toledo, Ohio. Smithson disappeared after he was shot."

Fred examined the folder. "I'll do it."

Hank gave him $5,000 in untraceable twenties and fifties, and a throwaway cell phone. "Use this only to contact me." He handed Livermore a piece of paper with the number. "We'll meet once a week for a progress report. I'll use the phone to arrange the meeting."

"I'll need to travel, how do I get you travel receipts?"

"Bring them to our meeting."

Chapter 26 Hank Strong Investigated

Monday, May 24, 2010

Helen Jenson prepared search warrants for Ed Davis and Hank Strong on Sunday using the information provided by Andrew Smithson. She presented them to the Sussex County judge on Monday morning, who approved the warrants.

Helen, accompanied by Detective Bill Norse, CSI Ben Johnson, and three uniform State Troopers, entered Hank's office at 1:00 in the afternoon and handed him the warrant.

While expecting this and having taken precautions, Hank almost panicked, but calmed himself. They wouldn't find anything incriminating. He said, "Here are the keys to my homes. I've got nothing to hide, but I'd rather you don't break the doors down."

Helen accepted the keys, "Thanks, I need your cell phone and the location of your safe deposit box."

Hank complied. "I'd want to stay with you while you're doing the search. I won't contact anyone, even my staff."

"Thanks for your cooperation. After we box the material here, we'll go to your Bethany Beach home, followed by your Middletown home. Ben Johnson will examine the material in your safe deposit box. Mr. Strong, you can travel in a squad car."

Riding in another car, Helen gave Hank Strong's cell phone to Bill Norse. "Copy the SIM card files, so we can return the phone to Strong later."

After they left Bethany Beach, Helen said, "Hard to accept we found nothing."

"Strong prepared for our visit. The place was too clean and neat," Bill Norse said.

"Hope Ben finds something in his safe deposit box, and we discover evidence in Middleton," Helen said.

"If he's as prepared with his house as he was with his office material, we'll find nothing," Bill said.

After three hours of searching the Middletown house, they drove south more dejected than before. They had found nothing and had received a call from Ben Johnson that the safe deposit box had no damning evidence either.

When the detectives arrived at State Troop Barracks 4 in Georgetown, Helen said, "Hopefully, we'll be luckier with Ed Davis tomorrow."

The squad car returned Hank to his office after 7:00 p.m. As he got out of the car, the driver handed him his cell phone.

The office had closed hours ago so Hank drove to his Bethany Beach home, dreading cleaning up the mess the cops had made. They damaged his mattress, pillows, and furniture by slashing into them with what appeared to be to Hank an enthusiastic abandon. He decided to take the next day off to clean the house and decide whether to stay or flee.

Hank realized his boss, CEO Jim Regan, would have to accept his immediate resignation. That evening he decided not to worry but to have a relaxing drink and dream about his future. He drank one Black Label scotch before his steak dinner accompanied by two glasses of red wine. He ended his meal with a snifter of Remy Martin VSOP brandy before retiring to his trashed bed and slashed pillows.

Hank awoke with a clear head. At nine, after preparing his monologue, he called Regan.

"Hank, I was about to call you. Heard about the search yesterday. Hope they didn't destroy your homes."

"No, they're okay, but they trashed the furniture and wall

hangings," Hank said. "I've trained my successor, Sam Willard, so well that now he is making all the decisions. Since I have over a month's leave, I'd like to make yesterday my last day so I can clean up both homes."

"Fine with me, but come in Monday, May 30, which we will make your last day. Hank, you'll need to visit Human Resources for an exit interview."

"Thanks, I'll be there at 10:00."

"Don't feel persecuted. The police showed up this morning looking for Ed Davis. They will search his home too. I wonder if they're going after every executive, and when will they issue a search warrant for me."

Hank felt a wave of relief surge through his body. "The police must not have a clue on who led the embezzlement. Perhaps, the searches will clear me and Ed."

Hank carried a cup of coffee to his study and thought about his departure. He wrote nothing fearing another search. He knew the police would not tell him if they found anything. Confident in his pre-search preparations, Hank knew he'd never get arrested. So he decided to leave on next Monday afternoon's flight from the Philadelphia International Airport to Salt Lake City where he would disappear.

Fred Livermore's chosen profession allowed him to stay up late and sleep until noon. While drinking his first cup of coffee, he turned on the local TV mid-day news. He almost dropped the coffee pot, when he heard the police had searched Strong's two homes yesterday and were searching the residence of Hank's colleague Ed Davis today.

Fred had always suspected Hank had taken part in the embezzlement, but perhaps the crime included all of Liberty's top management. It concerned him that the police might arrest Hank before he finished the job of locating Joann. He would lose $5,000 plus expenses. That afternoon Fred left on a flight to Toledo, Ohio, where Hank had told him he would find Joann's mother.

As they ate, Andrew told Joann, "While the first report you read concerning employee use of the Liberty Credit Card computers was interesting, the second study scrutinized the VP's private social media accounts. Several belong to dating sites. Normal, if they're single. We found nothing unusual, except for Ed Davis and Hank Strong. They both use Facebook, Instagram, Linkin, and belong to several travel clubs touting retirement in foreign countries. Strong belongs to several mystery book clubs, dating sites, and visited spy, medical, and forensic sites."

"Ed can't be involved," Joann said, knowing him as happily married, who championed qualified women, including her, in a male dominated company.

"Ed was a Facebook friend of George Belford. We learned from the Facebook Messenger App that he met with him several times, not recorded on the company's systems. Ed might be innocent, but we're interested in anyone conducting research on leaving the country."

"Ed and his wife love traveling. They've often talked of living in a different country for a few months every year after they retire."

"With Hank, his murder mysteries, medical websites, spy shops, and his Internet curiosity concerned us. Wonder if he studied how not to get caught committing murder?"

"I don't know about Hank, but Belford did spy on me, Joe Reynolds, Margaret Hoffman, and Paul O'Hare." Joann spent two hours reading the second report and concluded while boring for her, it might interest a detective.

Joann and Andrew worked through the evening news and cooked a steak at 8:00. "The third study is a continuation of the analysis Joe Reynolds performed on Liberty's IT system log data. We can discuss it tomorrow," Andrew said.

They kissed, went to bed, made love, and slept in each other's arms, so they missed the news of the search of Hank's homes. They entered the kitchen on Tuesday morning at the start of ABC news program.

Both froze when they heard Hank Strong's name.

"Didn't know it would happen that soon," Andrew said.

"Ed Davis's turn could be next. Hope they find enough on Strong and his accomplices so I can stop living in fear."

"Since you're here every day, I'm not sure I want it to end."

"Andrew, I'll stay with you after it's over," Joann said.

Andrew beamed and blushed.

Then he said, "A Delaware detective, Bill Norse, with computer smarts is arriving tomorrow afternoon to help us with IT system log analysis."

Tuesday May 25, 2010

After landing in Philadelphia Tuesday afternoon, Margaret and Paul took a limo for the drive home to Ocean View, Delaware. A few years ago, they would never have incurred this expense. Most likely they'd have used a slow airport shuttle that weaved its way south. Paul convinced Margaret they now had more money than they could spend before they died. This was one way to enjoy it.

The driver recognized the passengers as soon as they entered the limo, even before reading the passenger manifest. "Welcome to our limo service. Your drive will take two-and-a-half hours. The cooler contains complimentary juices, soda, water, wine, cheese, and crackers. The contents are for your enjoyment."

After opening the cooler, Paul said, "Thanks, we'll start with a glass of white wine. What's your name?" He opened the screw top wine bottle and handed a glass to Margaret.

"Jerry. I read about your adventures in Mykonos. That must have been exciting."

"More interesting than exciting. Just a day's work for an ex-cop," Margaret said.

"Did you hear the latest in the Liberty embezzlement case?" Jerry asked.

"No," Margaret said.

"The police conducted a search at Liberty Credit's Finance VP, Hank Strong's office and homes yesterday. A report on the search is on page 4 of the paper next to you. The noon TV news reported the police are searching Ed Davis, another VPs' office today."

"Thanks, we'll read the paper. We have jet lag so we will take a nap after we finish our wine," Paul said. "Please wake us when we arrive."

Margaret looked at Paul, "Now we know why Helen asked us not to call." She snuggled closer to read the paper Paul had opened.

Bill Norris arrived at the Duck, North Carolina safe house on Tuesday afternoon to help analyze the Liberty IT system logs. Andrew, who had been working with Norris remotely for a month, introduced him to Joann. Bill also carried copies of the files on Hank Strong's computers.

Helen had briefed Bill on what he could tell Andrew and Joann concerning the raids before he left Georgetown, Delaware. Bill parried their questions for a half-hour. Bill followed his boss's instructions summarizing the disappointing information. They had found nothing to incriminate Strong.

"Have you learned anything more than what Joe Reynolds found?" Bill asked.

"No, nothing new in the data during the embezzlement period," Andrew said.

"It must have taken them time to set up the illegal software. I suggest we examine at least the three months before December 4, 2009, when the embezzlement started," Bill said. Helen had agreed to his strategy the evening before.

"Typically, a programmer writes a new application on a development environment, verifies it on a testing environment, and runs it on production machines," Joann said. "Joe conducted his analysis on systems data on production machines."

Bill said, "Let's extend his analysis on the production environment back to September. That will tell us when they started developing the embezzlement programs." Bill and Joann spent the rest of the afternoon reviewing Joe's programs and the two written by Andrew's firm to understand and improve upon the initial systems. Andrew prepared each program to cover the new dates. Andrew submitted the long-running number-crunching programs to analyze three months of billions of system log data before 7:00 p.m.

Andrew said, "Let's go to the kitchen for a beer and let's order dinner. I'm famished."

Bill opened the fridge door, looked inside, and asked, "Bud Lite, Dogfish Head IPA, or Heineken?"

Andrew reached for the Dogfish Head IPA, the others chose Heineken. "We can eat anything we want, although it helps our driver if we use one restaurant." They agreed on seafood, and Andrew distributed four different menus between them.

"Andrew, you've been here the longest, you pick," Joann said.

Since Andrew knew Bill had to limit his expenses charged to the Delaware State Police, he chose the Black Pelican Seafood Company, one of the more moderately priced restaurants on the Outer Banks. Passing around the menu, Andrew said, "Order whatever you want, except beverages, we have those here."

"I'll need a separate receipt, and I'll have to pay with a state credit card," Bill said.

"Of course," Andrew replied.

Since they valued their bodies and health, they restrained themselves and did not order the calorie-busting meals. Andrew and Joann ordered the fresh grilled tuna while Bill chose shrimp and grits. He explained, "Grits in Delaware doesn't compare to Duck grits. I always eat shrimp and grits as least once on every trip to the Outer Banks."

On Wednesday morning they divided up the report. They found nothing on the production runs until the month of November that paralleled Joe Reynolds' findings. The embezzler submitted these production runs from untraceable remote sites on weekends or during second or third shift periods. Andrew and Bill concluded they must have been the final tests before the embezzlement programs ran. They decided to review the test system data next.

Since the test data archives were only a small percentage of the production data, the analysis program runs were completed by mid-afternoon.

They discovered test runs two weeks before the execution of the embezzlement programs, starting on Monday, November 22, 2010, very similar to those Reynolds had detected. The test programs ran on weekends on non-prime hours except on Wednesday and Thursday, December 1 and 2, 2010. The tests ended on December 3, 2010.

After they completed the analysis, Joann stated, "Since we know when the perpetrator ran the programs, I'll ask Liberty HR to compare those times with the IT staff's attendance. If we find partial or full matches, we'll know who ran the programs."

"Brilliant," Andrew said, thinking bringing back Joann not only made me happy, but she possesses a fine brain that may help us crack the case. "I bet HR will find George Belford matches the submission times."

Bill Norse nodded his head in agreement.

The HR report appeared in Joann's email Thursday morning, which she summarized for Andrew and Bill. "Only one IT employee had company attendance the inverse of the program execution times. It's not Belford. He matches only fifty percent of the time. We misinterpreted Steve Haven's role in the crime. Haven's absence mirrored one hundred percent of the program execution time. He wasn't a victim."

Silence engulfed the three.

"How could we have missed it?" Andrew asked.

"Haven's murder indicates he wasn't the leader. Someone killed him so he couldn't identify the leader," Bill said.

"We can assume the same person who killed Haven ordered

Belford to murder me. He or she could be a sociopath without a conscience," Joann said.

Bill Norse called Helen. "The team has made significant progress that changes the tenor of the investigation. By examining the computer log data and Liberty staff attendance data, we found Steve Haven wasn't a victim. He was an important criminal responsible for the embezzlement. He developed, tested, and submitted the embezzlement programs. We now have to discover Belford's and Haven's crime boss."

"I had hoped the search on Strong's homes would have helped. But we came up empty. Unfortunately, your recent findings set us back to the beginning of the investigation. We'll have to start by looking at Belford's and Haven's relationships. Let me know by tomorrow what you are going to work on. No point in duplicating our efforts."

Chapter 27 Searching for Joann

Wednesday, May 26, 2018

Fred Livermore arrived in Toledo, Ohio on Tuesday evening, rented a car, and drove to a Holiday Inn. He spent the evening researching the sixty-two-year-old, Alice Cummings, who he found worked as a nurse at the Medical Center at the University of Toledo. Knowing most nurses worked twelve-hour shifts, three days a week, he drove by her dark home at 6:00 a.m. After stopping at McDonalds, he returned at 7:30 and discovered a car parked in her driveway.

Fred drove to his hotel, extended his reservation for one more day, and went to sleep. He woke up in mid-afternoon. At 4:00, he went to Alice Cummings's home and noticed the same car parked in the driveway. Fred drove down the street, crossed an intersection, and parked on the opposite side of the street from her house where he could see her car. After fifteen minutes, he drove and parked at another vantage point. This movement continued until 6:30 when Alice got into her car and left. Fred followed her to the hospital. When she did not return to her car within thirty minutes, Fred drove back to the hotel.

After 9:00 p.m., Fred went to the hospital and seeing Alice's car still parked, drove to her home. Dressed in dark clothes and wearing gloves, he surveyed the house and not finding alarm signs, walked to the back door and picked the lock. He stopped at each phone and installed a listening device. When Fred found Alice's laptop on a desk in her bedroom, he opened it and used a hacking program to bypass Alice's password. Fred copied her document files onto a USB drive and planted a Trojan Horse program, which would send copies of the emails Alice received or sent to his laptop.

On Wednesday morning, Margaret said, "Paul, since we don't know if Belford had accomplices, we have to be alert. It's been over a month since you last fired a gun. We are going to the shooting range to refresh your skills. From now on when we leave the house, both of us will be armed."

"I've had the same thoughts ever since the car chase," Paul responded.

Margaret watched Paul shoot and after fifteen minutes said, "You're just as sharp as before we left."

"Let's compare rifle scores. I think I beat you," Paul said.

Margaret retrieved the targets, comparing them she said, "You did. You're almost shooting at a sniper's proficiency level."

Thursday evening May 27, 2010

After work, Helen picked up a six pack of Dogfish Head IPA on her way to her meeting with Margaret and Paul. She arrived at her old boss's home a few minutes after six. They hugged while Paul poured the beer into glasses.

Helen said, "Tell me about your honeymoon. We can discuss the case after we finish the pizza."

"Sure, but much of the trip was intertwined with the case after we met Joann Cummings," Margaret said.

"I already know what happened to Joann. Tell me about the islands you visited. My husband and I are thinking of spending a few weeks there next summer," Helen said.

"Let me open the laptop and show you our photos," Paul said. After talking a half-hour, having only described Athens and Crete and looking at over fifty photos, Paul said, "I'm getting hungry." He turned on the oven to preheat it to 450 degrees and took two fourteen inch pizzas they had topped earlier and placed them in the oven. Helen liked vegetarian pizza, with peppers and mushrooms, while Margaret preferred pepperoni, sausage, and mushroom. Paul loved all pizza toppings.

They finished the first beer while the pizzas baked. Margaret refilled everyone's glasses, during her description of their visit to Santorini. After Margaret and Paul completed their trip review Helen started her update. "Bill Norse, Joann Cummings, and Andrew Smithson are in Duck, North Carolina in a safe house owned by the Berkley and Jones accounting firm. They completed an analysis extending Joe Reynolds's work and comparing the program submission time with Liberty staff absence from work. The analysis did not find George Belford as the hacker. Steve Haven fits that role."

Margaret and Paul looked at each other. "We missed the beginning of the story," Paul said.

"Yes, we'll have to restart," Margaret said.

"Haven's murder completely fooled us. We were thinking it occurred because he had discovered who committed the crime. Whoever killed him, if it wasn't Belford, that person ordered Belford to murder Joe Reynolds, and tried to kill Joann, and both of you. He wants to hide all connections between himself and the crime," Helen said.

"If Belford masterminded the crime, we're done. If not, we have to continue investigating. My guess is Hank Strong," Paul said.

"True. Since you're civilians, I can't ask you to investigate. But, if you do, please keep me informed so I can avoid assigning duplicate resources to the same topics," Helen said.

"We'll look into Steve Haven and see if we can find any connections he had with others in the embezzlement," Margaret said. "Helen, you could help us by sending us Haven's contact information, restaurants, and bars he patronized, and his personal habits."

"I'll email you a copy of his case file which should have enough information for you to start conducting interviews."

"Even though you found nothing during the Strong search, I still think he's involved. Please send us his photo," Margaret said.

"Will do. It's close to 9:00. I have to be getting home to my family. Thanks for the great pizza."

Helen awoke refreshed on Friday morning, thankful Margaret and Paul would investigate Steve Haven's past. Helen called Bill Norse when she arrived at her office, "Bill did you decide what to work on next?"

"We'll continue to review the Liberty IT data and to investigate Hank Strong's IT activities outside the Liberty system."

"Both tasks sound reasonable. Update me on your progress by 5:00 p.m.."

Margaret opened Helen's email containing Haven's case file and photos of Haven and Strong. They used the file to help discover Steve Haven's private life. Helen's file identified twenty family and work contacts and four bars and restaurants he frequented.

Margaret called Joann, "Hi, Paul and I are on speaker phone. We have returned home and will investigate Steve Haven's murder."

"How can I help?"

"Can you give us a list of his friends at Liberty and where he hung out socially? We're searching for background information."

"I'll email you in a few minutes?"

"We look forward to reading it," Paul said.

After Joann hung up she turned to Andrew, "Margaret and Paul want to know about Steve Haven's friends and habits. What do we know?"

Within thirty minutes, they emailed Margaret eighteen names, and five establishments frequented by Haven. Margaret found Joann's list duplicated eleven of her case file names, but increased the list to twenty-six names and seven bars and restaurants.

They agreed they'd learn more by visiting the bars and restaurants than by interviewing his contacts, although they needed these interviews for the book. Their main priority was identifying Haven's killer.

At noon, Paul drove them to Jimmy's Grill, Haven's favorite

breakfast restaurant, in Bridgeville, Delaware. After they were seated, the waitress gave them menus and asked, "What would you like to drink?"

Both answered, "Ice tea."

When she returned and gave them the drinks, she asked, "Are you ready to order?"

"I'll have a Caesar salad," Margaret said.

"Medium hamburger for me," Paul replied.

As she started to leave, Margaret asked, "Do you work the breakfast shift?"

"Yes. Wednesday through Sunday. Why?"

"We're authors of true crime books. You might have heard about our book on the skeleton murders," Paul said.

"No, but I don't read that much."

Margaret reached in her handbag and handed her a paperback copy of the book. "You might enjoy it. It's a murder mystery and takes place in southern Delaware."

She took the book, "Thanks."

"We're looking into the murder of Steve Haven. You know this was his favorite restaurant," Paul said.

"I remember him, especially after they found his body."

Margaret showed her Haven's picture. "To be sure we're talking about the same person. Is this him?"

"Yes, he came in several times a week and usually on Saturday."

"Have you ever seen him with this man?" Margaret asked showing her a picture of Hank Strong.

"Yes, during the fall, almost every Saturday for a month in November. I can't forget him since he flirted with me and left great tips. Was he involved in the murder?"

"We don't know. But his meeting with Haven is interesting. Can we have your name so we can properly quote you?"

After she responded, placed their order, and served them, Margaret and Paul couldn't help smiling throughout their meal. They left a twenty-dollar tip.

Since only one establishment on the list served breakfast, they returned home, later visiting a restaurant in the evening in Georgetown, Delaware. While the staff remembered Steve Haven, because of the publicity of the murder, they had never seen Strong with him.

On Saturday, they tried to visit two restaurants, one at cocktail hour and the second for dinner. The wait staff was too busy at cocktail hour to be interviewed, so Paul and Margaret decided to stay for a meal. While the waiter remembered Steve Haven, he did not recall Hank Strong. After the questioning, Margaret said, "Haven's murder had so much publicity, everyone who met him remembers him."

"True, we'll just have to keep at it until we find a second person with a great memory who recognizes Hank Strong's picture," Paul said. "Only four more restaurants to visit, before we call his contacts."

"Let's go to lunch and dinner on Sunday and Monday and finish them."

"I agree. No more cocktail hours."

On Sunday afternoon, they ate at the Blue Water Grill, a seafood restaurant in Millsboro. Once again the waiter recognized Haven, but had never seen Strong.

That night they went to the Hang Out bar in Long Neck, Delaware. A rock band played eighties songs. As the hostess walked them to a table, Paul saw several men staring at Margaret.

She noticed Paul's determined look and wondered if it bordered on jealousy. "I like this place. We should come here again."

Paul surprised, said, "Why?"

"I think you know. The men appreciate me here."

"Margaret, they don't appreciate you as I do," Paul said knowing he frequented this bar before meeting Margaret. He had behaved the same as the lecherous men staring at her. He decided not to tell Margaret this part of his single life. "Let's taste the food before we decide to return."

Margaret said, "That sounds reasonable."

After the waitress placed glasses of Chardonnay in front of them, she asked, "Would you like to order?"

"Before we do, we want to ask you a few questions," Margaret said, showing her Haven's picture. "Have you ever seen him?"

"Yes, that's Steve Haven. He used to be a regular here. Someone killed him."

"One more picture," Margaret said, as she showed him a picture of Strong's face.

"Yes, he met Haven here one night in the summer, and they drank most of the night. After Haven left, Strong paid the bill and left a forty dollar tip."

"How do you know his name?" Paul asked.

"He told me, gave me his business card, and asked for my phone number. I told him I had a live-in boyfriend, and it wouldn't work. He told me to keep the card in case we split up, so I did. But we stayed together."

After they placed their order, Margaret said, "Despite how smart Strong has acted, his weakness for women may have doomed him."

"No crime is perfect, no matter how smart the criminal thinks they are, especially if they have a fatal character flaw."

The writers enjoyed their food and danced a few times before leaving at 10:30. On the drive home, Paul said, "I enjoyed the meal and the dancing. We should go again."

"I had a good time too." Margaret guessed Paul had overcome his fear of her straying which made her happy. She expected her husband to act confidently in their relationship.

Since they arrived home after 11:00, they decided to call Helen in the morning.

After 9:00 a.m., Helen picked up the phone, "Hi, it's Margaret and Paul on speaker phone. We had a few interesting days investigating Haven and Strong."

"What did you find out?" Helen asked.

"Strong had at least five meetings with Haven in two restaurants before the embezzlement started. While it's not enough to arrest him, it tells us we should keep observing him," Paul said.

"I agree. We'll keep pursuing him until we collect evidence of his direct involvement."

Thursday, May 27, 2010

Fred returned to his hotel near 10:00 p.m. on Wednesday. He examined his copy of Alice's hard drive, searching for Joann's name.

Fred copied the emails he found to a file named Joann. He learned she had returned to the U.S., but her location wasn't identified. Fred accessed Alice's email and found those related to Joann were already on the USB drive.

Fred crashed near 2:00 a.m. and woke up at 7:00, turned on his laptop and waited for Alice to turn on her email. Her email app opened a few minutes before 8:00. She had received an email from her daughter, also addressed to Margaret. It summarized her trip home and hints to her current location. She was staying in a four-story house in Duck, North Carolina in a gated community. Joann did not give the street address but did describe the cars and the security of the location.

Fred left Toledo that afternoon and flew to Norfolk. He drove a rental car to Manteo on Roanoke Island near the Outer Banks where he had reserved a hotel room. He accessed the Google Maps road-level view to examine the homes in Duck. He discovered six that fit the description in Joann's email. Fred visited them and found only two in gated communities.

The next day Joann sent another email to her mom, saying they didn't leave the house, but yesterday ordered a great meal from the Black Pelican Seafood Company.

Fred staked out the restaurant and on the third day saw a car similar to the one Joann described pull up to the Black Pelican at 6:30. He followed the car but could not enter the gated community. Fred watched the car drive to a house that matched Joann's description. He took several pictures of the house and the gated entrance and left.

The next morning Fred checked out of his hotel and drove for five hours home to Annapolis, Maryland.

Saturday May 29, 2010

Fred called Hank, "I've located Joann. On Sunday, I want to meet to deliver my report."

"Let's meet at Trap Pond on Sunday at noon, where we met last time," Hank asked.

"No. Too isolated. Let's meet at the Cracker Barrel on Route 1 in Rehoboth at 1:00."

Hank thought he's right to be suspicious, but I'll get Joann's location. "See you Sunday."

Hank arrived five minutes early, settling into the crowded restaurant and ordered coffee and a chef salad. Fred joined Hank at his table, preferring a coke and a tuna sandwich with fries. Three tables of diners surrounded them so they had to guard their conversation.

Hank did not mention Fred's fear and the change in venue. "Fred, good to see you again. How did you like Ohio?"

"Very much. My aunt told me I should investigate Duck, North Carolina, for a retirement home for you. The detailed information is in this envelope," which Fred had placed next to his coke.

"Let's enjoy our food before you show me where I might live for the next twenty-five years," Hank said as he started chatting about Major League baseball. Fred picked up his intent and the sports conversation on baseball continued for a half-hour, until the customers near their table left.

After the last one departed, Hank said, "Fred, you have something?"

"Yes, but you owe me a fee. I suggest we exchange them simultaneously."

"I want to look at what you have before I pay you."

Fred shook his head no. "Since the cops searched your homes, the police could arrest you this afternoon. I don't want to take that chance. The envelope contains $1,105 in itemized expense receipts."

Hank realized Fred would withhold the information, unless he paid him. "Okay, I'll give you your expenses later." He handed Fred a business envelope and grabbed the letter size manila envelope from Fred.

"It includes the location of Joann, Andrew Smithson, Joann's boyfriend, and Bill Norse, a Delaware State Police detective. Please send my expense check here. Fred handed him a piece of paper. He put $10 on the table for his food and prepared to leave. "You know how to reach me if you have another assignment."

Hank paid the bill. He walked out, sat in his car, opened and examined the material.

He thought Fred is good, I may have to use him again.

Now I can take care of Joann, but also three others investigating me. Hopefully, if I destroy the house, I can destroy much of their evidence. Sitting in the car his rage over George's death seethed. He thought he could assuage it and safely leave the country satisfied.

After reviewing the hard copy with its exact geographical description, he examined the USB drive, finding it had the same information. He drove to his Bethany Beach home, left the Duck location document in his car. He smashed the USB drive with a hammer and buried it in his back yard near the wrecked laptop he had buried in January. He assumed since the police had already searched his home without finding the laptop they wouldn't return.

On Monday morning, Hank Strong arrived at work before 10:00, with his luggage packed. He went to HR for his exit interview, which lasted half an hour. He then walked the halls saying goodbye to his staff, thanking them for their work, and wishing them well with their new boss.

At 11:00 he entered Jim Regan's office. His boss said, "Hank, thanks for stopping by. It's unfortunate you have to leave under these circumstances. The Board had to let you go to quiet the stock market."

"Yes, it also helped me since much of my 401k is in Liberty stock. I've always wanted to retire early and this gave me the opportunity."

"Perhaps, this check might help you enjoy your retirement," Regan said as he handed Hank an envelope.

Hank opened it, glanced at the $2 million severance check, and said, "Thanks, it sure will. I've wanted to spend a year traveling around the states. With this check I can see the world."

"Hank, you earned it, not just for your excellent work over the years, but how you trained your successor."

"I enjoyed my stay here, and now I'm ready to travel."

"Where do you plan to go?" Regan asked, curious as to how retired executives spend their time.

"In my youth and as a young adult, I skied at Snowbird, Utah, but I never toured the rest of the state with its desert, mountain, and canyon scenery." Hank removed his plane tickets from an inside suit jacket pocket and showed them to Regan.

That afternoon, Strong deposited his bonus check in his regular checking account. He drove to his hidden safe deposit box and retrieved his new passport and identity cards. He drove to the Philadelphia International Airport, checked his luggage, boarded the 4:15, and flew to Salt Lake City.

Hank stayed in Salt Lake City for the evening. The next morning he rented a car, and drove to Moab, Utah at the southern entrance to the Arches National Park, named for its more than two thousand natural sandstone arches.

He drove slowly extending the normal three and a half hour drive to five hours to enjoy the reoccurring beauty of the mountains and canyons of Utah. Hank wondered if he would regret his flight overseas, never to return and see the exotic geographical sites of the U.S. He rationalized that with his new identity, he could pass undetected in the States too.

Further thought convinced him of the need to leave. He had

murdered Steve Haven, was indirectly involved in the murder of Joe Reynolds, and had masterminded the Liberty embezzlement. If caught, he would spend the rest of his life in jail. Enough deterrent to complete one more task, the elimination of Joann Cummings, who he believed was the only individual who could connect him to the crimes. He registered at the Springhill Suites by Marriott, located just a few miles east of the park entrance on Route 191, for a three-day stay. His room had a view of the Colorado River.

The next morning, Hank entered the park. After driving around for several hours, and stopping and taking pictures of the major natural sites with his cell phone, he parked and spent an hour hiking, talking to as many park visitors as he could. That evening he ate in a restaurant in downtown Moab and spent a few hours in the bar introducing himself to other tourists.

Chapter 28 Hank Strong Disappears

Tuesday, June 1, 2018

Helen called Margaret and Paul, "I'm sending you a timeline we have developed. It's missing the early events you discovered about Strong's meetings, plus the details of Belford's activities. Since you will need a detailed timeline for your book, I'm asking you to update ours."

"We've started," Margaret said.

"When you finish, I need you to present it to the team on the Outer Banks. When can you come here?"

"Is Friday okay? We can be there by 1:00."

"That's too early. Can you make it Friday evening? You can stay at the Duck location," Helen said, hoping the meeting would generate new ideas for collecting evidence of Strong's involvement.

"We'll see you Friday evening."

"I'll send you the address with the table," Helen said.

Margaret opened the email, the timeline table, and commented on its form, "It has four columns: the date, event, order discovered, and source of the information."

After reviewing it, Paul said, "It's comprehensive and even includes our involvement. It shouldn't take us long to update it."

"Let's put our additions in italics so Helen can recognize them," Margaret said.

In a half hour she returned the following table to Helen.

Table of Liberty Credit Card Co. Embezzlement Events Known to Margaret and Paul

Event date	Event	Order and date discovered, if different from event date	Source
9/19/2009	*Hank Strong and Steve haven meet often at jimmy's grill in Bridgeville, Delaware*	*19* 5/26/2010	*Margaret and Paul interview waitress at Jimmy's Grill*
10/1/2009 to 12/1/2009	Writing and testing the embezzlement program	18 5/26/2010	Andrew Smithson, Bill Norse and, Joann Cummings examine log files
12/5/2009 to 1/2/2009	Performing the embezzlement	10	Joe Reynolds examines log files from 3/15/2010 to 3/30/2010
12/9/2009	Discovery of fraudulent credit card purchase	1 1/8/2010	Jean Baker client analyzed by Joann Cummings
1/16/2010	Federal trade commission ask Delaware State Police to run the investigation	2	Commission accepts Senator George downing's recommendation
2/4/2010	Joann briefs operations manager on potential problem. Security chief called in to analyze situation	3 2/4/2010	Joann Cummings and Operations Manager - Ben Davis
2/5/2010	Security chief states problem is external hackers, Joann believes it's internal fraud.	4 2/5/2010	Joann Cummings and George Belford
2/10/2010	Discovery of the large extent of the crime	5 2/10/2010	George Belford, Joann Cummings, and Ben Davis
2/18/2010	Discovery of Steve Haven's body	6	Ken Staple and family, investigated by Helen Jenson
3/8/2010	Andrew Smithson of Berkley and Jones hired by Hank Strong.	7	Andrew Smithson, Joann Cummings, and Hank Strong

Event date	Event	Order and date discovered, if different from event date	Source
3/12/2010 3/13/2010	Helen Jenson interviews Joann Cummings after Andrew Smithson shooting	8	Andrew Smithson, Joann Cummings, Helen Jenson
3/13/2010	Joann Cummings hides out in WV cabin	9 4/24/2010	Margaret Hoffman, Paul O'Hare briefed by Joann Cummings
3/29/2010	Joann Cummings decides Margaret Hoffman and Paul O'Hare would be perfect for solving the case	10 4/24/2010	Margaret Hoffman, Paul O'Hare approached by Joann Cummings
4/3/2010	Joe Reynolds contacts Joann Cummings about his research on the liberty credit card computer system log data	11	Joe Reynolds and Joann Cummings
4/15/2010	Margaret Hoffman and Paul O'Hare fly to Athens	12	Margaret Hoffman and Paul O'Hare
5/4/2010	Joe Reynold's presents work to Joann, Margaret and Paul in Naxos, demonstrating the crime had to be internal embezzlement. Belford murders Joe Reynolds	13	Joe Reynolds, Joann Cummings, Margaret Hoffman, Paul O'Hare, and George Belford
5/15/2010	Belford dies in an auto accident	14	George Belford, Joann Cummings, Margaret Hoffman, and Paul O'Hare
5/23/2010	State police search of hank strong's homes, safety deposit boxes	15	Hank strong and Joan Cummings
5/23/2010	Andrew Smithson, Bill Norse, and Joann Cummings meet in Duck, NC to conduct research	16	Andrew Smithson, Bill Norse and Joann Cummings
5/25/2010	Steve Haven found to be embezzler. Not murdered since he had discovered the crime	17 5/25/2010	Helen Jenson briefs Margaret Hoffman and Paul O'Hare

After hearing Strong had met with Haven, Helen renewed her investigation of him. She directed the Duck group to examine Strong's computer files hoping to discover information directly related to the embezzlement. They found out he was as careful with his computers as he was with his home.

Helen had decided to bring Strong in to question him about his contacts with the murdered Steve Haven.

Margaret and Paul continued shooting practice, in the mornings of the days they conducted interviews. Paul's skills increased impressing Margaret, who arranged for him to practice on a range simulating concealed attackers in both an urban and rural settings. Shooting accurately at a fixed target had the same difficulty as sinking foul shots, but hitting popup and moving targets was similar to hitting three-point shots while being guarded.

Wednesday June 2, 2010

On Wednesday, he returned to Arches National Park to begin his hike carrying a small backpack. Three miles into the park, hidden by the hilly terrain, he dropped his wallet and cell phone on a deserted area. Hank removed a wrinkled dirty t-shirt, one sneaker from the backpack, and placed them next to the wallet and cell phone. Before leaving the scene, he retrieved a red wig from the backpack and placed it on his head. He left, carefully placing his feet on rocks wherever possible, so as not to leave a trail, walked back to Route 191, and then followed the road into Moab.

Using his new identity and a credit card, he took a cab to the airport and purchased a ticket to Salt Lake City arriving in the evening. Hank rode the shuttle to the Double Tree hotel near the airport. That evening he ordered room service and did not visit the bar.

On Thursday morning, he took a van to the airport and boarded a mid-morning flight to Dulles International Airport in Virginia an hour west of Washington, DC. He left the plane and took the airport van to the long-term parking where he had left a car two weeks earlier, filled with clothes, cash, and several international airline tickets all in his new identity.

Thursday, June 3, 2010

Park Rangers noticed Strong's car parked overnight on Thursday. The Hampton Inn cleaning staff discovered Strong's room had not been vacated but the bed not slept in on. Both incidents were reported to the Moab, Utah police.

That morning a hiker found Strong's cashless wallet, cell phone, and shirt. She called a Ranger. The search began late Thursday afternoon and resumed on Friday morning.

Helen drove to Hank Strong's home in Bethany Beach on Thursday afternoon with Detective Tony Portelli. As she rang the doorbell, a neighbor, John Tompkins, walked over to her and said, "Hank's not home. He left on Monday and told me he's spending at least a week in Utah hiking to celebrate his retirement."

"Did he tell you when he'd return?"

"He said he might spend more time out west since he has no obligations in Delaware."

"Thanks for the information."

Tony looked at Helen. "Perfect set up for him to disappear."

"Hope not," Helen said as they returned to the State Trooper Barracks in Georgetown.

She contacted Bill Norse and told him Strong had gone to Utah.

"Do you think he'll leave the country like George Belford did?" Bill asked.

"It's possible. I'm going to send a BOLO to Utah after I ask the TSA to verify he flew there," Helen said, sharing Tony's and Bill's fear.

The Utah police received the BOLO and replied to Helen on his status. The Park Rangers concluded someone might have mugged him on the trail, and disposed of his body in the park.

Chapter 29 Planning to Attack the Investigators

Thursday, June 3, 2010

Hank Strong's plans vacillated between leaving the U.S. or staying to end Joann's threat to his freedom. Sitting in his hotel in Fredericksburg, Virginia drinking scotch, he convinced himself he had to eliminate Joann Cummings, Smithson, Hoffman, O'Hare, and records of the investigation before leaving the country. If he didn't, Cummings would discover his connection to the crime, and he'd be caught, before he moved to a foreign country. Strong feared she might already have made the connection, and the FBI, the TSA, and other police agencies were looking for him. He didn't know if his disappearance in Utah gave him enough time to elude capture.

Hank recalled Fred's report, and knew it wouldn't be easy to kill her, since Joann never left the Duck house. He suspected they might arrest him if he were caught and identified on the gated community's grounds. He had to destroy the house from outside the compound. His military experience told him a rocket-propelled grenade with its high-heat explosive was the ideal weapon.

He knew he could not buy an RPG device and the grenades, both classified as Destructive Devices by the National Firearms Act over the normal web, even with his false identity. Fred had given Strong a contact on the dark web willing to provide the armaments at a high cost with no identity verification required. Hank also purchased an automatic weapon, AK-47 plus ammunition and night-vision binoculars. After transferring the funds to an overseas account, he received the location of a shipping company, in Rocky Mount, North Carolina.

Hank had to wait two days before picking up the weapons on Saturday. This left only five days before his scheduled flight to freedom.

Chapter 30 Hank Strong's Role in the Conspiracy Identified

Friday, June 4, 2010

Earlier in the week Margaret and Paul had interviewed six of Strong's contacts. The last interview early Friday morning with Shelly Vaughn, Strong's next-door neighbor, an attractive thin blond woman in her early fifties, promised to be fruitful. She worked as a lawyer in Washington and only visited the beach during the off season once a month to check how the house fared during the winter.

Margaret and Paul introduced themselves and explained their mission. "We're investigating Hank Strong's possible involvement in the Liberty Credit Card embezzlement. We're authors and intend to write a book about the crime," Margaret said as she handed Shelly a copy of their earlier book.

Shelly looked at the first few pages of the book, and said, "I've read it, but I noticed you signed this copy. Thanks. How can I help?"

"Do you mind if we record the interview?" Margaret asked.

"No, go ahead."

Paul showed her Hank Strong's picture and said, "We want to verify you know Strong."

"That's him. I don't know him well, just enough to say hello when we saw each. He usually stays here during the week while I visit on weekends."

"Have you ever seen him with this man?" Margaret asked as she showed her Steve Haven's picture.

"No, I don't think so."

Paul displayed a picture of his car. "Have you seen this car? It's an old 2002 banged-up Silver Toyota Celica."

"Yes, in January. I came here to check the house and saw Hank leave the garage in that old car around 6:00 p.m. I remember it because Hank only drove expensive late-model cars. Strange, I normally stay up late, and around 11:00, I was sitting in my front room and saw him walk past my house under a street light. I didn't recognize him until he walked up to his stoop under the porch light and entered his house. I wondered what had happened to the car."

Margaret and Paul glanced at each other with a self-assured look. They now had a witness directly connecting Strong to the murder of Haven. After the interview, they left the house and Paul said, "That's what we needed."

"I agree. After the police arrest Strong, the case will be over," Margaret said.

"That still means it's too early for us to celebrate," Paul said.

Margaret called Helen at 11:00 a.m., "We have found an eye witness who directly connects Hank Strong to Steve Haven's murder. I'll send you an audio file of the interview." After she provided details, Helen smiled knowing they had almost closed the case. Helen told Andrew, Bill, and Joann.

Helen said, "I sent Tony Portelli a copy of the file."

Helen called Tony and told him, "When you receive an audio file from Margaret I sent you, use it to make an affidavit and go to Shelly Vaughn's house and get her to sign it."

Tony called Helen at 2:00 in the afternoon stating he had just emailed her the affidavit.

She instructed him, "Use it to get a warrant for Hank Strong's arrest."

Helen told those at the Duck house, "While we now have a warrant for Strong's arrest, the hard part will be finding him, since he disappeared in Utah. I don't believe someone mugged him on a trail. I think Strong set the scene to look like it and then disappeared.

220

Hopefully, he didn't go overseas."

The crew at Duck waited for Margaret and Paul to arrive that evening. They left Dagsboro, Delaware at noon and drove south on Route 113 until it merged with Route 13 and drove over the scenic Chesapeake Bay Bridge and Tunnel to reach the western shore of Virginia. Then drove onwards to North Carolina.

Both carried weapons, hoping not to use them, but ready for any eventuality.

Five hours after leaving they arrived in Duck and entered the gated community. When they walked into the house, their fellow investigators greeted them with a standing ovation.

Friday evening, June 4, 2010

Helen summoned the investigators at the Duck house into the dining room. She said, "Since Margaret and Paul have collected direct evidence of Strong's involvement in Haven's murder we will celebrate tonight with a pizza, beer, and wine party."

Margaret said, "We're glad to help."

Paul wondered if she referred to the case or the party.

"Besides the food and drink, we need to catch Strong, since he has disappeared," Helen said.

"We caught Ralph Cohen on the Outer Banks after he disappeared while investigating the skeleton murders. I suggest we use the same approach for Strong," Margaret said.

"We had an easier search for Cohen since we restricted it to a limited geographical area and concentrated on marinas," Bill Norse said.

"True. Strong disappeared in Utah and could be anywhere in the U.S., or he could have left the country," Paul said.

"It differs from the Cohen search, where we identified him as a person of interest, and asked cops finding him not to arrest him, but to notify us. We have a warrant for Strong for murdering Steve

Haven and participating in the Liberty Credit Card embezzlement. We'll authorize his arrest by any police agency," Helen said. "I'll start with the FBI and the TSA. Enjoy yourself while I write the BOLO. But don't get drunk. I'll need a few of you to proof the document."

"Warn the police he might be wearing a disguise as Cohen did," Margaret said.

"Okay, I will, and state he's believed to be armed, dangerous, and a flight risk," Helen said.

"We might have missed something," Andrew said. "We'll review his electronic information to see if we can narrow the search. I suggest the Delaware State Police revisit both his houses. You might have missed something hidden in the furniture, a secret safe, buried in the ground, or another hiding place."

"Agree. I'll write a modified search warrant based on the new information and have Tony Portelli deliver it to a judge tomorrow," Helen said.

Saturday, June 5, 2010

At Helen's request her boss, Lt. Ray Fuller, led the search of Strong's home in Bethany Beach, accompanied by Ben Johnson, the lead Forensic investigator. Captain Walter Nelson headed the search on his Middletown, Delaware home. Detective Tony Portelli accompanied Captain Nelson since he knew more about the case than Nelson.

The State Troopers used Saturday morning to plan the raids, identify the personnel and equipment they needed. Since they had found nothing significant in the earlier normal searches, Helen told them, "Strong might have hidden material in the walls, the cellar floor, or buried them in the grounds outside the home. Suggest you use wall-scanning radar to scan the walls, ceiling, and floors of the buildings. Ground penetrating radar will help to find any buried items."

They hired a radar consulting company to provide the equipment and the technically skilled personnel to operate it.

The Bethany Beach house search began at 11:00 a.m. The regular uniformed officers repeated the earlier search of the rooms and furniture, reexamining the cut up upholstered furniture, beds, rugs, and cushions. They found nothing new.

The scanning radar company split into two groups. One examined the walls and floors, and the other concentrated on the yard. The outdoor scanning group discovered the buried remains of a laptop under a group of Crepe Myrtle trees in his backyard. The Forensic staff packaged the remains of the laptop and USB drives and took them to Georgetown for further examination.

The indoor group had no luck for the first hour until they found a small internal wall safe overlooked in the first search. The safe was empty.

The Middletown house search began at 4:00 and the police found nothing new. However, the indoor scanner team found travel documentation and ticket receipts in a previously unidentified safe. The Forensic staff removed them for analysis on Monday.

Initially, the remains of the laptop perplexed the investigators. They couldn't find a full or partial company ID code on any of the PC parts, and concluded it had to be privately owned.

Forensic investigator Ben Johnson became ecstatic when he accessed a damaged USB drive at 7:30 p.m. He grimaced as he read Fred's report. Ben was concerned when it identified Joann's Duck location, knowing Strong's proclivity for killing his enemies. Ben called Helen Jenson to warn her of the danger. "I found something very disturbing on the USB drive we discovered." He summarized his findings and fears for the Duck team's safety.

"Thanks for the warning. We need to evacuate since Strong has had enough time to travel to Duck since he disappeared in Utah. I won't tell you where we're going since Strong could intercept our email or phone communications. Please don't call us again. I'll contact you after Strong is captured or killed, if he decides to visit us."

Helen summoned the house's guests to meet with her at 8:00 p.m. in the dining room and discuss the situation.

Andrew said, "I agree with leaving. Do you have a place to go?"

"Not yet. Just drive away and find a hotel."

"My company has another safe house twenty miles south of here in Manteo on Roanoke Island. They have enough room for us. I suggest we go there," Andrew said.

"Can we leave in ten minutes and arrive there without notifying them?" Margaret asked.

"Yes, we can leave in two cars, if everyone packs light and takes only cell phones and laptops. But don't use them, until our IT staff can change the IP addresses and SIM cards," Andrew replied.

"Good, everyone meet here in eight minutes," Margaret said.

Chapter 31 The RPG Attack

Saturday, June 5, 2010

Hank Strong left Fredericksburg at sunrise to drive to Rocky Mount, North Carolina to pick up his weapons. To avoid being identified by pursuers, he wore blue contact lenses, a blond wig to cover his shaved head, and a pillow in front of his stomach adding weight. He could not be sure if the RPG attack would kill the house's occupants, but it might be his last chance to eliminate his major adversaries before leaving the country.

On his drive south, a fleeting worry entered his mind. Could the weapons delivery be an FBI sting? Since he had used the same dark web source to get the gun for George Belford in the first attempt on Joann's life, he dismissed these thoughts. He had to trust someone.

After picking up the package, Hank drove to a half-empty parking lot in a shopping mall and examined the weapons. He found them satisfactory and proceeded east toward Duck, North Carolina, arriving at mid-afternoon. He drove around the development searching for the optimal location. Hank needed clear access to fire into the house, and to be able to escape safely.

After finding a spot hidden from view, he drove away, filled his car with gas, and stocked up with food and water for his drive to freedom.

At dusk he returned, scanned the house's exterior carrying his weapons and wearing binoculars. After placing the AK-47 on the ground, he armed his launcher with a grenade and kept the other three ready. Now was the time. Hank decided to shoot the cars under the house, the front door, and one window each on the second and third floors.

Strong had success with his first salvo, hitting and destroying two cars which exploded and ignited the other cars and the carport ceiling. The second shot blew the door off its hinges as the foyer ignited. The next two shots hit and shattered the windows, charring the walls. When finished, Strong looked through his binoculars for a damage assessment. He beamed at the flames and assumed everyone in the house would die.

Since the group congregated in the kitchen, in the back of the house, they did not see the RPG's exploding flash, but they heard and felt the explosion. The impact shook the home, throwing those standing to the floor, and those sitting holding onto their chairs. Next the flames lapped outside the front windows. The heat soon reached them. They listened to the fire extinguishers activate.

The room remained quiet as Helen evaluated their options. She asked, "Is everyone okay?"

A chorus of "Yes, I'm okay," and "What happened?" responded as she gazed at the group. No one was wounded, except for a few cuts and bruises.

"The building's safety design had prevented any injuries," Andrew said.

Helen asked, "Andrew, have your staff bring their guns to the kitchen."

"Margaret and Paul have guns. There might be another attack. We have to stop them. Bill and I, Margaret, and Paul grouped by twos, will go to the left side of the house. Your staff should do the same on the other side. Stay low and behind cover, just as they trained you in the service."

They left by an undamaged back door.

Strong gazed in satisfaction as he viewed the burning building. He gloated no one could have survived that attack. His face turned into fear as he watched two armed men scan the area from the side of the house.

Strong thought of running to his car, but saw a man and woman crawling from the other side of the house toward him. The woman had a pistol and the man a rifle. Hank knew if he ran they'd shoot him in the back. Picking up his AK-47 and without aiming he sprayed the area occupied by Margaret and Paul.

"I'm hit," Margaret cried.

Strong changed his aim to the other side of the house releasing a hail of bullets in that direction. No one cried out.

Paul looked at the muzzle flashes and saw a man firing. Not knowing if the shooter wore body armor, he aimed at the head.

Only ninety feet away, Paul couldn't miss. Just to be sure he fired three quick rounds. The attacker's head snapped back as one of the bullets went through it, knocking off the wig. The attacker fell to the ground. Paul looked at Margaret, who even though she bled from her left calf, gave him a thumbs-up after she watched the shooter collapse.

Paul's well-trained associates kept low waiting for the next shots. He moved next to Margaret. "Where are you hit?" Paul whispered.

"Left leg."

Seeing her calf bleeding Paul undid his belt and fastened it as a tourniquet below the knee. He tightened the belt until the bleeding slowed. "How do you feel?"

"The tourniquet hurts, and I'm little nauseous. Christ, a veteran of two foreign wars, a Marine and cop for thirty-four years. Never been shot. Didn't expect it to happen in beautiful Duck."

Andrew, who had remained in the house, had called the police and an ambulance. He assumed someone would be hit. Paul also called for an ambulance on his cell phone and was told it was on its way.

"Margaret, the EMTs will arrive in a few minutes. You should be okay," Paul said, hoping her injuries weren't serious.

After three minutes of hearing no shots, Helen yelled, "Stay down. I'll investigate." She carefully crawled toward the body staying behind cover. When she reached it, she said, "It's Hank Strong. He's alone and dead, it's over."

When she finished talking, she heard the sirens of the police and two ambulances. After they arrived, Helen directed one set of EMTs to help Margaret and sent the others to the house.

They carried a stretcher to her.

Ann the female EMT. seeing the bleeding and the guns, asked Margaret, "What is your name? How bad is the pain on a scale of 1 to 10?"

"Margaret Hoffman. Nine."

Ann injected a painkiller, "This should help. You might go to sleep. Are you hit anywhere else besides the calf?"

"No."

"Who applied the tourniquet?"

"I did. I'm her husband." Paul said.

"We will leave it on until we get to The Outer Banks Hospital. We'll give you the belt back then. Do you know where the hospital is?"

"No. We're visitors."

Ann handed Paul a business card. "The address is on the card. It's south on the coastal road in Nags Head, a half-hour away. Go to the emergency room, and ask for your wife."

"I'd like to, but he destroyed our cars in the attack," Paul said pointing to the burned-out shells of the cars below the house.

The male EMT said, "Ride up front with me."

The second EMT team reported no serious injuries in the house. They treated three people with superficial cuts.

After everyone, except Margaret and Paul, returned to the house and assembled in the kitchen, Helen said, "Andrew, it's too bad this beautiful home got destroyed."

"I doubt it sustained major damage. Nothing happened to this room, except a few glasses and dishes broke when they crashed on the floor. Most rooms have automatic fire sprinklers while the computer rooms have water-free automatic extinguishers which will put out any fire. The walls are reinforced with two inch thick steel, so I assume your luggage and electronics survived, as long as they didn't get wet," Andrew said.

Joann said, "I wonder if I should stop helping, since this is the second time I've almost lost my life working with Margaret and Paul."

"Belford would have killed you, if you hadn't contacted them. With Strong dead your problems should be over," Andrew said.

"Perhaps," Joann said, "I guess I'll thank Margaret and Paul for giving me scary memories which I'll remember in my nightmares for the rest of my life."

Andrew said, "I called Mateo. Told them what happened. They're sending cars to move us to the safe house."

While waiting, Joann said, "Andrew, I'd like to visit Margaret and thank her. Can you get me a ride?"

"Yes. We'll use one of the Mateo cars."

"I'll get Margaret and Paul's luggage and drop Paul's laptop off at the hospital, so he can write while the events are fresh in his mind," Joann said.

The EMT Ann repeatedly took Margaret's vital signs and transmitted them to the hospital as they drove and that she might need a transfusion.

When they arrived, they wheeled Margaret into an examination room. Paul followed her. The physician examined her leg and replaced the makeshift tourniquet. He ordered a transfusion. He concluded the shot damaged the blood vessels and called a surgeon.

The nurses prepared Margaret for the surgery while she and Paul talked.

"Sorry, I couldn't ride with you. How is the leg? I hope it doesn't give you an excuse when I start beating you in tennis?" Paul asked.

"Everything was fine after the needle. We'll see about tennis, but you'll have to cook for the next few weeks."

"No problem, I love cooking, but it is more fun when we do it together. Lucky Andrew's company built a re-enforced fort for a safe house."

"Everyone would be dead if it was a normal house. I liked the way Helen took over after the attack, and thanks to your marksmanship, Paul, you saved many lives," Margaret said.

"I had a good teacher. I wish I had my laptop to write up what happened before I forget."

"Call Andrew and ask him to bring it."

"I don't have his number."

"I'm glad we emailed the latest version of our draft to each other. If the attack had destroyed the laptop, we'll have a duplicate draft waiting for us," Margaret said.

"I don't know the status of the laptop."

The nurses had completed attaching the sensors for body vitals to Margaret when a new physician entered the room. "I'm Doctor Blake, your anesthesiologist. I will administer the painkillers and monitor you during the operation. I'm giving you a local, so you'll be awake while the surgeon repairs your leg. Are you allergic to any medication?"

"No."

The nurse said, "Mr. O'Hare, I'm taking your wife to the operating room. I'll have someone direct you to the surgery visitor waiting room. We'll get you and take you to the recovery room when the doctor completes the surgery."

Joann and Andrew arrived twenty minutes after Margaret went into the operating room. "We came to see how Margaret was doing and to drop off your laptop and cell phone," Joann said.

"Margaret is in surgery. They are repairing damaged blood vessels in her calf. Thanks for the laptop. I've been so worried waiting for Margaret to be taken to the recovery room. Now, I can get my mind off the operation and write about the attack."

"We've moved the group and your luggage into the Mateo safe house," Andrew said.

"I'll be staying here overnight while Margaret recovers. They told me she should be released tomorrow if the surgery goes well."

"The Duck police are taking statements from everyone. I told them they could find you here. The old house will need renovations before we can occupy it. Fortunately, the Mateo site has the same IT infrastructure as Duck. We use it to back up the Duck files, so we have lost nothing. Joann, Helen, and Bill will return to Delaware tomorrow. I'll follow them in a few days. One of our staff will drive you and Margaret back to your home when she is ready to travel," Andrew said.

Paul said, "Thanks for the laptop, cell, and transportation."

Andrew and Joann left and drove to Mateo. Paul opened the laptop and began writing.

After two hours, a nurse took Paul to the recovery room.

Margaret beamed seeing him. "Hi, my hero. I survived, and feel no pain."

"Hon, you look great, but a little tired. Did they tell you how long you'll be incapacitated?"

"I'll be in the hospital for a least a day and have to use a wheel chair until the leg heals. So we won't be playing tennis for a while."

"That's too bad since I'm finally in shape. Your injury will help us complete the book earlier, since you won't be running around. Andrew and Joann came to visit you. They gave me the laptop and moved our luggage to the Mateo safe house."

"What's happening with the others?"

"Helen and Bill are returning to Delaware tomorrow. Joann will go with them. Do you want me to read what I wrote about the attack?"

Chapter 32 The Crime's Aftermath

Sunday, June 6, 2010

The Duck police removed the driver's license from Strong's wallet. It was not Hank Strong's. It showed a man wearing the attacker's disguise. A detective took the corpse's finger prints and sent them to the Integrated Automated Fingerprint Identification System (IAFIS), maintained by the FBI. The prints confirmed Helen's initial identification, the body was Hank Strong's.

Helen felt relief after the long investigation, glad the threats against her, her associates, and friends had ended.

The next morning Helen, Bill, and Joann stopped by the hospital to visit Margaret, "It's over. Now you can resume your honeymoon. How is the leg?" Helen said.

"My leg is starting to hurt. I've already called the nurse for a painkiller. Thanks for coming."

Paul said, "We decided earlier to finish our first draft, before we go back to Greece."

"We'll return in September, when it's not as hot and has fewer crowds," Margaret said.

"I'm available for interviews for the book whenever you want. Dinner at your house is a great interview location," Helen said. "The case is not completely closed. We still have to recover the money Strong embezzled."

"If he sent it overseas, and if his account isn't found, it will be lost forever," Margaret said.

"I'm also ready to help you on the book any time. Andrew's firm will help find the money," Joann said.

The three left for the drive back to Delaware

"Margaret, we'll have to be more careful in the next book we write. I don't want to get shot at again," Paul said.

"Then we'll have to write tourist books. The excitement that comes with police work has it risks."

"Speaking of excitement, when will you be healthy?"

"The doctor said, I've recovered enough to go home tomorrow. I hope I'll be ready for the type of excitement you want soon."

****

Thank you for reading *The Billion Dollar Embezzlement Murders*. If you liked the book, or my other books, please write an Amazon review to inform other potential readers they will enjoy the book. Please open my Amazon author page to access the forms to write your review.

https://www.amazon.com/Frank-E.-Hopkins/e/B0028AR904

Check on the book cover of the book you want to review and the review option will appear toward the bottom of the page.

Second in a Series

The Billion Dollar Embezzlement Murders is a sequel to *Abandoned Homes: Vietnam Revenge Murders*. The Maryland Writers Association awarded *Abandoned Homes: Vietnam Revenge Murders* first place in the mystery/thriller in their 2018 novel contest. A description of this novel is presented on page 230. This sequel does not continue a discussion of the crimes in *Abandoned Homes: Vietnam Revenge Murders*, but follows the lives of the two main characters of the book: Margaret Hoffman, Detective Delaware State Police, and Paul O'Hare, retired professor.

In the first novel, the couple meets and falls in love as Detective Hoffman leads the State Police team that solves the murders. Hoffman and O'Hare write a best-selling book about the revenge murders. In the second novel, they marry and after Detective Hoffman retires from the State Police, they participate in solving the embezzlement and become targets of the murderers in Greece and the Outer Banks of North Carolina.

A third novel in the Margaret Hoffman and Paul O'Hare series is in the planning stages. The two detectives witness the death of three close friends from tainted prescription drugs. Further research indicates their friends' deaths are part of a larger tragedy, including the demise of over a thousand individuals from the same drug, and over fifty thousand from other drugs. The detectives vow to solve the cause of the deaths of their friends and end the practice of the Federal Drug Administration not adequately testing drugs, and inspectors and politicians accepting bribes from the drug industry.

About the Author

Frank E Hopkins (http://www.frankehopkins.com) writes realistic crime novels and short stories portraying social and political issues.

Frank lived in the New York City area while attending Hofstra University in the 1960s, the location and time period of *Unplanned Choices*, a novel about illegal abortion and murder. As a consultant he managed proposals in response to Federal government solicitations, the background for *The Opportunity*, a story of crime in the Federal Government contracting industry set in Washington, DC and Rehoboth Beach, DE. Frank's collection of ten short stories, *First Time*, is set in East Coast locations he visited that inspired the book's stories. The Delaware Press Association awarded *First Time* second place for a collection of short stories by a single author in their 2017 Communications Contest.

Frank is active in the Rehoboth Bay Writers Guild, the Eastern Shore Writers Association, and participates in writers' critique groups in both organizations. He is also a member of the Berlin chapter of the Maryland Writers Association.

His Facebook profile is http://facebook.com/hopkinsfe and his author page is http://www.facebook.com/frankehopkinsauthor

His author email address is frank@frankehopkins.com

Abandoned Homes: Vietnam Revenge Murders

ABANDONED HOMES: VIETNAM REVENGE MURDERS
IS A SUSPENSEFUL SERIAL KILLER CRIME NOVEL

U.S. involvement in the Vietnam War ended in 1975 when the U.S. abandoned its Embassy in Saigon. However, the hate developed during the war years, especially at major universities continued. Proponents of the war, fierce opponents of communism, acted during the war years to remove potential traitors from our society. Those against the war continued their opposition, begun in the 1960s, culminating in the riots and student killings at major universities, including Kent, Maryland and Wisconsin.

Paul O'Hare, a retired history professor, uncovers a long-hidden domestic impact of the Vietnam War thirty-five years after the war ended when he finds a skeleton in the crawl space of an abandoned home in southern Delaware. The Delaware State Police investigation team, headed by Detective Margaret Hoffman, discovers two more skeletons and the quest for a serial killer begins. Hoffman soon discovers the three skeletons had been graduate students at the University of Maryland during the 1970s as had Paul O'Hare. He becomes a major suspect. Eventually the State Police clear him and he begins a romantic relationship with Detective Hoffman that includes conflicts between his anti-war sentiments and her experience as a Marine veteran.

The search for a serial killer reveals a complex web of interrelated former students, a crusading newspaper reporter, and CIA agents and double agents, in this fast-paced suspense novel.

The Maryland Writers Association awarded *Abandoned Homes: Vietnam Revenge Murders* first place in the mystery/thriller category in their 2018 Communications Contest.

What readers say about
Abandoned Homes: Vietnam Revenge Murders

A Mystery on Many Levels
Frank Hopkins spins a tale that begins one place and takes you to another as the story unfolds. A photographer finds interest in old houses in the countryside where properties are low value and the houses are forgotten and left to decay. He steps on rotten boards exposing a skeleton and discovering the source of a deadly virus. So, we have an outbreak menace story, right? Wrong. As a smart, tough policewoman becomes involved, we have a cold case story about who the skeleton represented and now have a murder mystery. The murderers are alive and remain dangerous. The photographer and the policewoman begin a relationship and you want to know where that goes. Jack Coppley on November 4, 2017.

I fell in love with the two main characters
Once I started this book I could not put it down. I fell in love with the two main characters. The story moved fast so you don't have time to get bored. The characters, the locations and the events were all believable. This is the third book of Mr. Hopkins that I have read and am now starting on the fourth. This gentleman is definitely my new favorite author. Bonnie P Cashell on January 4, 2018.

Good Story, Especially for Delawareans!
This was a fast moving mystery and easy to read, with no dull chapters. I found the subject matter enlightening as well. Carol70 on February 5, 2018

Skeletons in the basement and closet

Frank Hopkins has managed to reach back in time to rekindle old hates and awaken fears in his latest novel, Abandoned Homes: Vietnam Revenge Murders. Beauty, skill and toughness in the person of State Police Detective Margaret Hoffman, retired U.S. Marine, combine with modern police forensics to solve decades-old murders involving the CIA. Threading her way through the trail of skeletons, she falls in love with Paul O'Hare, a retired history professor, who initially discovered the skeletons, only to become a murder suspect. Follow the trail of mystery, motive and murder that abounded on college campuses of the 1970s. Amazon Customer on October 13, 2017.

Unpredictable...Informative...Entertaining

Abandoned Homes: Vietnam Revenge Murders is a complex murder mystery which holds you captive from the onset. Hopkins' hero begins an unforgettable journey into the unknown with the discovery of a skeleton in an abandoned home. The story unfolds as he works in tandem with the Delaware State Police to ascertain the identity of the victim. It soon becomes clear that the political unrest of the Vietnam War is a pivotal piece of the puzzle. College campuses were a focal point of the peace movement and it was determined that the victim was a student at The University of Maryland during the 1970s. As a witness to the protest of the Vietnam War while attending the University of Maryland in 1970 Hopkins lends a personal aspect to his narrative, which is relevant in all of his books. Brimming with twists and turns! A Must Read! Linda D. on October 6, 2017.

Another good read from Hopkins

Hopkins shows us his versatility with a murder mystery this time. The story develops when a retired college professor stumbles across a dead body in an abandoned home he's researching. First, he's a suspect by the investigating female State Police officer, he then

238

becomes her lover. They follow leads across the Mid-Atlantic States to uncover a long-buried plot that began in the political unrest of the Vietnam War. Each chapter takes the reader deeper into this complex tale of intrigue. William Kennedy on October 21, 2017.

Hatred between factions for and against the Viet Nam war didn't end when the war did

In Frank Hopkins' new murder mystery *Abandoned Homes: Vietnam Revenge Murders*, a retired history professor pursues an unusual but innocent hobby-investigating and photographing abandoned homes in rural Delaware. His discovery of skeletons in the abandoned homes sets off a search for a serial killer that endangers his life as it reawakens the raging conflicts that took place on college campuses during the Viet Nam war years. Carole Ottesen on November 17, 2017.

Hard to put down!

Such a devious mystery! Frank E. Hopkins has a way of weaving an intriguing story along with characters that stick in your head. Kari on January 5, 2018.

I enjoyed this captivating tale

Mysteries are not normally my genre, but the author kept my attention throughout. Can't wait to read his next book! Diana M. on January 5, 2018.

Another great book by Frank Hopkins

Frank Hopkins' intriguing book *Abandoned Homes: Vietnam Revenge Murders* is a step-by step murder mystery. From the first page to the last, it is a fast paced story that is difficult to put down. The book starts innocently when Paul O'Hare, a retired history professor, stumbles upon skeletons in an abandoned house which he is photographing. Paul meets Detective Margaret Hoffman who is on the case using modern day forensics. Even though he becomes a suspect, Margaret Hoffman and Paul become lovers. Not only is this book a riveting tale of murder, but also has a great romance. Something for everyone! If you want an entertaining and unpredictable book, then this is definitely for you. S. Scarangella on March 11, 2018.

Mesmerizing Murder Mystery

Mesmerizing is the word for this book. The mystery story line was exceptionally creative and from the beginning draws the reader in one direction, and veers off smoothly into others before its surprise ending.. One could not help but sympathize with the corpses and surprisingly the culprits. The book brought back memories of our confused country over the Vietnam anti-war movement and my own College Park experience. My only complaint is that the "lovely" heroine policewoman's food choices were entirely too healthy!!!! Kathy H on March 15, 2018.

Stirs your curiosity

If you are looking for a mystery that stirs your curiosity throughout, *Abandoned Homes: Vietnam Revenge Murders* is definitely one to purchase. From the beginning, Mr. Hopkins sets the stage with vivid images of rural Delaware through which he skillfully creates an intricate web of characters and plot twists that connect skeletons found in deserted houses to polarized views of the Vietnam War. You, too, will enjoy reading how the pieces of the puzzle fit together. A great read! JD an avid reader on April 15, 2018.

Great mystery murder investigation.

Excellent mystery with a strong female lead character. The Delmarva location setting and description are an interesting backdrop for this novel. A book you will not want to put down until the mystery is solved. Kathy L. on March 25, 2018.

Abandoned Homes: Vietnam Revenge Murders **is a page-turner!**

In the late 1960s and early 1970s college campuses across the United States were sites of anti-war protests sometimes accompanied by violence as students and the country divided over the war in Vietnam. In 2008, when retired University of Maryland history professor, Paul O'Hare stumbles upon two skeletons in an abandoned home he's photographing in lower Delaware, he suddenly and inexplicably finds himself at the center of an intense and long-ranging police investigation. Paul is eventually cleared, but as the police uncover more and more evidence leading to the identity of the real killer, old enmities and enemies emerge from the shadows of Paul's past, making him a target right up to the story's dramatic conclusion. *Abandoned Homes: Vietnam Revenge Murders* is a step-by-step police procedural page-turner. Recommended for fans of realistic detective fiction, with a bonus if the reader is from Delaware and can recognize locations and landmarks! JM Reinbold on June 22, 2018.

Nicely crafted murder mystery

A masterfully written police procedural, with finely defined characters and a well-paced plot. Hopkins has clearly done his research. And, as a Delawarean, I enjoyed his many references to lower Delaware and the beach area--many locales of which I recognize and have visited. The scenes of violence are handled with precision and with modicum gore. Two thumbs up. F. Weldon Burge on October 10, 2018

Many of the locations in this book are easily recognizable to readers in the Mid-Atlantic area

Frank Hopkins' book, *Abandoned Homes: Vietnam Revenge Murders*, looks back at the turmoil, deception, intrigue, and anger of the late sixties and early seventies in this engrossing, hard to put down mystery. It won first place for a mystery/thriller novel in the 2018 Maryland Writers' Association novel contest. It is a thought-provoking, exciting mostly police procedural with a little romance thrown in. Many of the locations in this book are easily recognizable to readers in the Mid-Atlantic area. Eileen Haavik McIntire on July 5, 2018

Stirs your curiosity

If you are looking for a mystery that stirs your curiosity throughout, *Abandoned Homes: Vietnam Revenge Murders* is definitely one to purchase. From the beginning, Mr. Hopkins sets the stage with vivid images of rural Delaware through which he skillfully creates an intricate web of characters and plot twists that connect skeletons found in deserted houses to polarized views of the Vietnam War. You, too, will enjoy reading how the pieces of the puzzle fit together. A great read! JD an avid reader on April 15, 2018

Engaging

Very engaging story and believable characters. This is also a Maryland Writer's Association winner, and Frank did a great job. F. J. Talley on June 17, 2018

First Time

First Time is a collection of ten short stories by Frank E Hopkins. The Delaware Press Association has awarded First Time second place for a collection of short stories written by a single author in their 2017 Communications Contest. While each story has separate characters they are linked by the theme that each story exposes the main character to the first time they experience an event participated in by all. The stories include anticipation of the happiness they expect; the dismay and wonder they feel during the event; and the surprising ending.

The stories include anticipation of the happiness they expect; the dismay and wonder they feel during the event; and the surprising ending. The stories cover a wide range of events in childhood, coming of age, romance throughout life, recovery from divorce, and disappointments in the declining years.

The collection includes:

"Passages South" – male college students in search of excitement on a trip to Florida during spring break;

"My First Four Days in Sorrento" – romance by a mature man, that perplexes his children;

Two college freshmen who meet and start a romance in "My First Psych Class", taught by professors behaving strangely, who appear in need of counseling;

"My First Car" – purchased from a Mafia-connected used-car salesman;

"My First July 4 Rehoboth Beach Weekend" – parties and misguided fireworks;

"Steve's First Woman" – self-explanatory;

"The Romance Life Cycle" – danger, danger do not eat yourself out of love;

"Santa Claus Stories" – why parents lie to their children;

"The Ski Trip" – two friends offer to introduce a recently divorced man to the single life at Sugarbush, VT, illustrating the validity of the theory of unforeseen consequences.

The last story, "My Trip Alone", relates the bittersweet recollection of a widower who adjusts to his wife's earlier death by revisiting their favorite fall trip to see the autumn foliage in the mountains of West Virginia.

What Readers Say about *First Time*

There is something for everyone here
First Time contains a variety of stories beginning with four dopey college students driving to Florida for spring break and ending with my favorite, a touching story of a widower re-tracing the last vacation he took with his beloved wife, Anne. It's a good collection and an excellent way to get to know the author, Frank Hopkins. R. E. Reece on August 15, 2016

...book of short stories entwining each one together...

I enjoyed reading how you can relate to past experiences in some way to your own life...I certainly could especially...Santa Claus Stories and My Trip Alone...these stood out for me. Judith L. Kirlan on July 29, 2016

First Time **is nostalgia at its best.**

The variety of stories touch on some part of a reader's own life, from a spring break trip to an exotic love. Frank E. Hopkins does a fine job of weaving the stories that, at first seem to stand on their own, but then all come together. Each story taps into the emotions of events throughout life in a way the reader can relate. All-together, *First Time* makes a great beach read with each story taking just a little of your time. I recommend it. Jack Coppley on June 13, 2016

First Time **is a witty, eclectic, entertaining collection of memorable times**

Author Frank Hopkins' creation *First Time* is a witty, eclectic, entertaining collection of memorable times in the lives of ten individuals. First impressions are always the lasting impressions and *First Time* will make a pleasant dent in your enjoyment psyche. Amazon Customer on May 17, 2016

...being reminded of similar firsts from my youth

… fond memories as a student or the traditional Spring Break trip to Florida. The bitter sweet memories of my first car and a trip alone. But by far was a memory I didn't have but could live through his writing, the trip to Sorrento. Beautifully written, through his words, I enjoyed the walk up from the beach, the breeze from the sea and the aromas coming from the multiple restaurants he visited. I could feel the charm of the city in his writing. William Kennedy on April 13, 2016.

The Opportunity

The Opportunity is Frank E. Hopkins second novel. It is a suspenseful crime novel set in the high powered competitive environment of federal governmental contracting in Washington, DC and the fast-paced professional networking social life of Rehoboth Beach, Delaware in the beginning of the twenty-first century.

The novel portrays corruption in the Federal Government, and includes the relationship between a Federal agency, its contractors, and members of Congress. The corruption involves exchange of confidential information for sex between the Contracting Officer and the marketing representative related to bidding on a government contract. The Contracting Officer's former girlfriend exposes the corruption to a newspaper reporter, who publishes a series of articles that initiate an investigation by the Federal agency and the FBI.

The Opportunity provides a glimpse into the intriguing quid pro quo relationships between federal government officials and the corporate executives that compete for government contracts.

What Readers Say about *The Opportunity*

Well-written fictional exposé on government contracting
...provides an insightful look at government contracting seamy underbelly, with sharp and cunning characters and themes of corruption, morality, and accountability. From the political front offices, backrooms, and bedrooms of Washington, DC to the flashy satellite singles scene of Rehoboth Beach, *The Opportunity* gives the reader an insider's look into a money-and-sex driven world that,

sometimes simultaneously, operates both in the shadows and in the public eye. Brent Lewis on January 30, 2016

The Opportunity: **A Must Read**

I recently had the pleasure of reading Frank Hopkins' latest novel, *The Opportunity*, which I highly recommend to those interested in a novel which documents how government corruption could occur in Federal Government contracting. The novel faithfully explores how government contractors approach winning a major contract and the single life scene in the Rehoboth, Delaware area. Carl Pergler November 14, 2014

Hard to put down. Hopkins has a sense of ...

the Washington scene and its corruption. His heroes are those persons who wade through the paperwork to find the culprits. Journey along with the author ... and find out more than you ever imagined about how our government works and doesn't work. The issues of women using sex to get information are all too common in our government. Tom the Baker December 26, 2014

I really enjoyed the book The Opportunity

..fast paced and exciting. Someone once asked me what I read for, I responded "I love local color". The book certainly contains it with realistic descriptions of scenes set in the Washington, DC and Rehoboth Beach, Delaware areas. I recommend The Opportunity to all readers interested in a read which holds your attention about the government contacting industry. Nancy Oppenheim December 22, 2014

This fictitious example is entertaining and fun to read

A description of a federal procurement life cycle. Fictitious? Maybe not! Well done story about marketing, competition, personal goals, and Government review of a competitive. The Opportunity by Frank

Hopkins was one of those stories for me even though I have lived in the Washington, D.C. area and have been close to government life in many ways. The competitive and sometimes grim real world of the contracting game was an unknown. This book, exciting and readable and is written with enough intrigue to keep the interest going until the very end. Amazon Customer July 26, 2016

Contract work with a twist of intrigue
A rare book that takes you into the details of government contract bidding, but adds a twist of intrigue. Jack Coppley June 28, 2016

Read it!
Once you pick it up it's hard to put down! Frank Hopkins did an excellent job in bringing the characters to life and creating a fabulous storyline! a real must read! Lisa on August 12, 2016

Another Winner by Frank Hopkins
…it seems to be the goal the principal characters in *The Opportunity* to retire rich as early as possible; nothing much is acknowledged of the intrinsic value of their work. Rather it is a means to the end of acquiring wealth, and to the extent it does not do that, it has no value. Frank Hopkins' experience as an economist and as a consultant in both government and business shows in his precise descriptions of the contracting process. Along with everything else, readers gain a good understanding of how things work (and don't work) in Washington. That may or may not be a good thing. …if you get the opportunity to read Frank E. Hopkins' newest novel, *The Opportunity*, do not fail to do so. It is another winner... Robert J. Anderson November 15, 2014

Intriguing Fictional read....Hopkins nails it!
Excellent, *The Opportunity* by Frank E. Hopkins keeps you reading, anticipating how the book's discussion of corruption between the

U.S. government, its contractors and Congress is brought to justice. The stories of sexual misconduct, spying on the Government and its competition, favors to enhance careers, create entwining twists and turns that excite the reader from the beginning until its tragic ending... I highly recommend this book a great summer beach read. Judith L. Kirlan July 4, 2016.

Seductive and Engrossing!
Once again Hopkins' delivers ....*The Opportunity* is a compelling story, exposing unscrupulous characters who are employed in the business of Federal Government Contracting. Hopkins addresses the breach of trust, immorality and irresponsible attitude while attempting to win a contract. As a reader unfamiliar with the intricacies of government contracting Hopkins brings his characters to life by detailing the strategies involved for winning a contract: starting with an RFP (request for proposal), capturing the contract, identifying a capture program manager, producing a team prior to the "bid" and writing the proposal. His experience as a consultant in Government and Business lends credibility to the narrative. The book continues to draw you in from beginning to end. An unforgettable read. Linda D. on July 28, 2017

Unplanned Choices

What will Happen if Abortion is Outlawed?

Anyone born after 1956 would not understand the fear of pregnancy and death from a botched abortion felt by those achieving sexual maturity in the 1960s and 1970s.

Unplanned Choices is Frank E Hopkins' first novel. It is a coming-of-age romantic historical drama, is set in the late 1960s and early 1970s in New York City and Long Island during the turbulent period of the Vietnam War, the Civil Rights struggle, the sexual revolution, the women's movement, and the struggle for legalizing abortion.

The novel is the story of Steve Lynch and his first love, Anna Marino. Both Anna and Steve are raised in the Roman Catholic faith and struggle with the church's prohibition of sexual activity and their growing sexual drives. They meet in college after both abandon the church. Anna becomes pregnant and then dies during an abortion, before abortion on demand becomes legal in New York. The novel describes the impact of the abortion on Steve, on the abortionist, on Anna's family and friends, and on a NYPD investigator.

If Anna could have legally had an abortion, she would not have died and the impact on the other characters in the novel would not have been so tragic.

Situations similar to that portrayed in *Unplanned Choices* could occur hundreds of thousands of times in the future if abortion were to become illegal or heavily restricted again in the United States.

What Readers Say about *Unplanned Choices*

Filled with high drama and a book that I highly recommend

Unplanned Choices is set in the late 1960's-early 70's at the height of the Vietnam War. At this same time the sexual revolution and Women's Rights Movement are moving to the forefront. The struggle for legalizing abortion has begun. ... The author paint a vivid picture of the challenges women and girls faced as they struggled with choices regarding their own sexuality. This brilliant author takes the reader to a period of time in our country that we hope will never return. ruthziemniak on February 4, 2020.

Couldn't put it down.

Incredible. A historical novel that outlines the never-spoken-about sexual revolution and restrictions of women's reproductive rights. The book was so realistic, the characters the same. Easy to get to know them. I wanted to read more and more since I too grew up in that era. Lou on October 5, 2013

Unplanned Choices is a gripping book.

Unplanned Choices explores sexuality, religion, abortion, and culture in a stimulating, gripping manner. I read it whenever I could until it ended. I want more from it, and I want more of it. Robert J. Anderson on December 1, 2013.

I could not put it down it left such an impression.

I had to reread it again. I encourage everyone to read to see how far we have come with our rights as women Please don't let them take it away from us. I was impressed that a man could write so openly and honestly with such insight on the issue of abortion. I will definitely put Mr. Hopkins books on my reading list. Verified Amazon Customer on December 9, 2015

It's a page turner from page 1.

I really enjoyed this book and found it hard to put down... The story line was fascinating and the relationship it has to our present political climate is frightening. Every congressman and senator should read it along with every justice sitting on the Supreme Court. The thought that Roe v. Wade is even a matter for discussion let alone reversal is archaic and barbaric. They need to read this book for an accounting of what could happen if a woman's right to choose is taken away. I loved the courageous spirit of the women (and men) in this book. I think that style lends itself to a fast read and one that keeps you on your toes. It is now making its way around our office. I will definitely purchase this writer's second book. Verified Amazon Customer on January 12, 2016

Awesome read

I can relate to this book, as a young teenager and young adult in this era when abortion was illegal. The book shows the doubt of a young woman back in the 60s who did not have a lot of choices in having to deal with a unplanned pregnancy. They had nowhere to turn except to find someone to help in their turmoil who did not have the skills of a professional physician. Some paid with their life as so well portrayed in this book. Judith L. Kirlan on October 10, 2016

Compelling and Informative

I recently experienced the pleasure of reading Frank Hopkins first book *Unplanned Choices*. It proved to be quite provocative, a real "page turner," always educating while inspiring serious thought. Hopkins probes abortion through the lens of Catholicism, re-introducing us to Margaret Sanger an early feminist, women's rights activist and nurse who coined the term "birth control," ultimately opening the first clinic in the United States. Additionally, he explores civil liberties and the Vietnam War. The narrative flows developing the characters while analyzing their choices. I would highly recommend this book. Linda D. on June 6, 2017

Loved It

Unplanned Choices is the first book written by Frank Hopkins that I have read. I can promise that it won't be the last. I have the other 3 books already on Kindle. I stayed interested in the story from the beginning. The characters seemed real and easy to relate to. The very best part for me was when the story took a surprising turn. I highly recommend this to anyone that loves to read. I expect to see many more books written by this talented author. B. Cashell on December 12, 2017

He writes a very interesting story and it is even more interesting for people like myself who lived and experienced those times – remembering ...

Just finished reading *"Unplanned Choices"* by Frank E Hopkins. I could not put it down. He writes a very interesting story and it is even more interesting for people like myself who lived and experienced those times – remembering how things were, how we dated, what we did (or didn't do), all the songs he refer to. Most of all, our fear of unwanted pregnancy and the shame that it would bring to us and our families. The details were so vivid it really took me down memory lane... Gunther on February 14, 2018

The Abortion Issue Confronted

In Mr. Hopkins' novel *Unplanned Choices*, one of the topics he very openly tackles is the controversial issue of abortion. Mr. Hopkins has written an entertaining yet extremely thought provoking book which can serve as a springboard for deep conversations about abortion. This moving story may cause the reader to more thoroughly scrutinize a political candidate's stance on abortion which could influence how the reader votes. Dialogues, debates, elections and judges' decisions will determine whether Roe vs. Wade is upheld or overturned, affecting future generations. Put this insightful, easy read at the top of your list! JD an avid reader on September 8, 2018.

A Great Read!
Thoroughly enjoyed reading this novel by Frank Hopkins. The book was well-written and easy to read. I couldn't put this book down until I knew where next the book was going. Historically, fascinating dealing with a time well familiar to me. A great read! Sally Scarangella on March 1, 2018

A real page turner
I just finished the last half of Frank Hopkins' Unplanned Choices in one sitting and immediately wanted to read more from this author. He has captured precisely the background of a turbulent era when the Viet Nam War was raging on American television screens and Roe vs. Wade had not yet been decided. Promising young graduate students Steve and Anna fall in love and must struggle with the moral and mortal consequences of a terrible and unplanned choice. Carole Ottesen on October 26, 2017.

Read this book for a wonderful perspective of a time gone bye but still relevant ...
While reading Unplanned Choices I was transported to my youth and the era of secret relationships. Many memories of the pressure of feeling guilty about natural impulses were resurrected. The characters are clearly defined and draw the reader into the story with enough tension to hold interest. Read this book for a wonderful perspective of a time gone bye but still relevant to today's social, political, and psychological issues. Shellie Steinberg on June 11, 2016.

Made in the USA
Monee, IL
28 October 2021